HOLD BACK THE NIGHT

BOOKS BY PAT FRANK

Alas, Babylon
Mr. Adam
Forbidden Area
An Affair of State

HOLD BACK THE NIGHT

PAT FRANK

HARPER ⬤ PERENNIAL

NEW YORK • LONDON • TORONTO • SYDNEY • NEW DELHI • AUCKLAND

HarperCollins books may be purchased for educational, business, or sales promotional use. For information, please email the Special Markets Department at SP-sales@harpercollins.com.

Originally published in the United States in 1952 by J.B. Lippincott Company.

FIRST HARPER PERENNIAL EDITION PUBLISHED 2017.

ISBN 978-0-06-242181-4

17 18 19 20 21   LSC   10 9 8 7 6 5 4 3 2 1

For the United States Marines

ACKNOWLEDGMENTS

Encouragement, and advice, and factual aid provided by many people went into the writing of this book. I particularly want to thank Colonel J. R. Hester, Director of Marine Corps Public Information; Lieutenant Commander Edwin A. Fischer, USNR; Major Milton Maloney, Medical Corps, USAR; Captain Ned Carmody, who commanded a line company of the First Cavalry Division in some of the fiercest actions in Korea; and my friend Lieutenant Waldo Stockton, late of the heavy artillery, who first told me the anecdote of the battle of Scotch, which inspired the book.

Pat Frank

HOLD BACK THE NIGHT

Chapter One

CAPTAIN SAM MACKENZIE clung to his dream as long as he could. The dream was of his wife, Anne. She eased across the bed, and pulsed in his arms, but she was strangely cold, and he was bewildered. "Come closer," he whispered, and she moved tight against him, but she was still cold, and no relief to his desire.

Then in the half light that lies between sleep and consciousness he recognized, as if his mind stood apart from him and passed judgment, that it was a dream. Yet he retained hope that it was real, for he was sure he could feel her, and while it was not at all a satisfactory dream, still it was better than waking, and he tried not to awaken. Mackenzie shook his head and opened his eyes. He was embracing his carbine, under his parka. He had slipped the gun under the parka the night before, so the breech would not freeze and jam, in case there was an alarm and a fire fight in the blackness. Now the steel barrel lay against his cheek, a chill finger.

Mackenzie sat up and rubbed his shoulder blades against a knob of the rock wall towering straight up at his back. He looked about him and in the milky pre-dawn he saw the loom of his last two jeeps. He felt for his cigarettes, and he had none, and he spat the bad taste of night out of his mouth, and rubbed his face with his gloves. He discovered his knees would still bend, which was a surprise. A gaunt, old, old man of thirty, with sunken, bloodshot eyes and icicles growing from his beard, he walked stiffly over to the jeeps. He labored with them, and cajoled them, and prayed to them and God, but there was no answer.

The jeeps were frozen solid and the three wounded mercifully dead, so now Mackenzie counted those of his command he presumed alive, although they lay in their parkas like sacks embedded in the stiffened earth. There were sixteen, all that was left of Dog Company, which had been assigned the terrible duty of covering the regiment's retreat. For an endless haze of time, from the Changjin Reservoir to Hagaru, and from Hagaru to Koto-Ri, and beyond, they had fought off Chinese numerous as stones strewn on the Asian steppes, and with faces as hard and weathered and indistinguishable. Now, spent, the Marines had come to this scowling gorge. Captain Mackenzie tried to kick them to their feet.

All of them moved, or groaned, or uttered the meaningless obscenities of soldiers, but only two of them could rise. One was Ekland, his communications sergeant, a cocky and determined young man whom the captain had marked for decoration, and as officer material, even before Changjin. The other was little Nick Tinker, the youngest of them all, who claimed to be eighteen and was probably seventeen, and astonishingly beardless. "All right, you two," the captain said, "let's get things moving."

"Check the jeeps, sir?" asked Ekland. Mackenzie noted that Ekland was rolling on his heels like a punchy fighter. They'd had their last rations at noon the day before.

The captain shook his head, no. "I've done it already. Batteries dead. Not a spark. Oil's rigid. Always knew it was the wrong oil. Must've been ten, maybe twenty below last night."

"Must be twenty below now," said Ekland.

"It'll be better when the sun gets up."

The sergeant stared up at the sky and didn't say anything. Mackenzie knew what he was thinking. The sky was like gray-brown armor plate, and at this altitude it reached down to compress and crush them into the alien soil. There would be no sun this day, and no whistling jets and friendly Corsairs to harass and fend off the enemy. "We've got to get rid of those," the captain said. He nodded at the three burdened litters silent under the useless protection of the dead jeeps.

Nick Tinker, in a voice plaintive as that of a small boy dreading a household chore, said, "Do we have to bury them, sir?"

Mackenzie crossed the narrow, washboard road, and scuffed with his toe at the cracked mud of the ditch. It was like iron. "No. Just move them. Move them to a quiet place, out of the way."

Tinker and the sergeant lifted the bodies to a quiet place in the lee of a sentinel rock, and the captain knelt to see that their faces were covered, and sheltered from the wind.

Mackenzie did not want to look at these faces, for one was the face of Raleigh Couzens, the argumentative southerner who had been his friend, and tentmate, and the reliable leader of the Second Platoon. Yet he found it necessary. He peered at Couzens' face as if to pry from dead eyes what had not issued from live lips. Lieutenant Couzens had inexplicably been returned by the Chinese after capture. Then, carelessly and recklessly and for no good reason, Lieutenant Couzens had thrown away his life.

Back when they were staged at Pendleton, and Couzens had joined the regiment, his eyes had been the merriest at the "O" Club bar, and his tongue the sharpest. Couzens could, and sometimes dared, spit a senior major on the bayonet of his wit. Everyone agreed he should have been a trial lawyer, or perhaps a politician. Now the merry blue eyes were glazed by a patina of ice. In this distorted face, and in his own mind, Mackenzie could find no solution.

The captain rose. "Now somehow," he told the sergeant, "we've got to get these men up and going, because if we stay here we've had it." A glint from the hilltop on the other side of the gorge caught his eye. In the front seat of the lead jeep he found his musette bag, opened the clasps with fumbling, gloved fingers, and brought out his glasses, his fine, six power Zeiss glasses for which he had traded a Samurai sword in another war, and another life, a long time ago. He had trouble focusing. His vision wasn't behaving properly, and he steadied his elbows on the hood of the jeep.

For a moment a swirl of cloud hid the hilltop, but presently it thinned, and out of the scud, and out of the past, emerged two figures. They were strange figures with no proper right in this century—squat, armed men on short-coupled, hairy ponies—motionless as an old print of Red Indians spying on a wagon train.

Mackenzie was fascinated. These were not American Indians. Theirs was an older and more savage heritage. He knew he looked upon a patrol of Mongol cavalry, the lineal descendants of Genghis Khan, and Kublai Khan, and Timur and the Golden Horde that hundreds of years before had ravaged Asia and burst open the gates of Europe. And since he was a thoughtful and studious man, Mackenzie was frightened, for he also knew that from that dark day, until this very moment, the barbarians had not looked down on civilized man with such cruel hatred, and contempt.

Nick Tinker was squatting on the ground, sighting his carbine. "No, son," said Mackenzie, quietly. "They're not in range of that weapon." He was thinking of something else. If the patrol was fired on, and knew itself discovered, it would be quicker to report the Americans' presence in the pass, and bring another screaming mob down upon them. And he would have less time to organize the remnants of Dog Company for defense, not that he thought it would make much difference, but still it was a professional matter.

And then the captain noticed that Ekland was sitting on the ground, with his elbows on his knees and his head in his hands, and he was shaking his head slowly, as if something inside his head tormented him. "Ekland!" the captain snapped. "Did you see that? Did you see up on that hill? We've got to get the hell out of here!"

Ekland kept on shaking his head. "I can't go, captain," he said. "I just can't go."

The captain knew that if Ekland couldn't go, then nobody could go, except perhaps Tinker, and Tinker couldn't

5

go it alone. And the captain recognized that he had reached the end of his command. He could neither bury his dead nor save his living, and he knew that the time had come for him to open his bottle of Scotch.

Mackenzie groped deep into his worn, old-style musette bag and brought out what at first appeared to be a tightly bound bundle of long johns. This he unwrapped carefully as if unswaddling a baby, and at last held in his hand a bottle guard of soft, handsomely tooled Morocco leather. Stamped on the side, in faded gold letters, was "S.M.— A.L. '42." He took the glove off his right hand and rubbed the lettering tenderly with his blackened fingers, as if touching the face of a child, or a girl. He quickly replaced the glove. It was too cold, and there might be too little time, for overlong sentiment.

Tinker, who had been watching curiously, finally asked, "What's that, sir?"

"A bottle of Scotch."

"A bottle of Scotch!" Tinker's voice was shrill, and Mackenzie could hear the echoes bouncing across the gorge.

Ekland suddenly stopped shaking his head and swayed to his feet, and the captain noticed movement from the others on the ground. They had been watching, listening.

"Is that honest-to-God a bottle of Scotch in there?" Ekland asked.

"It is. Wonderful twelve-year-old Scotch. No. Older than that. I've had it since 1942."

"You been saving it all this time?"

"I have." The men were getting up now, one by one,

6

and gathering around him, regarding him in wonder and bewilderment. "I've been saving it for now."

"Why now, sir?"

"Well, I'll tell you, Ekland," the captain said, raising his voice a trifle so they all could hear. "This Scotch was given to me by a young lady and she told me to save it for a really important occasion, and I consider this an important occasion." He didn't feel it necessary to explain further. The most important thing that happens in a man's life is death, its conclusion. Now that they were no longer completely benumbed, they would understand that. It would sink into them. They would understand his words, and prepare themselves.

Tinker, with the tactlessness of the very young, asked, "Who was the lady, captain?"

"My wife." He added, "She wasn't my wife then, but she was my girl. It was just before we sailed for New Zealand to be staged for The 'Canal." He looked across the gorge. On the opposite side, the north, the hills rose in almost perfect cones, bare of vegetation and flying ghostly banners of snow. On his side, the south, were perpendicular cliffs. He was thankful that the road pressed close to the cliff, for it was his only flank protection, or had been thus far. The Mongol horsemen were still black specks on the hilltop directly across the ravine. He kept staring at them, but his mind was not in this bleak land.

He was in that penthouse cocktail lounge, "The Top of the Mark," on a spring night so perfect that the Bay bridges were pendants of diamonds, instead of pearls as they seemed on nights less clear, and every light in San Francisco was like a cut jewel. It was their last night together, and they were holding hands under the table, and whenever they didn't think people were looking, they kissed. He had been a senior at Stanford when she was a junior, and now that she was a senior he was a freshly created second lieutenant of Marines, his bars shining embarrassingly, like spurious gold.

And she had this package with her, wrapped in silver paper and red ribbon in the way of women, and he had been kidding her about it the whole evening, and then all of a sudden she was no longer gay, and she'd said, "Sam, I'm going to give you this now."

"Oh, it really *is* for me!"

"Yes, Sam, it's for you. Now, stop trying to grab it! Before I give it to you you have to promise me something. Promise not to use it until there is a really important occasion."

"Isn't this an important occasion? I'm leaving you. I'm going away. I'm going somewhere out there." He nodded towards the Pacific. "And it's the last time I'll ever leave you. All that's important, isn't it?"

"Sure, Sam, but there'll be bigger days. I can just look forward and see them. Can't you?"

"What's in it?" he joked, hefting the package. "Female magic charm to keep the boy from harm? Hand grenade, new type?"

"Don't unwrap it, Sam. Not now. There'll be times when you'll need it more. Wait and see. Promise me you won't take it out of the box until you're aboard ship."

He saw how grave she was, and promised, and kissed her without caring whether anyone watched or not. And they drank a last Scotch and fizz, and lifted their glasses to the stars, and he said:

"I cry warning.
"Night is falling.
"Sleep not, lest there be
"No dawning."

She said, "That's cute. Who wrote it?"

"I don't know," he lied. Sometimes he made up in his head little bits and pieces of verse, but at that time he never told anybody about them.

He drove Anne back to her home in Los Altos, and they tiptoed across the gravel in the patio, so as not to wake her parents, and he did not leave until dawn's first breath blew the morning's mists back into the sea.

That last night in Los Altos he would always treasure in the locket of his heart. Even now, watching the wind off Siberia whip plumes of snow from the hostile hill, he could almost see and feel her lithe and vivid dark beauty, and kiss the throb in the arch of her throat, and smell the rich jasmine which that night she had worn. Now, when he was bone cold, she warmed him with the thought of her body.

Then someone jostled his arm, and he turned in anger.

Beany Smith, the Jersey City boy who couldn't hold his liquor and had been in the punishment detail for seven days back in Pusan, and who even now should be in the brig for attempted rape at Ko-Bong, crowded forward, his eyes alight. "You goin' to divvy that up with us, captain?"

For a moment Mackenzie didn't speak. He hated any-one to touch him. He hated to be shoved. He controlled himself, and said, "Sure." He unzipped the top of the leather bottle guard with his teeth. From its safe bed of soft wool thick as rabbit fur peeked the top of the bottle, crowned by its black and gold foil.

Beany Smith counted heads. "Seventeen of us. That makes one good slug apiece, captain."

"I don't drink," said Ackerman, the quiet Pennsylvanian who was bazooka man and a corporal. "I'm an Advanced Adventist."

"So can I have your slug, Ack?" Beany Smith asked quickly.

"You'll be damn lucky to get a smell of it, Smith," said the captain. "You've been trouble ever since I saw you, you son-of-a-bitch. I had to lose a hundred and sixty-odd men and still have you!"

Mackenzie stopped suddenly. It was ridiculous for him to be eating out Beany Smith at this time, and place, when he had accepted destruction and dissolution for himself and for all of them. He looked around at the circle of grubby faces and frost-cracked noses peering at him with interest from under the hoods of the parkas, and it was then that he realized that in the last few minutes there had been a definite change in the condition, and the morale, of Dog Company. His men were on their feet, and therefore they could march and handle their weapons, and he would be derelict as a commander if he did not use the capabilities of his company to the utmost, and inflict maximum damage upon the enemy.

This was his decision, and he instantly took under consideration the first tactical problem—the effect of one drink of Scotch on one completely exhausted Marine with a stomach utterly empty. It would start them moving, all right, and they'd feel hopped up and warm for forty-five minutes to an hour. But when the alcohol died within them there would come inevitable depression, and if they collapsed again, they were through. He determined his course. "You're each going to get a drink," he said. "But you're not going to get it until we're back inside our own lines."

He waited for their groans, and they came, and then subsided. Sergeant Ekland said, "Do you think it's far, sir?"

"Not too far," Mackenzie said, "and the poop is that there's an evacuation fleet waiting for us at Hungnam." He was not at all sure of this. Like most small unit commanders he had only the most general idea of the strategy of battle outside his own sector, and depended upon the Stateside short wave, or Armed Forces Network, for news of what he could not see with his own eyes, or learn from his patrols, or what he was told by Battalion and Regiment. But in the hazy past, during the fighting at the Hagaru air strip, Dog Company had saved the life of a Major Toomey, of the Division Staff, and the major had told him he thought there'd have to be an evacuation from Hungnam, and that was the poop of which the captain spoke.

He began to give orders. They were to take only light weapons, except for one bazooka, and Ekland's BAR, and one grenade to a man. They were to carry two litters, and two of the six jericans of gas still strapped to the jeeps.

"What're we going to need gas for," asked Tinker, "with no jeeps?"

"You'll find out," Mackenzie said, "and meanwhile you and Smith will carry them. Lay 'em in one of the litters. They'll be easier that way. Every man will take his turn with the jericans. Nobody's going to bugger off on this duty."

The captain looked up at the hilltop. The patrol was still there, waiting like human vultures. Well, the longer they waited, the better, and the further Dog Company might get. He eased himself into the seat of the lead jeep, removed a glove, took his map from his pocket, and tried to concentrate on it.

It was a makeshift map, issued in a hurry. This was understandable. The company had been living in the luxury of tents, and everyone knew the war was practically over, when the Chinese attacked. So the map was bad, but it did show, as a twisting, thin blue line, the secondary road over which Dog Company had fought to protect the regiment's flank and rear. To the south, winding through a parallel pass, the map showed the main road from Koto to Hamhung, over which the bulk of the regiment had retreated with its heavy equipment. Hamhung was the industrial city, and supply depot, six miles inland from the port of Hungnam.

"Ekland," Mackenzie called, "come over here." The sergeant walked to the side of the jeep, and Mackenzie shared the map with him. "Ekland, what do you think of this?"

Ekland looked at the map hard. "Sir," he said, "I'm not sure. This map is screwy."

One of the good things about Ekland, the captain thought, was his frankness. When he didn't know, he simply said he didn't know. Mackenzie attempted to estimate the distance Dog Company had progressed since Koto, but time was blurred by hours of marching minus hours of fighting, and somewhere he feared he had dropped a whole day. Still, allowing for the hairpin turns in the road that the map ignored, and the dips and humps of the terrain, they might have covered two-thirds of the distance to the coastal plateau, where he judged they would bump into Ten Corps' perimeter. Providing, of course, that Ten Corps still existed, and there was a perimeter. He had lost his radio jeep to an ambush of tanks and self-propelled guns in the first fight after Koto, and had not since been in touch with Battalion, or Regiment. So far as Mackenzie knew, his might be the only unit still fighting in Korea. Or the Eighth Army, over on the other coast, might have counter-attacked and put the Chinese to flight. Or everything might have been settled in UN. But all he knew for sure was that it was his job to get Dog Company over this road to Hungnam, if possible, and if that wasn't possible, then to kill as many of the enemy as he could.

He stuffed the map back in his pocket, and wondered how many things he had forgotten. The socks, of course. He reached under the back seat of the jeep and pulled out the last bundle of clean, dry socks. Two pair he took for himself, and then he tossed the bundle out into the road and shouted, "All right, men, come and get it!"

They moaned, and swore, and the big Swede from Minnesota, Ostergaard, wept, but there was nothing they could do about it, because he had ordered it. They took off their shoepacs, and the clammy socks they had worn through the night, and rubbed each other's feet for five minutes, and put on the clean socks. Mackenzie got out of the jeep and rubbed Ekland's feet, and then he got back into the jeep, and let Ekland rub his feet.

On that very first day when the colonel had sauntered into his area, and hinted that Eighth Army was in trouble, Mackenzie had taken a long look at the map of Korea, and had then gone scrounging for extra socks. When they fought their way out of the trap at the reservoir, Dog Company's vehicles carried five times as many socks as a company should need. But Mackenzie was determined of this, that he would accept wounds and death from the enemy, if he had to, but he'd be damned if he'd yield casualties to the weather. He'd be damned if one of his men would lose a foot to frostbite.

So every morning, and every nightfall, no matter what else happened, the men changed their socks. On the unexpectedly long breakout of Dog Company, the supply of socks dwindled alarmingly, but the attrition of personnel had been equally great, and it had come out even.

Sergeant Ekland leaned over the side of the jeep and said, "It's a long way to go without cigarettes, sir. We're out. All of us."

"So am I," the captain said. In Mackenzie's estimation the lack of cigarettes might be as damaging as lack of food.

The sergeant looked over to the side, where the bodies lay marked by the rock, and then shambled off the road. The captain watched him bend over the bodies.

When he came back Sergeant Ekland was grinning through his frosted red beard, and he held close to his chest three boxes of combat rations, and one full pack of cigarettes, and one pack half full. "I'd forgotten," the sergeant said. He began to slice open the cartons with his bayonet.

The captain didn't say anything, but he rested his hand for a moment on Ekland's shoulder. Then he announced, "Okay. Chow!"

Three rations split seventeen ways wasn't much. But it was something. It was something for the belly. The captain counted the cigarettes. Twenty in the full pack, nine out of the ration cartons, and nine in the opened pack. That made thirty-eight. There would be one cigarette for each now, and another for some time later on, when it would be needed, and a few to spare.

As he ate his minute share of cheese and chocolate and biscuit, the captain wondered how he could have been so stupid as to forget the rations on the bodies of the dead. Raleigh Couzens and the others had been hit the morning before, and so had needed no meal at noon, for they were so torn inside. Ekland had used his head, as usual. Mackenzie hoped that if any were saved, Ekland would be one of them. The Corps, and the world, could use men like that.

Mackenzie finished, and washed it down from his canteen. His canteen was almost empty, and he suspected that some of the others' would be completely empty. More than food, more than cigarettes, they must have water. He called Ekland. "We need water," he said. "Know how to get it?"

Ekland looked around at the world that held them, like a barred cell of rock and ice. "No, sir."

"I'll show you. Bring me those helmets." He gestured at the dead, and watched as the sergeant stripped the dead of their helmets. Then the captain walked to a ledge of rock from which hung ice daggers downward pointed, and began to knock them away with the butt of his carbine. The sergeant filled the helmets with broken ice.

The sergeant waited to see where the captain would make his fire. Mackenzie pointed to the four jericans they would not take along. "Pour these over the vehicles," he ordered. When the jeeps were saturated the sergeant set the three ice-packed helmets on one of the seats, and then set both jeeps afire. They burned hot and bright for ten minutes, and the captain allowed his men to crowd as close as they dared.

When the fire died he half-filled his canteen from the water in the helmets, and his men lined up and filled theirs. Then he shouted them into movement, and shepherded them into column as he wanted them, with Ekland and the automatic rifle in front, and Ackerman and his bazooka in the rear.

As they strung out along the road, stumbling in the frozen ruts of the ox carts, they bore no resemblance to a company of Marines, or even the remnants of a company. Nothing like them had ever been seen on the parade grounds of Quantico and Lejeune. Yet they were Marines, and armed, and on the move. They would fight, and they were dangerous.

Mackenzie took the lead, his carbine snug against his back and the bottle of Scotch tucked like a football under his arm. As they rounded the first bend of the road he shoved the bottle into the pocket of his parka, alongside the map, and glanced back at the crest of the hill across the gorge. The Mongol horsemen had vanished. He suspected he would see them again.

Chapter Two

ONCE THE MEN were in their stride, the captain timed their progress, counting the cadence in his head, and was surprised to find that their pace was as good as you would expect from boys still in boot camp, well-nourished, fresh, and strong, hiking over the Carolina hills. His men of Dog Company might be bedraggled, and sick with weariness and apprehension, but they had been tempered to an inner hardness by the blowtorch of battle.

He saw nothing of the enemy, but he knew they were there. This new enemy was not orthodox. This new enemy did not expose itself except on ground, and at a time, of its own choosing. Then it rose, as if birthed on the spot by the mud of Asia, in full strength and ferocity. A five-star general had discovered this, the hard way, in Tokyo, and Mackenzie had discovered it, the hard way, at the reservoir. This new enemy slithered around your flanks, and stabbed your rear, and ate at your guts. You could not put your hands on him. It was like trying to strangle a jellyfish.

At the end of an hour, when he reached a turn where

he had a clear field of fire on both flanks, and a precipice rising at his rear, he called, "Okay, take a break." His men halted, and carefully laid down their weapons, in the manner of veterans, and then propped themselves against the rocks.

Mackenzie busied himself building a small pyre of pebbles and what loose earth there was, and Sergeant Ekland, sensing the captain's intent, joined him and jabbed and scraped the iron earth with his bayonet. "Trick I learned from a fellow who was in the Aleutians," the captain explained. "No fuel there, either."

Then he called for the jericans, and emptied on the pyre a gallon from each. When the gasoline had soaked well into the stones and earth, he touched his lighter to it, and it blazed like a great torch. "Good for eight minutes, maybe ten," the captain said. He stripped off his gloves and flexed his lean hands before the fire, and pushed back the hood of his parka and took off his helmet and his alpaca pile helmet-liner, and scratched his itching scalp. Then he squatted on the ground.

The men packed close around him, and he overheard a whisper, "He's a hard bastard, but not dumb." The corners of his mouth smiled, and he looked sideways at Ekland, and he saw that Ekland too had overheard, and was smiling behind the red beard. While they were separated by the tricky chasm between officers and men, the captain found that he and Ekland often thought alike, and acted alike. And while they never spoke of it, it was the captain's belief that their aims and ideals were close kin—that both enjoyed the magnificent independence and occasional loneliness of free men.

Ekland said, "Sir, do you think we could split up a few of the cigarettes?"

"Okay," the captain agreed. He broke out four cigarettes. "One to four men," he said. He knew Ackerman didn't smoke. They crowded the fire and burned up the cigarettes, inhaling deep, and when their fingers scorched they impaled the yellow ends on sharpened match sticks for a last puff. Mackenzie shared his cigarette with Ekland and Ostergaard and Joe Kato, the lazy Hawaiian boy whose surprising agility with languages made him a valuable asset in the linguistic morass of Asia, so that he had become a PFC and the unofficial interpreter for the captain. Captains weren't assigned interpreters, but this captain, by the luck of orders, had one, and had found good use for him. Mackenzie had discovered America deficient in one technical weapon of war—the languages of other peoples.

Kato took the last drag on the captain's cigarette, and said, "Sir, tell us more about that bottle of Scotch. Weren't you ever tempted?"

"Yeah," Beany Smith said. "How come you never drank it? Nothing big ever happen?"

Mackenzie laughed. "Big things happened—at least they seemed big at the time. Lots of times I almost opened it. I almost drank it at Guadalcanal, after I was hit when the Japs attacked on the Tenaru. I had shrapnel in my back, and I could hear the Japs prowling around in the night, and I had to lay there quiet, in my hole, until morning, and I almost drank it then."

"Why didn't you?" Beany Smith asked, somewhat awed.

"I wanted it bad enough, God knows. I didn't have any

morphine syrettes, and I was afraid to yell for the aid men. Every once in a while, that night, I'd hear a scream and a scuffle, and I knew that a Jap had fallen into somebody's foxhole, and that one or the other was dead. I started to open the Scotch. I figured four or five drinks would put me out of pain. But I didn't open it because I was afraid I'd drink too much and pass out, and a Jap would slip into my hole and murder me."

"Like we were murdered at Ko-Bong," Ostergaard said, and then realized that he had said something clumsy, and wished he hadn't said it.

"Yes," Mackenzie said, accepting the blame, "as we were murdered at Ko-Bong."

Then Mackenzie told them of Guadalcanal, of the stinking jungle and the weird Banzai charges, and the uncertain days after the Navy lost four cruisers off Savo Island, and the thin-hulled transports fled the beach. He told how the lonely Marines lay in the mud while the Japanese battleships steamed past, hurling 14-inch shells down upon them, lording it over the night.

As Mackenzie talked he kept looking over the shoulders of his men, examining the cone-shaped hills on the other side of the gorge, and the road as far as he could see it. He noted that Ekland, like an experienced hunter in the field, always searching for signs of movement, did the same.

Mackenzie spoke of malaria, and dysentery, and jungle rot, and the crud. He told them of the foot-long centipedes that would creep between your belt and waistband in the night, and fasten on your thumb in the morning, and leave you screaming in agony like childbirth for a full day. He spoke of the leeches that fell from the trees to suck your blood, and the ants with a bite like hot pokers, and the wasps three inches long, and the three-foot lizards, and spiders big as dinner plates. He told of men brained by falling coconuts and rotten trees, and the stealthy crocodiles, and the stench of the enemy's abandoned dead, so you retched before your morning coffee.

He made it sound as bad as it actually had been. That was his intention.

"Jeepers!" said little Nick Tinker. "That must've been rugged!"

"Them wild Japs!" said Beany Smith. "They must've been awful!"

"They were pretty shrewd," the captain said, "and pretty tough. But we licked 'em on The 'Canal, and we won out in the end." The flame in the earthen pyramid was dying in blue spasms, each weaker than the last. "All right!" Mackenzie commanded. "Off your butts and on the way!"

Mackenzie, walking in the van with the bottle snug in the sack-like pocket of his parka, wondered if the crags and hills ever would begin to lose height, and give him hope of the coastal plains beyond; but as far ahead as he could see the truculent hills brooded over the gorge. Ahead the road veered from the protection of the cliff, and twisted out to touch the winter-paralyzed stream that in flood had so brutally eroded this tortured land. He did not like the looks of it. He called Ekland. "What d'you think?" he said.

"It looks chancy, sir," said Ekland.

"It does, doesn't it? But there's only one way to go, and that's ahead."

Yonder, where the road ran in team with the stream, Dog Company would be naked, exposed to fire and assault from every direction. But the point of danger was still a mile distant, and his mind returned to Kato's question. There'd been another temptation, not long after Guadalcanal, that he'd omitted.

They'd sent him out of the fleet hospital in Noumea with a Purple Heart and a couple of other ribbons pinned on a uniform so fresh it still bore its warehouse creases. They gave him two weeks' leave in Sydney.

Fairest city south of the line,
Sydney.
Women, whiskey; women, wine.
Bid me, Sydney.

Her first name was Kitty, and he was never quite sure of her last name and so he had not written her afterward. He met her on the last day of his leave. An artilleryman, hurrying back to the New Guinea front, introduced them during the lunch hour at Romano's. When you were on leave in Sydney you rendezvoused for lunch, or a late breakfast with martinis, at Romano's, just as you went to Prince's at night. Now that he thought of it, he was pretty sure her last name was Turcott. That was it, Kitty Turcott, "more white and red than doves or roses are," and stacked like a Venus in miniature to boot. It was strange that he should remember the name, after all the years, just now. Perhaps it was true that once you tucked a fact in your brain it was there for keeps, never truly lost.

He took her to Prince's that night. All the Aussie girls at their table—the table of the First Marine Division—were attractive, but she was the prettiest, and vivacious and gay, almost, he thought, to the borderline of panic. She laughed the loudest and drank the most. It didn't matter. He wanted her. They danced every dance in the tiny oval of the merry, noisy amphitheater, with the tables, immaculate in linen and silver and crystal, rising in concentric circles around them. She was a tantalizing, golden sprite, first pressing close to him, then fending him off with practiced grace. His share of the check was sixteen pounds, Australian, which did not seem exorbitant at the time.

At midnight the band played "The Star-Spangled Banner," and then, "God Save the King," and as they stood erect, her hand alive and warm on his arm, she whispered, "No more drink after twelve. Austerity, you know. I do wish I had another drink."

"Know any place where we can get it?" Mackenzie had been a child during prohibition, but he remembered his dad's tales of the speakeasies.

"We don't have any bottle clubs in Sydney. We aren't civilized. In London they have bottle clubs and therefore are civilized—so they say."

He whispered, "I've got a bottle at the pub." In Australia, you called your hotel a pub.

"Let's get it," she said, as the band rolled to its crescendo. "Let's get it and go up to my flat."

So they managed to find a cab in the brownout, and

they went to the Hotel Australia and picked up a bottle—this bottle. The captain pressed it close to his side. It seemed crazy now, but it had seemed important at the time. On his last night in Sydney, it was important not to lose that golden, rounded, sprite of a girl, for in the morning he had to catch a SCAT plane back to the Solomons. SCAT. It meant Southern Cross Air Transport, the wildest, coolest, most reliable airline that ever took off nonchalantly with a two-ton overload. He wondered whether anyone beside himself remembered, and blessed, SCAT now.

Then the cab took them to her flat, on Point Piper, overlooking Lady Martin's Beach and Rose Bay, and of course it had reminded him of San Francisco. It was not only the marine view. He remembered the advertisements in the San Francisco newspapers that always began, MARINE VIEW . . . A marine view in San Francisco might mean a slice of the bay an inch wide, but in Kitty Turcott's apartment the marine view meant the whole wide sweep, through a curved picture window, of one of the magnificent harbors of the world. It was not only the marine view, but the flat itself. Just such an apartment, furnished with a flair for style and still in good taste, you might find in the newest buildings on Telegraph Hill. If you were lucky. It was surprising that two cities, and two peoples, could be separated by the whole thickness of the world, and yet be as close, in spirit, as cities split by rivers only, like Minneapolis and St. Paul, and Omaha and Council Bluffs. They were very close, San Francisco and Sydney, bound together by ties of language and humanity, and common blood and aspiration that transcended geography. When you looked out across the bay from Kitty's flat, only the stars were different.

That's what the flying machine had done for the world. Distance was not measured in miles, any longer, but in time. One day when they solved the problem of fuel supply for jets, Sydney would be a one-night hop from San Fran.

Mackenzie prowled Kitty's flat, absorbing it, admiring it. There was a tricky bar built into the wall. When you touched a button it revolved and opened itself up. But all the bottles were empty.

The bookcases were full of books, and not merely used for knickknack shelves. They were books that a man enjoys in the shadow of the evening, or the insomniac hours just before the dawn. There were Maugham and Hemingway and Thomas Wolfe, and a beautifully bound set of C. S. Forester. There was Gunther and Pierre van Paassen, and Negley Farson, and the same edition of Kipling that Mackenzie had read from the time when he was twelve.

"Like it?" she asked. He realized that she had been following him, unobtrusive as a discreet sales girl.

"It's perfect. I don't want to leave."

"Yet tomorrow you must leave."

"Yes, tomorrow."

Her eyes were desperate. "Well, the bottle."

"Sure. The bottle."

He unzipped the leather case, and brought it into the open, and she took it in her tapered fingers, and held it up delicately to admire, and revolved it slowly before a soft light. "It's been a long time since I've seen one like this," she said. "You Yanks do all right by yourselves, don't

26

you? All the cigarettes you want, and all the drink, and the fine uniforms and ribbons."

"Oh, Scotch doesn't rain from heaven. This is a very special bottle." And he told her the story of the bottle of Scotch, but when he finished he found he'd spoken more of Anne Longstreet than of the bottle. He'd talked more of Anne than was proper or politic at the moment. Yet it was good for him. It emptied him. It was a cathartic.

Kitty listened well. She said nothing until all was ended, and then he saw she was crying, not loudly, but deeply. He took her hands. "What's the matter, Kitty?"

"She must be a splendid girl, that Anne."

"She's okay."

"Love her?"

"Yes. I love her."

"Going to marry her?"

"I hope so. Sure I am."

Kitty set down the bottle on the mirror top of the bar, and moved against him, and rubbed her perfumed, flaxen hair into his angular chin. "You're a good type, Sam," she said. "You're like my chap. Same size. Same eyes. Same mouth. Same hopes." She kissed him, delicately. "I don't think Anne will mind. If my chap was with Anne, I'd be happy for him."

He should have known there was another man involved. He said, "Your chap?"

She disentangled herself from his arms and went into the bedroom and came out with a photograph in a silver frame. "Here he is. Good, isn't he?"

The man in the photograph wore the peaked cap of an Australian officer, and his face was lean, and he smiled both with his eyes and his mouth, and there was a suspicion of a mustache, as if he'd just started to grow it. The Australian officer was six or seven years older than Mackenzie. "Looks like a nice guy," Mackenzie said.

"That's my husband. My husband, Tom."

Somehow this surprised him. He hadn't classified Kitty as either a good girl or a bad girl, but simply as a playgirl, a gay feather whirling in the excitement on the periphery of war, and not for the solidity of marriage. "Where is he?" Mackenzie asked, not that he expected her husband to pop out of the closet, or make an unexpected entrance through a rear door, but still it was best to know.

She sniffed and laughed. "Not here, Yank. Not in Sydney. He was with the Eighth."

"The eighth what?"

"The Eighth Australian Division. They were taken at Singapore—all of them—all who weren't killed."

Mackenzie said, "Ouch!" The thought of capture had always been more frightening to him than death. His worst fear, on Guadalcanal, had been that he would be wounded, and captured, and be slapped around and spat upon, and be afraid to fight back, and lose his dignity as a man. He said, "He's safe, of course?"

"I don't know. Nobody knows. Every night I listen."

"You listen?"

"Yes. Every night the Jap wireless gives the names of five prisoners. Australian prisoners. Usually from the Eighth. I tell myself it's silly for me to listen—that it's only a trick to get me to take in their propaganda. They're clever, those Japs. Yet every night I tune them in. I can't help it."

"What time do they broadcast?"

"There's a program at two in the morning for us Aussies. That's the one I always hear. Reception's best, then, and I'm loneliest. Usually I'm lonely, that is. I don't ask in every Yank, actually."

He found a corkscrew in the bar, and was about to rip the seal on the bottle when she put her hand on his sleeve. "Don't do it," she said. "It isn't necessary."

He felt relieved, but he said, as a matter of form, "Sure you don't want one, Kitty?"

"Not from that bottle, Yank. You hold that bottle fast." She turned her face away. "I drink too much anyway. Not that it makes me forget anything."

Just before two they went into the bedroom. Alongside the bed was a small, but powerful, Hallicrafter receiver, a present, she said, from someone in the OWI mission. They reclined on the rich, wine-colored satin of the coverlet, leaning back against the pillows propped against the wall, and tuned in JOAK, Tokyo, and listened to the smooth voice of a traitor. She was tense until the time came, at the program's end, when the names of five live prisoners were announced. Major Turcott was not among them.

Then she relaxed, and he took her, and it was delightful, in a gentle, casual way. In the morning he caught the SCAT C-47, loaded with companions sated by Sydney, back to Noumea.

Now that he recalled her last name, he felt that he ought to write to Kitty and find out whether her husband ever did come back. He'd always be thankful to Kitty, for a number of things, and the most important of these was that she had not allowed him to open the bottle of Scotch.

If he'd opened the bottle that night he'd have always felt guilty with Anne. A queer thought intruded. What if he had ever opened the bottle—ever, at all?

There was an alien and violent *whoosh*, the close crash of a shell like the snarl of an angry dog, and Mackenzie, even as his instinct and reactions forced him to throw himself on his face, knew that he was under mortar fire, and digging in was the wrong thing to do.

When they had you under mortar fire your only hope was to keep moving, and never give them a chance to zero in. He did not admire the Chinese tank tactics. Tanks shouldn't be used simply as mobile artillery, or conveyances for infantry. Tanks had a purpose of their own. And if he ever could bring their Mongol cavalry under the fire of heavy machine guns he'd soon teach them that horses were obsolete. And apparently they were novices at air war. But they knew artillery, and particularly they were adept with mortars, a simple weapon. They could plant a mortar shell in your hip pocket—if you stood still for them.

So the captain wasn't standing still. "Come on, you men!" he shouted as he bounced from the ground. He began to run.

As he ran he swore at himself for allowing the warm luxury of recollection to betray him, and rob him of his normal caution. Here was the point of danger where the road ran alongside the ice-clad stream which he had noted a mile back. Here was the point of danger, and he had approached it with his thoughts in Australia. Somewhere in the hills to the north, a mortar crew had him under direct observation. As they watched him run down the road they would be adjusting their barrels. Another mortar shell crashed in behind him, and he could hear his men pounding and panting and sobbing close at his heels, but his mind was on the exultant Chinese officer who must be laying those guns.

The Chinese officer would have them pinioned in his glasses, and be figuring out a range to interdict them. The captain searched for cover. Four hundred yards ahead the road veered from its alliance with the stream, and joined the cliffs again, and disappeared around a jagged shoulder of rock. If he could reach that shoulder, that abrupt turn to the right in the road, he would be protected by the defilade of the hill. So the captain read the Chinese mortarman's mind. It was necessary for the Americans to reach that point of safety. The Americans would stay on the road. Did not Americans always cling to the roads? So train the mortars to lay a barrage on the road, short of the cliff.

"This way!" the captain yelled. "Follow me!" He left the road and tore across the cracked alluvial flat, which was like an obstacle course, slick with powdered snow, where you didn't dare trip, because you would be dead. He swerved directly for the cliff.

Behind him the mortars laid a neat pattern on the road, where Dog Company should have been, but wasn't, and in a few minutes they were gathered together, gasping and wavering but there, under the protection of the hill.

Mackenzie leaned against a rock, his head cradled in his arms, breathing hard and trying not to let the men know that his legs were shaking, and weak, and he was about through. He did not wish to speak until he was more composed. Finally, he took a deep breath and turned and counted them. One was missing. Ackerman wasn't there.

Beany Smith said, "Is the bottle okay, captain? You hit the ground real hard."

Mackenzie reached into his pocket and brought out the bottle guard. He held it at arm's length. He was aware that they all watched him, numbly. He turned it upside down and shook it. It didn't tinkle or leak. "It's okay," he said, shoving it back into the parka. "What happened to Ackerman?"

"He was running right with me, sir," said Nick Tinker. "He stumbled."

"Hit?"

"I think so, sir."

This was disaster. Ackerman was the bazooka man, and the bazooka was all Mackenzie's artillery. It was his mortars, his 75-millimeter recoilless gun, and his other, lost bazookas all rolled into one thin tube. It was his sole effective weapon against enemy armor, or a road block, and he had no doubt that they would encounter armor, or a block, before they came out of this gorge. He rummaged in his musette bag, found his glasses, and crawled to a place between the rocks from where he could see, and not be seen.

First he swept the hills opposite, where the enemy was, but the enemy was invisible, as usual. In a way this was encouraging. If the enemy was assembling a force to storm his tiny party, then they had not yet gathered in what they considered sufficient numbers. The enemy was prodigal with men, as the Americans were with shell and bomb. Some thought the Chinese crazy, with their wild, bugle-heralded, chattering charges. He did not agree. America's arsenal was rich in matériel. Red China's and Russia's was crammed with expendable bodies. America considered people important, and munitions expendable, but it was different on the opposite side. It was simply a matter of viewpoint.

He shortened the focus on his glasses and examined the area where the mortars had come in on them. His glasses picked up what he sought, a lonely figure grotesquely sprawled in a patch of snow beside the road. He focused on it for a full minute, until he was sure he saw the bazooka under Ackerman. In that minute the figure did not stir. He called Ekland. "Sergeant, come up here."

Ekland crawled up until he was comfortable in a crevice just below. "We've got to have that bazooka," the captain said.

"Yes, sir."

"I'm going to send out one man. They may not want to waste a round on one man. Who do you think we should send?"

"Me, sir."

Mackenzie thought it through. "No, sergeant, you can't go. You know how to use cover, and I think you might make it there and back okay. But you might not. And I can't afford to lose you. You're too good with the BAR. And besides if anything happens to me I depend on you to take the company out."

"Nothing's going to happen to you, sir." Now that it seemed they had a chance, Ekland was dismayed by the thought that something might happen to the captain. Ekland was a technician, and had never commanded.

"Something could happen to me," Mackenzie said. "It happened to the others." This was a nasty thought at the moment—that every one of your junior officers, without exception, was dead; or a wounded prisoner perhaps craving death like a merciful drug; or in one case a probable coward and malingerer, skulking back to Tokyo and the warm safety of home. "Well, who do you think, then?" the captain demanded.

"Ostergaard," the sergeant suggested. "He has what it takes."

"Too big and unwieldy," Mackenzie said. "Not fast enough."

"Well, Beany Smith. He's a tough little monkey."

"I don't think Beany Smith could make it there and back. He's got guts, but how good are his legs? And can he hide himself? Do better, sergeant."

"Well, then, sir, you're going to laugh, but I'd say Tinker."

"No, I'm not going to laugh," Mackenzie said. "He's got more resilience, and stamina, than any of us." He called for Tinker, and Tinker scrambled up until he was beside Ekland.

Tinker looked, the captain thought, the way Tom Sawyer must have looked to Mark Twain, full of piss and vinegar, and excited and eager as if this foul and awful business was S.O.P. "Son," the captain said, "think you can make like a Red Indian?"

Tinker grinned. "That's the best thing I do. Out where I live, that's all us ever did, make like Indians. That's all there was to do, hunt, and trap."

"Where do you live?"

"Oh, it isn't any place much. It hasn't got any real name, but people call it Hickory Switch. It's near Hyannis, and Hyannis isn't very far from Alliance."

"Hyannis and Alliance what?"

"Nebraska, sir. In the sand hills."

The captain grabbed Tinker's shoulders, and pulled him up to where he could see the terrain through the niche in the rocks. "See Ackerman out there?"

"I think so. Yes, I see him."

"Think you can get out there, and back, without getting shot?"

"Sure."

Mackenzie had no way of knowing, but Tinker would without question do anything his captain suggested. The captain was Nick Tinker's god. Most of the others thought their skipper a hard guy, but Tinker did not think him hard—not when Tinker compared him with his father and older brothers. To Tinker, the captain was fair, and even on occasion kind.

"Okay, son, I want you to go out there and get that bazooka that's under Ackerman, and any rocket shells he may have strapped on his back. Be careful. Use concealment. Make like a Red Indian."

"And Ackerman, sir?"

"I don't think there's anything you can do for Ackerman."

Chapter Three

"The United Nations massive compression envelopment in North Korea against the new Red armies operating there is now approaching its decisive phase . . . if successful, this should for all practical purposes end the war, restore peace and unity to Korea, and enable the prompt withdrawal of United Nations military forces."—General MacArthur's communiqué of November 24, 1950.

As THE COMMUNICATOR for Dog Company, Sergeant Ekland had charge of all the radio equipment. After the regiment settled down at the reservoir, and the company was assigned security patrol at Ko-Bong, guarding a triangular spit of land extending into the frozen waters, he moved a radio receiving unit to his tent, and placed it between his cot and Ackerman's, so that he and Ackerman could listen to the news, and music, and Stateside shows broadcast by AFN.

Ekland and Ackerman had a number of things in common. They were older men. They were twenty-five. They each loved one woman. The four others in Ekland's tent talked continuously of women, but the women of whom they talked weren't their women. They were remote Hollywood beauties, or pin-up girls freshly clipped from *Life*, or high school steadies whom they now endowed with unmerited passion and sophistication, or the wise little tramps of San Diego and Norfolk dance halls and juke joints, who in warping memory acquired sincere lips and soft voices, and were no longer predatory. But Ekland and Ackerman really had women, Ackerman a wife and Ekland the girl he was to marry, if he ever got home. Time and distance, compassionate artists, were kind to all these women, painting over their defects, retouching their faces, and molding their bodies anew. So when the men told outrageous lies about their women, and boasted of their own sexual prowess, it was not that they lied, really. That was the way they remembered it.

After evening chow on November 24, Ackerman, Ekland, and the other four in the tent—Swede Ostergaard, Kato, Heinzerling, and Petrucci—listened to the six o'clock news and caught the MacArthur communiqué. Then Ekland clicked off the radio, for he knew that next to women, the men liked best to talk of the progress of the war, and their chances of getting home.

"What in hell does he mean?" asked Heinzerling. "Massive compression envelopment? Who's compressing who?"

"Us," said Ekland. "We're compressing. Not us personally, but those boys from the Seventh up on the Yalu River, and our other regiments, over on the other side of the reservoir at Yudam-ni."

"I bet they're sitting on their fannies, just like us, trying to keep warm," said Heinzerling, a dark, wide-shouldered man nurtured in the Youngstown steel mills.

"What a place to fight a war!" said Petrucci. "You could look all over the world, and not find a place like this. Why can't we fight a war in a nice, clean country like Germany, with running water, and real houses, and indoor heads?" Petrucci lived in Garden City, Long Island, and his brother had served under Patton, so he knew about these things.

"It's because we're Marines," said Heinzerling. "Where do they send the Marines? Either a jungle or a rock."

"Chateau Thierry," said Ekland. "Belleau Wood. Paris."

"What's that?" asked Heinzerling.

"You wouldn't know," said Ekland. "First World War."

"I guess you were there," said Heinzerling. "You weren't even a glint in your old man's eye."

Ekland estimated Heinzerling's age. "I was at a place called Iwo," he said, "when you were a junior in high school. That is, if you got that far."

"Well, what I would like to know," said Petrucci, "is who picked out this goddam icebox full of fleas and gooks and goons and Chinks in uniforms that look like those old-fashioned comforters they used to put on beds. Who did it? Who's responsible?"

"I guess MacArthur," said Ackerman.

"It wasn't MacArthur," said Ekland. "It was Truman." Petrucci made a rude noise.

"I don't think it was Truman," said Heinzerling. "I think it was that Republican, Duller, or Dullest, or whatever his name is, in the State Department."

And they argued politics. Both were too young to vote,

and their thoughts on politics were vague and juvenile, and based on faulty information, but still they wrangled, and got mad, and perhaps might have fought with their fists if Ekland had not told them to shut up.

Ekland walked over to the map they had tacked to the top of an ammunition case and nailed to their tentpole. He swung the light so he could see better. They had everything, there alongside the reservoir, everything except women. Everything had come up behind them from Wonsan, even the mobile generators. That was American efficiency. That was the way this generation of Americans liked to fight their wars—with all modern conveniences. If death came they could accept it, providing it was a clean, antiseptic death, preferably in the shining aluminum shell of a fighter plane in the clean sky, or the shining steel armor of a ship in the clean sea. The high command recognized that Korea was filth, the anal passage of Asia, which American foot soldiers would consider an unfit place to die in unless proper facilities were provided. Ekland looked at the map and said, "It doesn't look like much, does it?"

The map was a full page torn out of *Stars and Stripes.* It was a good map, for its size, just as Ekland was a good man, for his size. He wasn't large, nor were his shoulders particularly broad or his chest deep, although he was tidily constructed, as if nature had fashioned him economically, to get the most energy out of the least poundage. "It doesn't look like much," Ekland said, "but I say it is much. I don't give a damn who put us in here—MacArthur or Truman or the UN—I say it was right. Because if we lost Korea, we'd lose Asia. All Asia. India. The N.E.I. Hong

Kong. Malaya. Indo-China. The Philippines, and finally Japan. Know what would happen then?"

"No," said Heinzerling, somewhat awed. "What would happen then?"

"Then the Russians would have secured their Eastern flank, and they'd be free to pile it on the west. As it is now they don't dare move in the west. We're too close to Vladivostok and Khabarovsk. Those are their big bases out here. That's where they stage their supplies for the Chinese. If we'd folded without a fight here in Korea, we'd have folded everywhere. If we didn't fight here, then the French would know we wouldn't fight for Indo-China—or France —and the Italians would know we wouldn't fight for Italy, and the Germans—hell, they'd be speaking Russian. You know what Churchill said about the Germans—'They're either at your throats or your heels.' Well, they'd be at our throats again, if we gave up Korea."

"Where did you learn all that crap?" asked Petrucci.

Ekland wheeled on them. When Ekland began to speak, or move, as now, he increased in stature. Until then he had appeared simply an average young man with close-cropped red hair who had been an assistant engineer for NBC in the Merchandise Mart, Chicago. He started to explain where he had learned it, and then he realized that being much younger, and without his sophistication, they wouldn't understand. You couldn't explain the long, early morning seminars in Al's Diner with Si Cooper. Si had been a foreign correspondent until his paper merged, and the new management considered foreign correspondents a useless luxury. Now Si covered Chicago crime, or tried to, for NBC. Nor could Ekland explain the long talks with

Molly, and how stubborn she was for a girl of twenty-three, insisting that their only real security lay in a stable world. He remembered one phrase. "When we have babies," she said, "I want to be pretty sure they'll grow up. That's the kind of social insurance I want." And he couldn't talk of the nights in the control room, when everything ran smoothly and there was time to read the fascinating books on the Balkans, and India, and Afghanistan, and the Middle East, that apparently nobody else wanted to read because you could buy them from publishers' overstock in any book store. He and Molly joked about what she called his "nineteen-cent education," and yet he always knew she was glad the walls of his two-room apartment were lined with such books, because she had plans for him. All he said to Petrucci was, "Never mind where I learned it. Logical, isn't it?"

"Maybe," said Petrucci. Petrucci would never dare talk to a platoon sergeant, or the Marine Gunner, like that, but Ekland, after all, was only a technical man, and a private could talk to a technical man who did not command troops. Men who commanded troops were different. They knew everything, and you didn't dare dispute them.

"Not only that," said Ekland, "but if the Russkies got Europe, then they'd have the Med too. They'd have the steel of the Ruhr, and the oil of the Middle East, and steel is the muscle of war, and oil is the blood of war. And when they got Belgium they'd get the Belgian Congo, and its uranium, and England would be helpless. We'd have isolation, all right. We'd have it!"

"Well," said Ackerman, polishing his spectacles, "that

made sense back in June, but what's the sense in going on, now that we've won it?"

"Look, Milt," Ekland said, "I'm not so sure we've won it."

"That's what you think," said Ackerman. "What's the scuttlebutt? What's MacArthur say? Home by Christmas." Ackerman took the sergeant's buckboard from its nail on the tentpole, found a pencil, and radio dispatch blanks, sat cross-legged on his sleeping bag, and began to write.

"I suppose you're telling her we'll be home by Christmas," said Ekland. "Well, you're nuts. If we all started right now we couldn't get home by Christmas. Not even with an air lift."

Ackerman looked up from what he was writing. "No, I don't say we'll be home Christmas. I'm just telling her to go ahead and buy the car, because we'll sure be home soon. She ought to get a good used car, say 'forty-nine Chevvy or Plymouth, for under thirteen hundred, don't you think?" The Ackermans had been wanting to buy a car ever since they were married in 1948, but Priscilla wouldn't have a jalopy, because she said it would be bad for their morale. And Milton didn't believe in buying things on time. But now, with everything going so well, and the allotment money piling up, now was the time to buy one.

"Sure, I think she ought to get a car," Ekland agreed.

"When I get home," said Petrucci, "I'm going to get a convertible. Cream-colored."

"I think she ought to get a car right now," Ekland went on, "because I think this thing is going to last a long time, and it's going to get worse, and pretty soon it'll be like last time. No cars."

"MacArthur says it's all over. Ekland says it's just starting. Who knows more, Ekland or MacArthur?" said Petrucci.

"About some things, MacArthur. About other things, me," said Ekland. "MacArthur hasn't been home in a long time. Years. He doesn't know what the people are thinking. He remembers how it was after the last war, everybody screaming to bring the boys home. So it's smart, politically, to talk about bringing the boys back home. That's what he thinks, but he's operating on past performance, and this is a different horse. Nobody wants us to come home this time. They want us to stay out here and fight. They'd rather have us fight on the Yalu than on theMississippi."

"Personally," said Petrucci, "I have fit enough."

"Look," said Ekland. "Nobody stuck a bayonet up your ass and said, 'You're a Marine!' "

"Now don't get sore, sarge," said Petrucci.

"I'm not sore. But we're all here because we wanted to be here. Maybe for different reasons. Milt, he stayed in the reserve. Maybe he wanted that Navy gravy." The Marine Corps reservists got their checks from the Navy Department. "You others, you all volunteered. I don't know why. I don't give a damn. But you know why. And this is where you wanted to be—right here."

"Not me," said Petrucci, a slim, olive-skinned boy over six foot. "I want to be in a cream-colored convertible driving out the Parkway."

"With a broad," Heinzerling added.

"Yeah, with a broad. Now I know a real hot thing who lives in Jackson Heights, and she—"

"I tell you what," Ekland interrupted. "You may get a drive out the Parkway—in a box—with your dog tags on it instead of a license plate. Because these Chinks aren't through. Their top guy, Mao—I can't pronounce it—he isn't through. He wants you, Petrucci, and he wants me."

Vermillion, one of the captain's runners, stuck his head through the tent flap, his breath steaming in front of his face as if he had come in a hurry, and said, "Kato here?" He saw Kato, flat on his back on his sleeping bag, with his eyes closed. "Kato. Skipper wants you. Right now!"

Kato lifted his head. "Yeah? Why?"

"He's got Beany Smith up at mast. Some gook woman claims he tried to rape her."

"Who'd want to rape a gook?" said Kato, lifting his head. "Particularly a Ko-Bong gook." Kato, whose ancestry included Polynesian, Japanese, Chinese, and New England missionary, or so he believed, was undisturbed by the fact that sometimes gooks mistook him for a fellow gook.

"Beany Smith, he'd want to rape a gook," said Heinzerling. "And maybe me, maybe I'd want to rape a gook, right now."

"Kato, scram out of here!" Ekland commanded, suddenly serious and authoritative. If the captain was kept waiting, somebody's hide would fry, and Ekland didn't want it to be his.

Kato came to his feet in a lazy and yet lithe motion, and was gone.

"Now in Pusan," said Heinzerling, "I saw some gook women who weren't too bad. But I hear tell these Japanese girls, they're terrific. Now, if I get leave in Tokyo, the first thing I'm going to do is . . ."

And they went back to their talk of women.

Geography is the scorecard of war, and so there were thousands of maps among the American forces in Korea, in addition to the one tacked on Ekland's tentpole, and one of the most detailed of these was in the war room of the group which called itself JANAIC, in the South Korean city of Taejon. JANAIC meant Joint Army Navy Air Intentions-of-the-enemy Council. Of course this was a name that nobody could remember, and that is why it called itself JANAIC.

JANAIC had been established, when the war matured, to speed analysis about what the enemy intended to do. If news and information and intelligence about the enemy followed the long and twisting chain of command, with usual military rigidity, then everything from Korea would have to be funneled through Tokyo and Washington before it came back to Korea. JANAIC had been set up to short-circuit these attenuated communications. It sounded like a good idea at the time, but like all councils on what everyone calls "the very highest level," it had no troops, and no authority.

JANAIC could analyze, JANAIC could deduce, JANAIC could ponder, and JANAIC could recommend. But JANAIC could not act, and so when the Red tide receded, JANAIC found itself in a backwash. Who cared about the enemy if the war was practically over? What was really important was the shipping schedule, Stateside-bound.

Nevertheless, on this evening JANAIC met as usual in its room in the modern brick schoolhouse. Unless JANAIC was in session, the map was covered with black curtains, and the room was guarded. For this map held all the secrets—the movements of fleets and air groups and divisions, the locations of headquarters and ammunition dumps and prospective airfields, the crayoned black circles on the acetate overlays that told of friendly forces operating in enemy territory.

The map dominated the front wall of the schoolroom and hid the blackboards. There were only four men in the room, each cramped in a child's desk, attentive to the map as if it were the teacher. Two of the men were drinking coffee from paper cups, and all were smoking. There was an admiral, an air general, a general with paratrooper's insigne on his chest, and a major, his oak leaves drab under all the stars around him.

The admiral and the two generals, Air and Infantry, comprised JANAIC. They were selected for the job because they were, in Army slang, "brains." The headlines, and quick promotion, usually went to the swashbuckling fighters, like Patton. But recently "brains" had been doing better in the military services. Eisenhower was a "brain," and so was Gruenther. Marshall had been a "brain," and so had Zacharias.

Sometimes these three men reached a conclusion, and this conclusion was transmitted to Eighth Army, and Ten Corps, and Seventh Fleet, and Fifth Air Force. Often they were bewildered, and could not agree, for the enemy's tactics were rubbery and his political and military maneuvers seemingly erratic, although his strategic objective was always clear—the isolation and destruction of the one power that stood between him and hegemony over the world.

Major Toomey, freshly arrived from the United States and attached to Staff, First Marine Division, had been invited to the council because, reputedly, he knew a good deal about the Chinese. In spite of the Tokyo communiqué, JANAIC was still worried about the Chinese. The Chinese were quiet, yes, but the red goose eggs on the map, representing new enemy units, had been multiplying daily, until now they interlaced into a solid mass all along the front.

Further, something stirred in Manchuria, disturbing as the rustle of leaves when there is no wind. From Saigon and Hong Kong and New Delhi, gathered by intelligence, and funneled through Washington to Tokyo and finally Korea, were coded cables that the Communists had massed new armies above the Yalu, and Mao Tse-tung had bent the bow, and nothing could stay release of the arrow. When air reconnaissance is impossible, not because of weather but because of policy, and patrols bloody their noses against the foe, and the communiqués of the theater general conflict with the reports of intelligence, then is the time to be wary, and call in an expert. So JANAIC had called in Major Toomey.

When he wasn't a major of Marines, Toomey was a history professor at Berkeley, and he gave a weekly lecture in psychology. The major told himself he must be steady. He must not make a speech. He must not exhibit too much knowledge. Like a child among his elders, he must not speak until spoken to. He kept his eyes on the towering situation map, frowned in pretended thought, waited, and listened.

The admiral had opened the discussion. "The way I see it," he said, "is that Army is getting a full week's rest, and Blaik will have cooked up a whole new offensive system, so even if we are pointed for this game, I don't think we've got too much of a chance."

"The game I'd like to hear," said the air general, "is Kentucky-Tennessee. Probably the two best teams in the country."

"What about Princeton?" asked Infantry.

"Ivy League stuff," said Air. "Good amateurs."

The admiral turned to Major Toomey, as if out of courtesy to include a guest in the discussion. "How do you figure it, major?"

"I don't know much about football," Toomey said. "I don't follow it."

They all looked at him in surprise, as if he had admitted some curious thing about himself, like having six toes, or that his grandmother was a Romany gypsy. Toomey felt an explanation was necessary. "You see, my father was in the Foreign Service, and I went to school abroad."

"Oh," said Infantry.

"College, too?" asked Air.

"Yes," said Toomey. "The American University in Istanbul, and then the Sorbonne."

"Thought you might have studied in China?" said Air, hopefully.

"Not formally," said Toomey. "Just language school, when my father was consul in Shanghai."

"Well," said Air, "let's take off." Air was slender and

handsome, with just enough gray lacing his blond hair to disqualify him from jet fighters. "What's your evaluation of the ground situation?" he asked Infantry.

Infantry looked at the map, and his eyes, bright, cold blue in a face leathered by the campaigns of Africa and Italy, flicked from attack arrows to phase lines to sector boundaries to the squiggles that described terrain to the red ovals above the Yalu. There were new red goose eggs, representing reports from Hong Kong, crayoned in within the last twenty-four hours. For a full minute he said nothing. It was as if he listened, and the map spoke to him in a language unintelligible to the ordinary ear. Then he said, "I don't like it. I don't like it worth a damn."

Infantry came out of his chair and went over to the map and plucked a limber, seven-foot pointer from the rack at the base of the blackboard. "Eighth Army is strung out too far," he said, whipping the pointer along the Korean west coast. "The road net above Pyongyang is in bad shape. Our own bombing." He acknowledged Air with a small, tight smile. "If Eighth Army is hit, it'll have a tough time getting out its transport. It'd be even worse trying to bring up support."

Infantry paused so that they could have time to absorb the immutable logic of supply. "Ten Corps," he went on, "is in an extremely hazardous position. Particularly the Marines around the reservoir. They're strung out worse than Eighth Army." His pointer touched Yudam-ni, Hagaru, and rested for an instant on the dot that was Ko-Bong. Nobody noticed the names. They were not important.

"Yes," said the admiral. "Admitted. But the Navy can

give direct support to Ten Corps. We can't to Eighth Army. That's the difference."

"That isn't the difference," said Air. "The most important difference is that the closer we get to the Manchurian border, the less space we have for aerial warfare. The Air Force has been deprived of its battleground. We have lost our principal weapon."

The admiral's face, ruddy from the winds of all the oceans and all the seas, turned brighter red. "Our principal weapon," he said, "floats. Guns and planes, both."

Infantry ignored them. He shifted his pointer to the mountains of North Korea. "Now this ROK Corps in the middle has been moving too fast for its own good. They've outrun their supplies, and maybe their artillery, and they're going to get hell kicked out of them. That is, if the enemy has the capacity to attack. I'm scared of that ROK Corps. If they break—watch out. If they break they'll unhinge all the flanks, and there won't be a regular line any more. There won't be any communications between Eighth Army and Ten Corps, except through Tokyo."

"No communications now," said Air. "Two commands. Private wars."

"I think it is sort of silly," said the admiral. "Here they are all unified, and everything, in Washington, and they ought to have a unified field command in a little place like Korea."

"Well, we suggested it," said Air. "We made a proposal. And look what happened."

They were all silent. Nothing had happened.

"But will the Chinese attack?" said Air. "That's the question."

Infantry returned the pointer to its rack, and took his seat, and scratched with a yellow pencil on the pad before him. "I don't know," he said. "But if they do, I'd say we were in a helluva spot."

Air nodded, and turned to Major Toomey. "That's where you come in," he said. "What's your evaluation of the enemy intentions? What's Mao Tse-tung thinking?"

Toomey wanted to say, "If I knew what Mao was thinking I'd have a couple of stars on my shoulders, like you birds." But he didn't say that. He said, a proverb bubbling out of his memory, " 'When the enemy advances, we retreat. When he escapes, we harass. When he retreats, we pursue. When he is tired, we attack.' "

"What's that?" asked Infantry, puzzled.

"A Chinese verse, written by Mao Tse-tung."

"Verse!" said the admiral. "What is he, a poet?"

"He's not only a poet," said Toomey, "but he's perhaps the best known contemporary poet in China. Of course Chinese poetry is all formalized, and lots of modern Chinese poetry is merely rewriting of the ancient Chinese poets, and I presume this is too. Still, it's significant."

"A poet!" said the admiral. "What are we worrying about?"

"Well, Mao sticks pretty close to his writings," Toomey explained. "So the question is, are our troops tired? Because if they're tired, then I think the Chinese will attack."

"They're worse than tired," said Infantry. "If they were just physically tired I wouldn't worry. They're worse than that. They figure the war is over, and they want to go home. I remember Italy. V-E Day, 'forty-five. There is nobody so alert and resourceful as the American soldier when the going is bad, and nothing disintegrates so fast as an American Army with a victory."

"Mao is smart," said Toomey. "Mao will know that. Furthermore, I wouldn't be at all surprised if he didn't have a couple of divisions of guerrillas stashed out behind our lines right now."

"Oh, come," protested Air. "If that was true, we'd all know about it."

Toomey reminded himself that he should not argue with all this rank. Yet he felt compelled to say, " 'Guerrillas should be as cautious as virgins and quick as rabbits.' "

"More Mao poetry?" asked Air.

"Yes, sir. He's a specialist in guerrilla warfare. When the Germans were pounding at Moscow and Stalingrad, the Russians adopted his guerrilla tactics. He's written manuals on the subject."

Air looked at his watch. He had another conference, Target Analysis, in twenty minutes.

Toomey felt there was more he must say. "Mao has expressed his intentions in writing," he said, "and I think I'd better quote him: 'We want to take the enemy's eyes and ears, and seal them as completely as possible. We want to make them blind and deaf; we want to take out the hearts of their officers; we want to throw them into utter confusion, driving them mad.' I think that's what he's trying to do to us, right now."

"Well, he won't get away with it!" said the admiral.

"As to his final intentions," Toomey persisted, "I think you'll find a remarkable parallel with Genghis Khan. Genghis Khan said, 'A man's greatest joy in life is to break his enemies, and to take from them all the things that have been theirs.' Like Genghis Khan, Mao accepts war as glorious and inevitable. And he doesn't care how long a war lasts, for he has limitless time, and unlimited lives. In the history of China, a hundred years is like a single year to us, and a hundred dead is like one dead."

The three of the Intentions Conference now examined Toomey, silently, evaluating him as he had evaluated the enemy. Toomey was not impressive. Had they seen him in the Burma jungle in 'forty-four they would have categorized him as a good, tough officer, tan and lean. But he had eaten too well at Fisherman's Wharf, and Dinah's, and Omar Khayyam's, so that now he was a bit paunchy, and he wore spectacles, and his color was not good. Malaria, and atabrine, would always be in his veins, but they did not know this. It was simply that his color was not good. "Where did you learn all this crap?" asked the admiral.

"I was in China, sir, when people were just beginning to talk about Mao. And later I was on one of General Marshall's peace teams. But I've never seen or met Mao. All I know about his personality I got out of books."

"Books!" the admiral snorted. "I never read books. Don't have time. Why there isn't a day my desk isn't eighteen inches deep in intelligence reports, all classified secret, or tops." For a moment the admiral was thoughtful. "You know," he said, "sometimes I think the people in the lower echelons put a high classification on their documents, just so everybody will read 'em."

Major Toomey saw that the conference was drifting, and that it was necessary to bring it back on the track. It was his duty. "In my opinion, gentlemen," he said, "Mao will attack very shortly." He paused, so JANAIC could

realize the importance of what he had said. "He's in a perfect position. As the general said—" he turned to Air—"we
no longer have aerial supremacy, because there is no battleground for our planes. Because of political considerations, we cannot hit the enemy where he lives. So long as
Mao's lines of communication, and his supply dumps, and
airfields are immune from attack, he can stage troops for
an offensive. Mao knows that. He's no dummy. He'll take
advantage of it."

Air leaned back in his chair. "Well, gentlemen, what do
we do?" he inquired. "Do we draft a message to Eighth
Army, and Ten Corps, saying we believe an attack is coming? Or do we let things rock along for a few days until we
have more definite information?" He looked at his watch
again. "Personally, I think we ought to frame some sort of
message, if only for the record."

"Doesn't Tokyo have the same information we have
from Saigon and Hong Kong and New Delhi, and from the
Corps and Divisions?" asked Infantry.

"Well, I would assume so," said Air. "Tokyo ought to
have more than we have." Then Air remembered Pearl
Harbor, and how everyone had assumed that everyone
else had all the intelligence, and it turned out that nobody
had all of it, although everyone had a piece of it. Air
decided to hedge. "It wouldn't hurt if we just drafted a
caution message, nothing absolutely definite, but just what
we've discussed here."

"Wouldn't it be a bit presumptuous?" asked the admiral.
"I mean, in view of today's communiqué?"

"Think you're right," Infantry agreed. "Take me. If I
were in Tokyo, and I'd just announced we'd won it, I'd be

pretty sore if someone way up here in Taejon said, 'Signals over. The enemy is going to attack.' "

"Still—" Air began, and then realized that the vote would be two to one against him. "Yes, Tokyo must have better intelligence than we have." He looked around at all of them. Major Toomey started to say something, but nothing came out of his mouth. "Well, gentlemen, that's all, I guess," Air said. "We want to thank you, Major Toomey, for a most enlightening report. I'll see that air transport is arranged for you back to your division."

"Thank you, sir," said Toomey.

After Dog Company was assigned security patrol around the hydroelectric plant on the little peninsula at Ko-Bong, Sam Mackenzie and Raleigh Couzens had set up housekeeping, and established a Command Post, in the efficient manner of soldiers who make the best of every respite in battle. In the plant office Mackenzie had discovered a substantial steel table, and steel chairs. During the day this table served as the captain's desk, and during the night it was for company officers' poker. But on this evening it was the bench of a court of military law, and Mackenzie was the judge.

Kato entered the captain's CP, and saluted. The tent was crowded.

"Kato, come over here," said the captain, returning the salute.

Kato slipped between two big regimental MP's, and past Kirby, gunnery sergeant of Dog Company and perhaps the oldest man in the regiment—older than the colonel, even. Kato glanced at Kirby's face, square and forbidding as a concrete blockhouse, and it frightened him. Behind the captain, fondling his rifle as usual, sat Lieutenant Couzens. Directly before the desk stood Beany Smith, and the woman.

Mackenzie was now ready to proceed. He had heard the story of the MP's. They had been patrolling the single street of Ko-Bong, walking cautiously so as not to step into what the orientation pamphlets primly called "nightsoil," freshly emptied and foully steaming on the frozen slime, when they heard a woman scream. In a clay hut they had found this woman struggling with this private on her straw pallet. The private was drunk.

Beany Smith had been sick down the front of his jacket, and the stink of him filled the tent, and his eyes were puffed and swollen. Although he weaved with weakness from the dregs of the liquor, he was now sufficiently so-bered by vomiting, and fear, to be questioned, in the opinion of the captain.

Mackenzie looked at the woman. Her face was flat, and one cheek was raw and darkened with dirt, and she was flat-chested and dressed in a shapeless and filthy garment. Her eyes were bright black buttons, and she was so fright-ened that she sweated and trembled. The captain turned to Kato. "Ask her what happened?"

Kato began speaking to the woman in the even sibilants of Japanese. She looked at the ground, silent. Kato re-peated a question. The woman began to speak, haltingly, and then in flood.

As he turned to the captain Kato tried to avoid the eyes of Beany Smith. "Sir," Kato said, "this civilian says that she was standing in her doorway, just before dark, when she saw Smith come down the street. When he saw her he offered her a can of peanuts. When she took them he grabbed her, and dragged her into the house. Then he—" Kato hesitated. It was one thing to talk like this to the men, but it was another thing to use the ordinary verbs in front of the captain.

"He what?" Mackenzie demanded.

"Well, he tried to lay her," Kato said, hoping it was the right word.

"Did he?"

Kato addressed another question to the woman, and she replied in a single syllable, and followed it with a string of sentences.

"No, sir. He didn't."

"Did he use violence?"

"I can't quite make out, sir."

Mackenzie turned to Beany Smith. "What about it?" he asked, his voice flat and metallic, like the dull click from a forty-five when the hammer is drawn back.

"I didn't do nothin', sir. I thought she wanted it. I didn't rape this gook."

"You bastard! You swine!" Mackenzie exploded, and then he controlled himself, but only for a second. "You call this poor creature a gook! You're worse than a gook, Smith! I'd like to see you shot. Right now!"

Mackenzie stopped. He realized they were all shocked by his outburst. He had not meant to expose his feelings so. It would be all over regimental Headquarters by morning, how he had blown up. He pressed the palms of his hands to the underside of the table, so they could not see how he trembled. "Smith," he said, bringing his voice back to normal, "do you know the penalty for attempted rape, under the Articles of War?"

"No, sir." Beany Smith was now entirely sober.

"You can get twenty years."

"But, sir, I honest thought that she—"

"Pipe down!" Mackenzie leaned back against his chair. It called for a General Court, or at least a Special Court, of course, but this was not the place and time for formal trials, which would necessitate the summoning of officers from other companies, or Battalion. Any of them might be ordered to move out, any minute. And the regiment had no clerks to be tied up in court proceedings. There was another thing that troubled him. He had taken the time to look through Beany Smith's 201 file, when it was obvious the man would be a problem, and from what was in the file he had deduced it was early environment, as much as anything else, that had twisted this bandy-legged little bastard with the pushed-in face. And while a company captain had no time to practice psychiatry, still he believed that background should be considered in punishment. Mackenzie addressed the MP corporal. "I have decided to handle this right here on the deck, as Summary Court."

"Yes, sir," the corporal said, his face wooden. The MP's saluted, pivoted, and were gone.

"Smith," said the captain, "you're fined a month's pay. That isn't all. You're going to get every dirty job there is. You're going to look at your ugly face in the bottom of a latrine every day until you're ready to act like a human being."

Mackenzie turned to the gunnery sergeant. "Sergeant, I

want you to handle this man's punishment, personally."

"Aye-aye, sir." In thirty-six years as a Marine, Sergeant Kirby had seen much shipboard duty, and he used strictly Navy talk, as the regulations prescribed.

"Take him away."

When there were only four left in the tent Mackenzie looked at the woman, and she shrank away from his glance as if she expected his anger to lash out at her next. "Kato, tell her the man is to be punished. Tell her that I am sorry for what has happened. Tell her—" He was going to say that he was sorry for her people, and her country, but it sounded too theatrical. "Take her back to where she lives."

"And give her this junk," said Raleigh Couzens. In the rear of the tent he had located an empty carton, and half-filled it with C-rations, and chocolate, and sugar, and a can of hard candy, and as an afterthought two bars of soap.

Kato took the box under his arm, and led her away. She was smiling, and for the first time the captain noticed that she was quite young. This surprised him, for it always seemed that Korean women skipped a generation, and were transmuted from pot-bellied children into bent hags in an instant. You hardly ever saw a young woman.

When the gunnery sergeant was out of earshot of the company CP Kirby clamped the iron grapple of his fingers on Smith's elbow and spun him around. Without a word, he smashed him in the face with the heel of his left hand, calloused by the barrel of his BAR. Smith crumpled to the ground, moaning. "Get up!" Kirby said, and Smith got to his knees, shielding his face.

"Up on your feet, scum!"

Beany Smith got to his feet, his hands pressed to his mouth.

"When I get up in the morning I want to see this whole area policed," Kirby said. "If I find so much as one butt on the ground, I'll really hit you. Then report to the cook tent, to stow slops." He turned his back on the man and walked to his tent, an uncompromising figure of strength. Mackenzie was a good skipper, for his age, the sergeant thought, although perhaps a little soft. Mackenzie shouldn't be concerned with scum like Beany Smith.

At midnight the captain's field phone rang at his elbow. He had trouble unzipping his sleeping bag, and it rang again. Finally he wrestled an arm out of the bag and picked up the phone. It was Ekland. "I just got a message from a friend of mine at Regiment," Ekland said. "We've got a sort of private code. The colonel's coming up to inspect us tomorrow. I thought I'd better tell you, sir."

"Thank you, sergeant," Mackenzie said. Marine Corps sergeants were a strange race. They held together tight as a fist, a fraternity possessing secrets that no officer could penetrate, and practicing rites outside of regulations, law, and the rules of war.

"One other thing, sir. For the last hour all I've been able to get on our radio net has been Chinese. They're jabbering on all the high frequencies."

"Okay, sergeant, you can secure for the night."

The captain closed his eyes, but sleep would not come. He rose, dressed in the dark so as not to awaken Raleigh Couzens, and walked outside into the clear, still night. Now that the wind had died it did not seem so cold. He

walked briskly, a tall and lonely figure, to the line of foxholes Dog Company had dug across the base of his tiny
peninsula.

The midnight watch had just changed. He went from
hole to hole, stopping at each for a word with the shadowy
figure within. To each he said, in parting, "Keep awake
tonight, soldier."

When he reached the last hole he saw, far to the west, a
series of rockets bloom in the sky. He watched their green
and yellow and red petals arch across the horizon, and
fade into the gloom of earth. It was very beautiful, but he
recognized them for Chinese rockets.

Chapter Four

MACKENZIE AWOKE UNEASY. There was something left un-
done. For a minute he lay in his sack, hands locked behind his head, staring at the brown canvas, recalling all
his actions, so to clear his decks from the previous day.
"That son-of-a-bitch!" he exploded, sitting straight up.
"Where did he get his liquor?"

"Calm yourself," said Raleigh Couzens. "It's too early
in the day for excitement." Couzens was sitting on the
ground, cross-legged, before a Colman stove, a frowsy
Buddha entranced by the flame of an altar. Atop the jet
of flame was his steel helmet, filled with water.

Mackenzie leaped to his feet, his long johns bagging,
his wool socks curled around his ankles, and the OD shirt
which completed his night garb flapping around his
thighs. He snatched his musette bag from its nail on the
tentpole, plunged his hand to the bottom, and brought
out the carefully wrapped and protected bottle of Scotch.
He opened the bottle guard, and made certain the seal
was intact. "Thank God!" he said.

"Thought Smith had taken it?" said Couzens, who knew its story.

"Who else? Where'd he get the stuff?"

"Out of a jeep," guessed Couzens. "Out of the radiator. Alcohol."

"That stuff is poison."

"Not to Beany Smith," said Couzens. "Not much poison, anyway. Sam, if that bottle ever disappears, look inside me and you'll find it. Don't bother about anybody else."

"I'd brain you."

Couzens peered into his helmet, where the water was just beginning to swirl and steam. "You know when you'll drink that Scotch, Sam? I'll tell you." He spread his palms over the helmet, and pretended an incantation.

" 'Double, double toil and trouble; fire burn, and cauldron bubble,' " chanted Mackenzie. "Okay, swami, give."

"I see you sitting in your new home in Los Altos," said Couzens, making his voice deep and funereal. "You are out on the patio—the one with the swimming pool you are always talking about building. Your wife is by your side, and you are drinking a martini, very dry, with a stuffed olive. I can see your son. He is tossing pebbles into the pool. He is older. He is about eight. You are reading the *San Francisco Chronicle,* and you notice something peculiar about the front page. There isn't anything about fighting, or war, or black markets, or inflation. Joe Stalin has been dead a couple of years, the Russians have all gone back to Russia and the Chinese are all back in China and the Czechs again own Czechoslovakia and the Poles own Poland. Winston Churchill is Secretary General of the UN. He has taken up fishing, as well as painting. There isn't much for him to do. Everybody minds his own business. We have a new president, and everybody loves him. MacArthur is writing his memoirs."

"Cut it out," said Mackenzie.

"Wait!" said Raleigh Couzens, waving his fingers in the steam. "There is more. All the atom bombs have been taken apart, and the stuff inside them used to produce power, and we don't have any more coal mines, or coal miners, or strikes. Also we don't have John L. Lewis. Everybody has free electricity. Now on this evening—yes, I see it is evening—you have invited friends to dinner."

"Their names, no doubt, are Mr. and Mrs. Couzens, visitors from Florida," said Mackenzie. Now that he thought of it, he had never heard Couzens speak much of any particular girl, and he wondered whether there was a girl.

"Yes, their names are Mr. and Mrs. Couzens, and they are to dine with the retired colonel of Marines, and Mrs. Mackenzie. Suddenly Mrs. Mackenzie says, 'Sam, we're plumb out of Scotch. And you told me Mr. Couzens loves Scotch. Sam, this is most embarrassing.'

" 'Why, of course we have Scotch, dear,' you say. 'Remember that old beat-up bottle you gave me back in 'forty-two? There's no reason to keep it any longer, is there, dear?'

"And I see your wife kissing you and saying, 'Why, no, dear.' And you open the bottle of Scotch."

Mackenzie threw back his head and laughed. "So that's the way you figure it, swami? That's the way you think it will be?"

Couzens glanced up at Mackenzie, his bright blue eyes

for a moment wise and serious. "That's the way it's got to be, Sam. That'll be the most important day in your life."

Mackenzie stepped into his trousers, and put on another shirt over the one he had worn in the night, and sat down at his table. He made a note in the company log. It would be necessary to have the motor sergeant check the transport, to discover which vehicle was low on alcohol. He began to wonder about a morning report. They had been camped at Ko-Bong only three days, he reflected, and yet so quickly did he fall into the routine of the barracks.

Couzens' water had now come to a boil. He measured instant coffee and sugar into their tin cups, removed the helmet from the burner, protecting his fingers with a wadded shirt, and carefully filled the cups, wasting not a drop. This was a bond between them, their first morning coffee. It was a ritual begun on the transport on the way out, and practiced daily since, come the hell of phosphorus grenades or the high water of blown dams. It gave some continuity to a life that at best was nomadic and insecure.

Mackenzie sipped his coffee, and Couzens continued with their routine. He replaced the helmet on the stove, filled it to the brim again, and when it bubbled he poured half the boiling water into Mackenzie's helmet, and then adjusted the temperature in both helmets by adding cold water from the jerican, using a finger as a thermometer. When he was satisfied he said, "Okay, excellency. Your bath." They washed and shaved.

Then in mid-morning Ekland entered the CP. "Regiment just made a signal, sir," he said. "There's an air drop coming our way. Plane just flashed the strip at Hagaru."

"Air drop? What's up?"

"Turkeys. That's what they said. Turkeys from Japan."

"It must be Thanksgiving," said Mackenzie. "Is today Thanksgiving?"

Ekland said, "It's the twenty-fifth."

"I know. But what day is it?"

Neither Couzens nor Ekland said anything. Mackenzie grinned. They could keep track of dates, all right, because of the company log, but the days of the week nobody could remember, except that when a chaplain visited Dog Company, it was usually Sunday. You could get killed on Sundays as well as any other day, and there were no Saturday night parties. Come to think of it, Saturday night wasn't party night back home any more. Party night was Friday night, or at least that was when the parties started. Mackenzie took his wallet from his pocket, and in it found a celluloid calendar. "This is Saturday," he announced. "Thanksgiving was day before yesterday."

"I got another tip from my buddy at Regiment," said Ekland. "Colonel's jeeping up from Hagaru now."

"How's the area look?" Mackenzie noted that Ekland was clean-shaven, neat, and spruce. This was good, because he planned to speak again to the colonel about Ekland, and the colonel might want to meet him.

"Good, sir. Sergeant Kirby's been around again." The captain had warned his officers, and personally inspected, earlier in the morning.

They heard the roar of aircraft engines, low and close, and stepped outside to watch the drop. A fat C-119, that the Air Force called a "flying boxcar," and the Marines called "Pregnant Mame," thundered over their heads, banked in a tight circle, and coasted back. When it was directly overhead yellow parachutes spilled from its tail. There were two figures standing in the open cavern in the back of the fuselage. They waved.

"Oh, the Air Force has it tough," said Ekland. "I can just see them, rising from their Beauty Rest mattresses this morning in Tokyo, with geisha girls, or maybe even their wives, to bring their coffee and the morning *Stripes.* Then after a nice hot bath, and breakfast, they maybe remember they have a job to do. 'Oh, damn,' they say. 'We have to fly today. Korea.'

" 'Korea. How awful! That filthy place!' " Ekland's hands fluttered in what he considered was an imitation of an agitated female.

" 'Oh, we're not landing, dear.'

" 'Even so, I wanted you to drive me over to the commissary this morning. Remember, we're having a bridge tea this afternoon, and we're utterly barren of goodies.'

" 'Oh, I'll be home in time.'

" 'Well, alright, but you're going to miss your golf, dear.' Yep, the Air Force is rugged, real rugged."

Mackenzie looked down on Ekland, and his peculiar smile, which was hardly recognizable as a smile at all except for his eyes, touched the ends of his mouth. "You have a very short memory, sergeant," he said. "Remember that B-two-six?"

Ekland said, "Yes, sir," soberly. He knew he shouldn't clown like that before the captain. He'd never wear shoulder straps. "I remember that B-two-six, sir." In the fighting after the Inchon landing, a light bomber, flying too low for a bomber's own good, had saved Ekland, and perhaps most of the company. The company had run into armor, and Ekland had taken a BAR, and led a bazooka team in an attack, and he had pinned down the enemy infantry, but not the enemy tanks. And an Air Force ground observer had seen what was happening, and had called in the B-two-six, and the B-two-six had dumped napalm on the tanks. Then the plane had been hit, or anyway something had gone wrong, for it had nosed into a hill and dissolved in a pillar of greasy black smoke. It was for his part in this action, and the mop-up that followed, that Ekland had been recommended for the Silver Star and battlefield promotion.

"Okay," said Mackenzie. "Get back to your net. If you pick up any more Chinese signals in voice, call Kato and see if he can make anything out of them." Then Mackenzie prepared to meet the colonel, reminding himself to exhibit just the right degree of surprise when the colonel appeared.

It was said of Colonel Grimm that he would never make general, because he was too good a colonel. So far as anyone in the Corps remembered, he had always been a colonel. It was likely he would always remain a colonel, for he was in his upper fifties, and the Corps, like all the military establishment, was topheavy with brass. The Corps had been expanded enormously in the Second World War, and then drastically reduced. When that war was done, there was incentive for a young officer to accept discharge and make his way in the civilian world, but there was none for a general. When a general gets to be a general, even a buck general, he has reached the top of his profession. It was senseless for him to resign, and accept a bit more take-home pay as Vice-President for Sales of

Toasty-Pops, Inc., or Executive Assistant to the General Manager of Non-Rip Nylon. His prospects as a business man were as poor as the future of a man of middle years who has been drafted into the Army. Quite soon, the office force would stop deferring to him as General, and concentrate their attention and flattery upon younger men, with savvy and know-how, who were hep to the business. Of course, if he were a five-star general, or a four-star general with a Name, then it was different. In that case he sold his memoirs, or became Chairman of the Board, and lived happily ever after. So because almost every general wanted to stay a general, Colonel Grimm remained a colonel commanding troops in the field, which was exactly what he wanted to be.

When Colonel Grimm entered the lines of Dog Company he left his jeep at the first watch post, ordered the stiffened sentry not to announce his arrival, and took a good hard look at the foxholes and sandbags that stretched across the neck of the Ko-Bong peninsula to deny the encampment to enemy surprise. Particularly he viewed the siting of the machine guns and the disposition of the mortar platoon. He must have been satisfied, because he said nothing and began his inspection of the bivouac, on foot, and unobtrusive and inconspicuous as a second-class private skulking back from an off-limits area. The hood of his parka was pulled over the white eagle stenciled on his helmet, and his chin grated against his chest, so that the deep canyons in his face, that stamped him as an old man and out of place in Dog Company, were shadowed.

The colonel saw that the noon chow line was forming

up, and so he joined it. It is the custom of the Marines, when in the field, that the officers eat at the tag end of the line, and so the colonel, because of his rank, stepped behind the last man, who of course was Mackenzie. And Mackenzie, since he was accustomed to being last man, sensed something was wrong behind him, wheeled, and faced the colonel. "At ease, captain," the colonel said, instantly.

"Glad to have you with us, sir."

"Will you see that my driver is fed? My vehicle is at your last post."

Mackenzie spotted Kato, his mess kit filled, and gave instructions. The word sifted along the chow line. You could not hear the word. It was a soundless zephyr, but the progress of the word could be seen, as far ahead as the cook tent, by the straightening of the line, and of backs. The colonel was there.

As the line inched ahead Mackenzie said, "Is everything okay, colonel?"

"I'll talk about that later, in your CP," the colonel said. "But tell me, did you get the drop okay? The turkeys, I mean? We forgot about you, stuck off by yourselves here, until just as we finished Thanksgiving dinner. So I messaged Wonsan, and they messaged Tokyo."

"We got the drop fine, sir."

"So I'll have a second Thanksgiving dinner, heh?"

"No sir. We're having C-rations. The turkeys were frozen. They were shipped that way from the States, of course, and they were kept frozen in Tokyo, and they didn't get any warmer on the way here. Cooks say they won't thaw out for twenty-four hours. We'll have them tomorrow."

"Perhaps," the colonel said.

When they were in the CP, and alone, Colonel Grimm tossed back his hood, and unbuttoned his greatcoat, and laid his map case and helmet on the table, and sat down in one of the office chairs liberated from the hydroelectric plant. He eased his belt and said, "Your cooks aren't bad, Mackenzie. Wish I could be here for the turkeys."

"You're invited, sir."

"I doubt that I will be able to attend. I believe I will have other duties." The colonel's face was wry, as if he had made a prior date which he preferred not to keep; as if he had been invited to an all-male poker party, but was committed to address a garden club.

Mackenzie knew he dared not ask why the colonel couldn't have his turkey. He waited for the colonel to speak, and the colonel spoke, his eyes opaque as gunmetal and his mouth straight as the eye-slit of a tank. "This area is too clean."

"Thank you, sir," said Mackenzie.

"I said it was too clean. Know I was coming, Mackenzie?"

"Yes, sir," the captain admitted.

The colonel's face softened, for an instant, with inner amusement. "My headquarters must be insecure."

Mackenzie kept silent.

"But I didn't come over here to speak of turkeys, or the fact that communications are passing between headquarters and your company outside of regular channels." The colonel opened his map case, and spread on the table the map of the Division's sector, extending from the reservoir to the sea. Then, thoughtfully, he folded this map, and replaced it with a map of all North Korea. "I think there's hell to pay in the center," he said, tracing a brown finger along the mountain range.

Mackenzie remembered what he had seen in the night, to the west. "I saw flares last night. Chinese."

"They hit the ROK Corps. Nobody seems to know what happened, but there isn't any ROK Corps there any more. Know what that means?"

"Sort of leaves a gap between our Ten Corps and Eighth Army, doesn't it, sir?"

"Sort of does. Our regiment at Yudam-ni has been ordered to strike across the base of the Chinese attack, and we've been alerted for a move to support 'em. It won't work." The colonel looked at the map, spattered with cryptic symbols that he read easily as newspaper headlines. "I'll tell you what's going to happen, Mackenzie. If the Chinese have attacked in force anywhere, they'll attack everywhere. Our counter-attack won't get far, if it moves at all, and while I haven't been told to do it, I'm going to prepare to attack in another direction—to the sea. I probably ought to be back at Regiment organizing it now, but I wanted to see you first, because if what I think is going to happen, happens, you'll be cut off, and I want to give you your orders in advance."

"Yes, sir."

The colonel substituted the sector map for the map of North Korea. "In my opinion we will have to fight our way to the sea. We will use this road." The colonel's finger ran down the main road from Koto-Ri to Hamhung. "But we'll need protection on our northern flank. That's your mission, captain. That's the mission of Dog Company. I want you, whatever happens, to put your company on this secondary road." He traced it out. "See what I mean?"

"Yes, sir." Mackenzie saw exactly what the colonel meant. If the retreat was ordered, and it went beyond Hagaru and Koto-Ri, then Dog Company would protect the northern flank. It was a necessity. It was also, perhaps, the sacrifice of Dog Company. "I'll need tanks, sir," Mackenzie said, "and some guns."

The colonel shook his head. "Tanks won't go on your road. Your road won't hold them. But at Koto-Ri, if we get there, I'll assign you a recoilless seventy-five. Two, if I can spare them." The colonel folded the map case, and Mackenzie knew the inspection was over. He did not know whether Dog Company had been selected for the task because of its location, or because of other reasons. But he had one more question to ask.

"Colonel," said Mackenzie, "do you remember, after Inchon, that I put in one of my sergeants—Ekland—for the Silver Star, and battlefield promotion? I wondered what happened?"

"I remember," the colonel said. "Your communications sergeant, wasn't he? I read the action reports. Well, he'll get his Silver Star all right, but I'm afraid we can't make any more officers in the regiment right now. We've got a batch of lieutenants fresh from the States, and our TO won't stand it."

"He's officer material," Mackenzie protested. "He's better than a sergeant."

"There is nobody in the Corps better than a sergeant,"

the colonel said. "That is a fact, captain, and you keep on remembering it."

The colonel rose, and Mackenzie rose. "Goodbye, captain," the colonel said.

"Can I take you to your vehicle, sir?"

"No. I can find my own way." For no good reason, the colonel shook Mackenzie's hand.

Mackenzie watched the colonel striding down the company street, his back straight as a rifle barrel, and he saw Sergeant Kirby, as if by accident, meet the colonel, and he watched while they talked closely together, and for a moment the colonel had his arm around the sergeant's shoulders. Mackenzie sensed they were laughing, and he felt resentment, for he feared they were laughing at him. Then he realized they probably were laughing at something long past and done, an adventure on the China coast, an escapade in Port-au-Prince, or the remembrance of a girl in Havana. In this exclusive brotherhood, he was still a neophyte, he realized. He hoped, one day, to be a full member.

Mackenzie sat at his table and concentrated on what there was to be done. First he called in his officers, and briefed them on what the colonel had said. He decided it was useless to strike the tents, and go to ground, until a direct threat developed, or Regiment ordered a move. His men would now need all the rest and relaxation they could get.

He sent Lieutenant Sellers, his supply officer, to Battalion in search of better maps. Sellers, who had not joined the company until just before the Inchon landing, wondered whether he should not take along a squad to guard against guerrillas, or snipers, on the Hagaru Road. Mackenzie didn't feel this was necessary, but he told Sellers to do what he wished.

The captain dispatched Sergeant Kirby to the regimental supply dump with instructions to scrounge all the extra socks he could find. He had discovered that Kirby could come back with stores that generals and admirals could not command, or Department of Defense requisitions secure.

He ordered a thorough check on his transport, and extra supplies of gasoline lashed to the vehicles.

He talked to his medical corpsmen, and gave them instructions to distribute their supplies and litters, and not load everything on one or two six-by-sixes or jeeps.

He ordered his reserve mortar tubes emplaced, and zeroed in on ground not completely covered by the fields of fire of the machine guns. He wished to make it impossible for any living thing to cross the neck of the Ko-Bong peninsula alive.

He doubled the size of the night watch. The First Platoon would have the duty until midnight, and would be reinforced by Raleigh Couzens' Second Platoon from midnight on.

Then he cranked his field phone and asked that Ekland come to the CP. He might as well get it over with.

"Any news, sergeant?" he began, when Ekland stood before him.

"Yes, sir. Heard an AFN bulletin from Tokyo. Eighth Army is under heavy attack. The announcer said something about overwhelming numbers. And I intercepted a signal from some Second Division unit. In clear. They claim they're surrounded, and they're screaming for air."

"Sounds pretty rugged, doesn't it?"

"That isn't all, sir. Kato has been listening in on the Chinese frequencies. He says their radio traffic has stepped up enormously, and he thinks most of it is coming from headquarters of the Chinese Fourth Field Army. That's Lin Piao. He's young, and he's smart, and he's tough. Every hour they broadcast an order-of-the-day. The usual crap about driving us into the sea, and then they end it with, 'Strike down! Strike down! Strike down!' I heard it. It doesn't sound good, even in Chinese."

Mackenzie wondered why Ekland should know anything of General Lin Piao, or even remember the name, but he had tabbed Ekland as an unusual young man, and this knowledge of the enemy seemed to confirm his judgment. "Sit down, sergeant," he said. Ekland sat down on the edge of the chair. He felt apprehensive. It was not often that the captain asked one of the men to sit down for a talk in the CP. When he did, it usually was bad news, and usually it was bad news from home.

"I've got some good news for you, Ekland, and some bad news," the captain said. "I told you I'd put you in for the Silver Star, and promotion. You're getting gonged, okay, but no lieutenancy. Not now, anyway. Matter of the TO. However, my recommendation will always stay on your record."

"Thank you, sir," Ekland said. He knew that custom now required him to say, "Is that all, sir?" and then leave the CP. But the captain's face, composed and sympathetic, invited something more, and Ekland felt free to speak. "I guess I was a dope, captain. I had a good job. Real good. A hundred and fifteen a week from NBC. But when this thing started I rushed back in. I wasn't in the Reserves. I didn't have to do it. But Johnny Ekland was first in line. You see, my girl and I decided there was a future for us in the Marines. Guess we were wrong."

"I don't think you were wrong," said Mackenzie. "There is nobody in the Corps more important than a sergeant."

"Oh, sure," Ekland said. "A sergeant gets a good deal. But a sergeant's wife travels second class. She can't go to the 'O' Club, or swim in the pool, or even go to the movies with a girl friend who happens to be married to a second lieutenant. Just like you and me. Out here we eat out of the same mess kit. But when we get back Stateside, if we meet in a bar and want to talk, there has to be an empty stool between us."

Mackenzie tapped a cigarette on the table, carefully arranging his words before he spoke. This was the first time this embarrassing social problem, always present and always shunned, had been placed so directly before him. "No army is a democracy," he said. "If it was, it wouldn't be an army. There has to be unquestioned obedience, and therefore there is unquestioned rank. Rank, and what goes with it, is a necessity."

"I realize it's a necessity, captain. Maybe it's all right for me, but not for my girl. She isn't a second-class woman."

"Well, maybe the Corps isn't for you," Mackenzie said. "You're a technician. You do fine on the outside."

Ekland's face was freckled, and when he grinned and cocked his red head on one side, as he did now, he was gamin off a Chicago playground, taunting the law. "Right, captain! I resign! Think I'll fly back home right away. Like my travel orders now, if convenient."

They both laughed. "But seriously, sir, that's the trouble. My girl and I decided to give this thing a whirl. We figured that if I went in right away I had a good chance to make lieutenant, and if I didn't make lieutenant I could get out pretty quick. We figured it would all be over in a few months in a little place like Korea. Now we're trapped. This thing can go on forever."

The captain didn't reply immediately. Ekland felt that the captain was looking through him, and through the walls of the tent, and past the outcome of present battle and the confines of Korea. At last he said, "For us, for our generation, it might well go on forever. But our generation has the duty. If we win, our children are going to live."

"Yes, sir. If we win."

"We are going to win," the captain said, as quietly and certainly as if he were saying he was going to have a cup of coffee, and Ekland knew the interview was over. So he rose, and made his military manners, and returned to his tent.

And there in his tent Ekland crawled into his sack, and Milt Ackerman, his friend, frowning behind his spectacles, came over and said, "What's wrong, John? Sick?"

"I don't feel too well," Ekland said, and turned his face away.

"The GI's?" In Korea, even when you stuck strictly to American rations, and boiled your water or dosed it with the little white pills that presumably made it fit to drink, diarrhea was always possible, as if the men were infected by an effluvium rising from the pores of the fetid soil.

"No. I just feel bad."

"Anything I can do?"

"No."

Ackerman left him alone, and Ekland closed his eyes and buried his head in his arms and re-lived their Day of Decision. It was a Monday night, and they were partying on this unaccustomed party night because the next day was July 4, and Molly, who worked in the office of the University of Chicago's psychics laboratory, would have July 4 off.

It started with cocktails at Si Cooper's apartment, and then they had dinner at Luigi's, the little Italian restaurant off Division Street. The Chianti was domestic, the antipasto scanty, and the pizza passable. But Luigi's provided candlelight and an imaginative and sentimental violinist, so they often ate there, the four of them, when Grace Cooper could get a sitter.

Molly had started it, but Si Cooper had carried it through. Usually Si enjoyed his friends, and good talk, too well to try to drown himself in indifferent wine, but on this night he had jumped into the bottle.

Si talked a lot, and the gist of it, cutting through the rambling reminiscences of the Weisserhahn Hotel in Vienna, and the Astoria in Budapest, and the Parc in Istanbul, and the Athénée palace in Bucharest, was this: We fight for survival against the tide of barbarism. This is nothing new. It has happened before, many times. Consider Genghis Khan, Tamerlane, Suleiman, Hitler, and all the other egomaniacs with a passion for shoving other people around. "Sometimes we lose," Si Cooper said, "and sometimes we win. But so long as we keep on fighting, we move ahead a little. We always move ahead. One generation is"—he tried to say, "inconsequential," but the word proved too much for him, and the syllables rolled around in his mouth like loose marbles.

"You're not moving it much," said his wife, Grace, who was irritated.

"I tried," said Si, his bulk spreading across the end of the table. "I saw the beginning of it. I saw the League of Nations. Flopped, yes. The UN may flop too."

"Hush," said Grace.

"Won't hush," said Si. "But there'll be another UN. There has to be."

"Maybe."

"We're going to have one world," said Si, with the sagacity of the very drunk. "Maybe it'll be a slave world, or maybe it'll be our kind of world. But it'll only be one."

Molly looked across the table. "Do you believe that, Johnny?" she asked.

"I believe it," he said. "It's just plain logic."

"Then why don't we do something about it?"

"What can we do?"

"You did something before—the last time."

He examined Molly to see whether she meant it, and decided that she probably did. Molly was petite, and this night she wore her dark hair in schoolgirl braids, and her brown eyes with the gold flecks in them were clear and amazingly young, so that she looked about eighteen. "Know what I think you are?" he said. "I think you're nothing but a one-worlder, do-gooder at heart, and still a freshman."

"Do you love me?" she said.

"Sure. What's that got to do with it?"

"Nothing."

And they didn't speak of it any more until he took her home. Then they sat on the steps, because one of her roommates slept in the living room, and tried to be logical about it. First of all, what did they want out of life? They wanted something bigger and more exciting than what they were doing, didn't they? And if he went back into the Corps right now, there was sure to be promotion, because everybody needed technicians. This war in Korea wasn't going to last long. Who ever heard of the North Korean army anyway? As soon as MacArthur got a full division or two in there, they'd fold up and go back where they came from. Probably he wouldn't even see Korea. But the important thing was that there was going to be a real UN army, and of course the Marines would be part of it. So they'd travel, and see things, and really do the things they wanted to do. That's what they agreed.

"Okay," he said, "I'll be a sucker—this one time." And they'd laughed, and kissed, and they'd both known that he wasn't being a sucker at all, but was being real smart. That was the way they'd laid out the future.

Ekland raised his head from his arms and shook it as if the motion would rid him of these thoughts. He left the tent and went out to the radio jeep, sheltered by its tarpaulin and windbreaker. He had work to do. At 2300 hours Battalion called to relay a message that the regiment on the other side of the reservoir had hit heavy resistance north of Yudam-ni, and all units should be on the alert. Ekland passed on this report to his captain. Mackenzie called the reinforced squad he had posted in the plant, to the company's rear, just to be sure they were there, and awake. You couldn't ring the whole peninsula with a single company, and this squad was his sole protection from the west.

For a few minutes Mackenzie lay awake to smoke a cigarette and watch, silently, while Raleigh Couzens anointed his rifle, massaging the oil into the thirsty steel. Couzens treated his rifle like a woman. Well, in some ways rifles were like women. While they came out of the factories alike as dancers in the Radio City chorus line, still they were individuals. Some were mischievous and tricky and unfaithful, and some were sweet tempered and reliable and easy to handle. Couzens had discarded his regulation carbine after the Inchon landing, protesting that he needed a more accurate weapon. He explained that he did a good deal of shooting at his place in Florida, and he was used to a good gun. So he had found this M-1 somewhere, and made it his. Couzens cleaned it every night, but on this night he gave it especial care.

Mackenzie wondered whether there was anything more that he could do, and he decided there was nothing, but that he had better be fully dressed. So before Couzens took out his platoon he dressed, and then flopped down and slept again. The next thing he heard was a bugle call, not reveille as it should be, but disturbing and eerie as a siren's wail.

He was already groping for his carbine when he heard shots, and the bugle call again, and then cries of *"Sha!*

Sha! Sha!" far off. He knew what *sha* meant. Kill. Outside the CP he watched the green Chinese rockets ascending in a semi-circle around his bivouac. His ears were attuned for the steady firing of Couzens' heavy machine guns, which he knew should now commence, and the thud of his carefully sited mortars, but he did not hear them and he realized, suddenly and sickeningly, that the Chinese had not attacked across the spit of land. They were pouring across the ice, and had taken Dog Company in the rear.

Chapter Five

WHEN RALEIGH COUZENS led the Second Platoon down to the line of foxholes chopped into the neck of the Ko-Bong peninsula, he disposed two rifle squads on the alert, and inspected the mortar emplacements. He discovered that the night's normal humidity, freezing on contact with the steel, had rimmed the tubes with ice, and he ordered this chipped away and the barrels kept clear. The foxholes were deep, and neatly shelved, so that a man could smoke, and lay out his gear, in comfort inside, and even light a little fire, when the circumstances permitted. On this night the circumstances, of course, did not permit.

He gave his sergeant the duty for two hours, and then curled up in his own hole and was immediately asleep. Couzens never suspected it, but his men were often puzzled by his able professional conduct in the field. When they were staged at Pendleton, they called him, behind his back, sometimes, "Our Playboy," and sometimes, "Little Whitey." Since he dressed meticulously and always had a girl on his arm, when off duty, and since it was usually a different girl each time, they speculated on his amours and his ancestry.

Some things about him they knew—that he had left college to join the Marines in the last war, and had been a second lieutenant in the fighting at Peleliu. He had graduated from the University of Virginia after the war, and then for some unfathomable reason had re-joined the Marines when obviously there was no need for it, for the poop was that at Quantico he had driven a Cadillac convertible. They also knew that he re-fought the Civil War loudly and endlessly with the Skipper, always taking the losing side. Once, so the word was, a Confederate flag had been discovered in his foot locker, and Mackenzie had been infuriated, but the flag had stayed aboard, so perhaps Couzens, in spite of his expensive uniforms and girls and cars, was a brave man.

When the sergeant awoke him at 0230 hours, Couzens took up his rifle, made certain the action was unfrozen, and then prowled his position, his senses tuned to the night. The moon was only two days past its fullness, and unobscured, so that anything moving in the white wastes around him should be easy to pick up. Couzens hoped this was true, for on just such a night the enemy could swiftly move an army that in daylight hid in the boondocks from the prying eyes of reconnaissance planes. He wished he had borrowed Sam's good glasses.

Directly ahead of his defense line the road twisted through half-ruined Ko-Bong, lifeless as a village in a crater of the moon. But was it dead? Or were ghosts playing in Ko-Bong? He could swear he saw ghosts floating in the village street, slipping from house to house. It was as if all the dead men of Ko-Bong were stealing back into their homes. "Now this is strictly imagination," he told himself aloud. But he saw them again, and this time he saw a shadow, and ghosts cast no shadows. He knew he had spotted something tangible, but logically it would be a white-clad Korean emptying his pot. Still, he would have to investigate. He nudged three men from their holes with the butt of his rifle, and in single file they started down the road to Ko-Bong, soundless except for the hiss of their boots through the powdered snow, Couzens in the lead.

It was like a stalk, Couzens thought, a careful, silent stalk for a chicken hawk you fancied hidden behind the Spanish moss in a tall cypress by the river. In Mandarin. Whenever he held his rifle in his hands, like this, he thought of his boyhood days when his father was alive and taught him the secrets of the hummocks and the swamp and the river. There seemed no possible point of meeting between Mandarin and Ko-Bong, except by the whim of war, and yet there was. There was the very name, Mandarin. It was said that one of his ancestors, a British sea captain who traded with the East, had brought the first Chinese orange seedlings to Florida, and these oranges, larger than the original Spanish oranges, were called Mandarin oranges. And this ancestor, this Captain Couzens, had planted the seedlings where the St. Johns curved around his property like a sinuous and protective arm, and thereafter the place was called Mandarin. China had given it the name.

And he remembered nights in Mandarin utterly quiet and still, like this night. The peace of Mandarin was so profound that the fall of pine needles on the warm and welcoming soil made a clatter, and Ko-Bong seemed just as peaceful. But Ko-Bong was dead and full of ghosts. His rifle was perfectly balanced, ready.

They were close to the first house of the village now, and Couzens raised his arm, and the patrol halted. Couzens listened. He subordinated every other sense to listening, as he had learned in the woods. He listened until he heard scratching sounds in the thatch roofs over the gray mud and dark clay walls, and he listened until he was sure those sounds were made by rats. And when he was certain he heard nothing else, he beckoned his men ahead.

There in the center of the village he thought he heard something else, a sinister snick, like pebbles touching, and he froze, his heart hammering. It was at that moment that the bugle sounded, far back, and was followed by the first burst of shots, tiny but sharp in the night. He and his men wheeled, and stared back towards their own lines, and Dog Company's encampment beyond. They heard the second bugle call, and more shots, and then the green flare, that identified the Chinese, curved into the night. Couzens estimated it as perhaps three miles off, in the vicinity of the hydroelectric station they guarded. Like Mackenzie, he immediately guessed what had happened. The Chinese had crossed the ice, and attacked Dog Company from the rear. "Come on!" he cried. "Let's get out of here! Let's get back!"

It was this impulsiveness that exposed him, although when he considered it later he decided he could not have fought the patrol out of Ko-Bong in any case. He had taken not more than a step when the vicious screech and spurting flame of a machine-pistol came from a doorway to his right. Korn, his tommy-gunner, collapsed into the muck directly in front of him. Couzens threw himself on his face and tried to swing his rifle on the doorway. He never got in a shot, but it was this action that saved him, for the concussion of grenade explosions blew across him, tearing away the hood of his parka. Then something heavy smashed into his spine, and he knew he was dead, or soon would be, but the fierce wish to live of one near death forced him to roll himself into a ball and cover his head with his arms.

He felt a foot on his back, and heard a laugh, and he was yanked to his feet.

He was in the center of a group of Chinese soldiers, their faces glistening in the moonlight, shoving and shouldering for a better look at him, one of them incongruously smiling. They wore white cloaks over their heavy quilted uniforms. This ordinary dress of the Korean civilian made a perfect camouflage in the snow and the moonlight. Couzens looked to see whether any of his men had escaped. They were all down, but one was still twitching. Presently a figure leaned over this one and fired a burst into his head and he was still.

Couzens waited to be killed. For a moment they stood like this, an island in a stream of troops that had flooded from nowhere, converged into the street of Ko-Bong, and finally debouched in frontal attack on the First and Second Platoons. Couzens heard the powerful *whop-whop-whop* of an American heavy fifty going into action, and it sounded like the unexpected voice of a friend when you are in deep trouble; but it was too late, and too far away.

The grinning one, the one with the machine-pistol,

moved his hand to motion the others aside, and raised his weapon, but another, in the background, said a word, and knifed through the ring and grabbed Couzens by the back of his head and looked at his helmet, with its single white stripe. Then he said something more, and from the way he spoke Couzens knew he was an officer, although he wore no insignia. Two men came forward and the officer gave them instructions, and they nodded seriously.

The officer asked a question. One of the men replied at length, and Couzens knew that he was repeating what the officer had told him, so there could be no mistake.

Then the officer, and the grinning one, and the others went on, and the two prodded Couzens in the other direction. Couzens knew he was a prisoner on the way to the rear. He was giddy with relief.

They marched in silence out of the village and then began to climb an ox-cart trail that led upwards into the hills. After a time, when no other troops were in sight, one of the two grabbed Couzens by the arm and halted him, and Couzens despaired, and again prepared for death. In every army soldiers sometimes find it personally inconvenient to bring back prisoners, and it is simple to explain, if anyone remembers and asks about it afterwards, that the prisoner tried to escape and it was necessary to shoot him. It is a very simple explanation and cannot be refuted.

But the Chinese soldier made the universal gesture, with two fingers to the mouth, for a cigarette. Couzens reached under his parka and into the pocket of his battle jacket and brought out a pack of Camels, trying to mask his fear, and his relief. There was also a lighter in the pocket, and another package of cigarettes in the other pocket, but he would keep these if he could.

He offered the cigarettes, first to one and then to the other, hoping that in the darkness they would not notice the trembling of his fingers. Then he took one himself. One of the Chinese brought out a box of wax matches. He lit Couzens' cigarette first, and then his own. He blew out a match and lit another match, and held it for his companion. Couzens wondered why the superstition of three-on-a-match should be observed by soldiers the world over. He spoke for the first time. "Speak English?"

Both of them shook their heads, no. One spattered in Chinese, pointing and gesturing. Couzens shook his head. He did not understand. They moved on.

Couzens began to notice what went on around him, and he discovered that the night crawled with life and movement, as they all had suspected. The enemy dared not use the roads by day, for fear of American planes, but the night was his. Bands of gray-clad soldiers, their backs lightly laden with small, square packs, and some with rice bags strung around their necks, passed them. Some of these groups sang—a weird, off-key chant. Couzens knew neither the words nor the tune, but to him it was innately menacing as the sight of a snake to a child. Some marched doggedly and in silence. Couzens noted that their weapons were motley, and he wondered how they solved the ammunition problem. Some carried Japanese Nambus, and others American carbines and Garands and Springfields, and some German burp guns, and some British Bren guns descended from Singapore, and there were rifles and machine-pistols he could not identify. But all the uniforms appeared well-made, comfortable, and warm, even if bulky, and the men were all freshly shod.

The artillery moved behind horses, and he was surprised at the bore of the howitzers, somewhat larger than the American 155. Ox carts passed, loaded with mortars and fodder and ammunition and sacks of rice. Once they were forced to the side of the road by a procession of self-propelled guns of small calibre. Occasionally an ancient truck or bus, obviously appropriated in Korea, rumbled past, leaving the odor of bad diesel oil in its wake. No vehicles showed a light, but through the doorways of some of the houses Couzens could see lamps or charcoal fires. Everything moved in a single direction—towards the reservoir. It was a strange army. It was something out of the Napoleonic wars. It was not of this century.

Couzens wondered when they were going to eat, and where. He stopped his guards, and gave them another cigarette, and then rubbed his stomach. They spoke to him in Chinese and pointed up the road. One of them held up three fingers. Couzens didn't know whether it was miles, or kilometers, but he knew they expected to eat. They walked until they came to a line of houses strung along the road, and in these houses fires burned, and from them came the smell of cooking. His guards selected a house, talked together for a moment, and then one went inside. When he came out again he beckoned to his companion, and Couzens.

The house was a windowless double-room affair, smoke eddying under the eaves, and rich with stenches new and ancient. Squatting on their heels around the fire at one end were five soldiers, while on a crate sat a smaller, older, wiry man, resting stringy hands on his knees. Painted in faded red on one side of the crate was a label, "Singer Sewing Machines." Whoever had lived in the house was not there now, but on the wall was a 1945 Japanese calendar with a bright picture of a young lady in an orange-colored kimono.

The older man was a non-com, perhaps an officer, Couzens guessed. This man said nothing, but looked at Couzens with cold hatred shining out of jet eyes sunk in his wizened face. The five around the fire stared at Couzens curiously, and one of them said, " 'Ello, Yankee sonabitch," and smiled in greeting.

"Speak English?" Couzens said.

" 'Ello, Yankee sonabitch," the soldier repeated, still smiling, and Couzens realized that was all the English he knew.

Hanging over the fire was an iron pot. One of the soldiers stirred it at intervals, and then lifted the ladle to his lips, sniffed and tasted. It wasn't rice only, Couzens saw. It was some sort of stew. Then he saw three opened C-ration cans on the earthen floor, and he knew what it was, and he could guess how it came to be there. These were veterans of the surprise offensive of the month before, when Chinese troops were first committed to the war—the offensive that had been bloodily thrown back by the GI's, and the Marines.

His two guards squatted like the others on the floor, but Couzens remained standing, although his legs were so weary they trembled. It was a silly part of his heritage. He could not sit down until his host asked him to sit. Nobody asked.

The soldier stirring the stew finally nodded, and another brought a stack of wooden bowls from the other side of the room. The first bowl he gave to the officer, who filled it with care, seeking the meat from the C-rations. When he seated himself again the others filled their bowls and ate, lifting the bowls to their faces, and ladling the stew into their mouths with flying fingers.

There were only six bowls, so Couzens and his guards could not eat until the others were finished. The bottom of Couzens' bowl looked unappetizing as an ash tray in the morning, when he finally got it, but the stew was hot, and pretty good.

One of the guards touched his arm, and they had started for the door when the older man rose and gave a command. The two guards stiffened, erect. The older man walked over to Couzens and opened his pants. Then he deliberately urinated on the edge of Couzens' parka, and on his boots. The five soldiers slapped their thighs and howled in laughter, and the older man turned away and took his seat and gestured them out with his thumb.

Couzens did not remember much of the rest of the march. His humiliation sickened him until he staggered, and the tides of anger that rose and fell inside him finally gave him cramps, and he had to sit for a while at the roadside, pressing the heels of his hands against his rigid stomach muscles. His guards twice tried to explain to him, a puzzled pity in their faces, but of course it was in Chinese, and anyway it was useless.

At first light they came to a village, and from his memory of the maps Couzens guessed it could be a place called Pukkok, and he saw at once that it was a headquarters.

There was a radio van artfully camouflaged, and much wiring, and the guns of a heavy flak battery pointing arrogant fingers at the morning sky, and light flak, which looked like Bofors, in twin mounts on new half-tracked vehicles, and American and Russian jeeps carefully hidden. He was startled when he saw that three houses were not houses at all, but Russian T-34 tanks with thatch roofs cleverly attached.

Around a larger central building, heavily constructed of field stone and concrete, that might once have been a rural factory or warehouse, were sentries armed with American tommy-guns. Couzens reflected that we had given standard equipment to Chiang Kai-shek, and Mao must have got all of it, or almost all. His guards straightened their uniforms, and themselves, and marched him to the door of this building.

There was some questioning of his guards at the building's gate, and then a tall young man appeared, wearing the same quilted gray as all the others but with the authority of a staff officer apparent on his shoulders, and gave orders. Couzens' two guards shuffled away to where a fire burned and a pot of rice boiled, in the manner of soldiers relieved of a tedious duty, and the officer turned to Couzens and said, "You are a lieutenant of the Marines. You will come with me, lieutenant." He spoke in what Couzens had learned to call missionary-school English. It was stilted, and had queer inflections, but now it sounded good. Still, there was the disquieting feeling of being expected. This was not routine treatment for prisoners in anybody's war. There should be preliminary screening, and questioning, and days in a stockade before a prisoner was taken to a place like this, at least a Corps headquarters, and perhaps the headquarters of an Army.

The tall Chinese led him down a flight of steps. The headquarters, prudently, was in the cellar. They walked down a corridor, and Couzens glimpsed a map room and a communications center through open doorways. It was surprising that they could be so backward in the field, and so advanced at headquarters. It must be the Russians, he thought, but he saw no Russians.

The Chinese staff lieutenant led him into a small room. What furniture there was seemed comfortable. If this building had been a factory, the furniture probably came from the office of the Japanese or European manager. There was a polished desk and a matching executive chair, and a smaller chair with somewhat lowered seat facing it. Behind the large chair were three lithographs of equal size, Stalin, Lenin, and Mao Tze-tung, all idealized, with compassionate expressions on their faces, as if they were about to give a blessing. Covering most of one wall was an operations map, with the Chinese and North Korean formations marked in red, and the United Nations outfits in blue, just like the maps on the other side of the line. There was a steel safe, and atop the safe a tray with bottles and glasses and a decanter. "You will please sit down here," said the young officer, indicating a chair.

"Thanks," Couzens said. He relaxed in its comfort, the nerves of his legs jumping pleasantly. The Chinese officer left. Couzens thought it curious that they would leave a prisoner unguarded, but there was probably a guy with a burp gun just outside the door, and besides there was no place to go, even if he could jump out of the window, and there wasn't any window. The room's light irritated him. A large bare bulb, behind the chair opposite, was reflected directly into his eyes. He realized that whoever occupied that chair could observe every muscle twitch in his face, while the interrogator's own face would be shadowed, and they would have him at a disadvantage. Couzens shifted his chair quietly towards the end of the desk, changed its angle, and the glare wasn't so bad.

The door opened and a man came in. He was a stocky man, in his middle forties, his ivory face unlined. His thinning hair was freshly clipped close to his head. Heavy, steel-rimmed glasses enlarged his eyes, and endowed his round face with an expression of naïveté. He wore a dark blue woolen uniform of excellent cut, the tunic buttoned high on the throat. Couzens had never seen a Chinese uniform, or any uniform, like that before. He wore one decoration, a small red star of shining porcelain. As he closed the door behind him Couzens rose, which was correct military courtesy, but he didn't know whether to salute or not. The round man stepped towards him and held out his hand, and it was then Couzens decided to salute. He certainly couldn't shake hands.

The man returned the salute, casually, and said, "Do take off that heavy coat, lieutenant. You'll find it uncomfortable in here." He pronounced it "left'nant," in the British manner.

Couzens took off his coat, and found a hook for it. It was a relief.

"Now," the round man said. "Have you eaten?"

"I ate on the way," Couzens said, the memory of his degradation acid in his mouth.

"Doesn't appear that you enjoyed it much," said the round man, perceptive. "Well, our field rations are quite spartan, compared with yours, as you know. We aren't so rich." He smiled, but as if nothing were funny, and then he looked at Couzens' chair, and carefully placed it back where it had been, in the full glare of the light. "Please be seated, lieutenant."

Couzens sat down and waited, and the round man took the chair behind the desk, adjusted his bottom until he was perfectly comfortable, folded his soft, clean hands over his middle, and said, "I'm Colonel Chu. I'm political officer for the Fourth Field Army."

"I'm Raleigh Couzens, lieutenant, United States Marine Corps. Number O-7980655."

Colonel Chu tilted his head, and smiled, and this time he really seemed amused. "Name, rank, serial number. Oh, I say, you Americans should be able to do better than that!"

Couzens didn't say anything.

"You don't have to worry, lieutenant. I'm not going to ask you about the disposition of your forces, or how to make an atom bomb, or anything military whatsoever. I just simply wanted to have a chat with a Marine. Remarkable force. Remarkable tradition."

"That's very nice of you," said Raleigh Couzens, glad that he knew practically nothing about the strategic situation. He was certain that this was a polite prelude to torture, and he wasn't at all certain how he would behave under torture. It was fortunate that he had nothing to tell.

Colonel Chu swiveled his chair. "If you look at that map, you will see there is nothing about your army that we do not know."

Couzens inspected the map, and shivered inside. Couzens didn't know much about the positions and deployment of the United Nations units and headquarters, but everything he knew for sure was accurate on the map. They had the CP's of the three Marine regiments pin-pointed, and there was a neat blue circle around Ko-Bong, with red arrows thrusting into it from two directions. The Division's line of communications and supply from Wonsan was accurately plotted. The vulnerable territory between Ten Corps and Eighth Army, held by shaky South Koreans, was indicated, and this territory was split by a broad red arrow. Also on the map were secret things, like headquarters of the Joint Tactical Air Staff way back at Taegu. And there were things of which he had not even heard scuttlebutt, like the commitment of the Turkish Brigade, the Twenty-seventh Anglo-Australian Brigade, and the British Twenty-ninth Brigade to plug the breakthrough. Raleigh Couzens kept silent.

"You see, old chap," said Colonel Chu, "there's hardly anything you could tell me."

Couzens remembered a story of how German interrogators pumped captured American fliers during the last war. They'd convince a man they knew everything. They'd tell him the name of his group commander, and his squadron commander, and the date his outfit left the States, and how many aircraft it had lost since. And when the American was satisfied the Germans knew everything anyway, then he'd talk freely, and perhaps supply one small bit of information that the Germans had despaired of ever getting. So Couzens didn't say anything.

"We have a saying," Colonel Chu continued patiently,

"a proverb written by our leader, Mao Tze-tung. You have heard of him, lieutenant?"

"Of course."

"Our leader wrote a poem which has become famous. 'Know enemy, know yourself. A hundred battles, a hundred victories.' Good, what?"

"Pretty smart," Couzens admitted.

This answer seemed to please Colonel Chu. He opened the top drawer of the desk and brought out a package of Luckies. "Smoke, lieutenant?"

"Thanks very much."

The colonel lit one for himself. "We are well supplied. You Americans are really a remarkable people. You produce enough not only for yourself and your allies, but for your enemies too. Ha-ha. Not that we are enemies, actually. Not the people of China and the people of the United States. We have the same objective, actually, to remove from our backs the weight of the capitalists and the imperialists who would destroy us. Now, it is obvious that we have much in common, you and I. We enjoy good food, good drink, a Lucky Strike, and all these things we can have in abundance if we have peace. And you can go home to your wife. By the way, where is your home, lieutenant?"

"Mandarin, Florida."

"Florida." Couzens could see that Colonel Chu was mentally assembling a map of the United States. "Florida. One of the southern states, right?"

"The most southern." Couzens meant geographically.

"My word!" The colonel sat upright and stared at Couzens, fascinated, like a naturalist who has turned up a rare grub. "Tell me, lieutenant, have you ever lynched a Negro?"

Couzens was astonished. "Lynched a Nigra! Man, are you nuts?"

"Oh, come now. You must at least have witnessed a lynching."

"I've never even heard of a lynching in Florida," Couzens said truthfully. "What d'you think Florida's like? Ever been to Miami?"

"Well, perhaps you don't personally know of such things," Colonel Chu said. "No doubt news of such incidents is suppressed by your capitalistic papers. But the world knows of them. Asia knows. In a way, lieutenant—and now I speak as a professional in political warfare—you southerners have been our allies. Frankly, your treatment of the Negro has been our most consistent weapon. The lynching of a Negro, or any report of persecution, in—we won't say Florida—we'll say Georgia or Alabama—may be of no consequence to you, but to all with skin like mine it is the most important news of the day. It is flash news in Saigon and Singapore and Mukden and, yes, I should think even Tokyo. The Japanese have not forgotten your Exclusion Act."

Couzens was silent. He was thinking. He was learning something.

"There are lynchings in the southern states, are there not?"

Couzens didn't think much of his chances of getting out of this building alive, in any event, so he might as well speak his mind. If the commissar wanted a debate, he'd get one. "Yes, there have been lynchings," he admitted.

"But they don't happen often any more, and they don't go unpunished. Decent people deplore them—just as you must deplore the murder of your countrymen who don't agree with you politically, Colonel Chu."

Colonel Chu's eyes were round and surprised behind his thick lenses. "Oh, my dear chap! Those are not murders! We simply execute enemies of the people."

"Oh, I see," said Couzens.

"Why, of course. It is an entirely different matter."

"Natch."

"What's that?"

"Natch, for naturally."

"I've always had trouble understanding your American-isms. I've met quite a few Americans, you know, in Shanghai and Singapore. Haughty lot. Arrogant."

"So I've heard," said Couzens. "A buck goes a long way in those places, and they have more servants, and liquor, and women than they ever knew existed back home, and it inflates 'em. They become Big Time Operators. But you've never been in America, have you? Or England, either?"

Colonel Chu wriggled uncomfortably. It was not usual, or fitting, that a prisoner question the interrogator. Nevertheless he decided to answer, because the Marine was talking freely, and might yet confess something of real value. In the colonel's safe were coded cables from Peking for any prisoner interviews that would show deterioration of morale among the Americans, and particularly in the American elite units, such as the Marines. The interviews would be valuable, not only for Peking's propaganda, but for Radio Moscow. There was a large party in America which wished to abandon Korea, the cables explained, and this movement would be accelerated if it could be shown that American troops were demoralized, and out of sympathy with the war.

"Well, no, not actually," Colonel Chu replied to the question. "But I received part of my education at a British school in Hong Kong."

"You speak English perfectly," said Couzens.

The colonel inclined his head. "Thanks so very much. You are very flattering. And, in addition, I have read American books, and I have seen many American cinemas, which are most enlightening."

"What books?" asked Couzens.

"Oh, I have read *The Grapes of Wrath*. Conditions are pretty dismal among your farmers and farm workers, aren't they? And I've read *God's Little Acre*, and some of the works of Jack London and Upton Sinclair."

"And movies?"

"I've seen a great number of them. Some in Yenan, and some in Peking. In Peking on several occasions I was privileged to attend the cinema with our leader."

"Yes, but what movies did you see?"

The colonel squirmed, impatient. "Oh, a good cross section, I should say. The gangsters and the cafés and the gambling casinos and the music hall shows and comedians and life in your West with the pistol fights."

"You didn't, by any chance, see *Battleground*, or *The Sands of Iwo Jima*, or *The Best Years of Our Lives?*"

"Are they new?"

"Not so new."

"I haven't heard of them. Your blockade, I fancy."

"Well, Colonel Chu, you really ought to see them. Yes

you ought. That is, if you want to really know your enemy."

Colonel Chu considered that he had wasted enough time. Either this arrogant young man would answer the questions in the desired way, or he would not, and he would be sent to rot in the stockade. It would be best to lubricate his tongue. "Have a spot with me?" the colonel asked, rising. "Scotch or bourbon?"

"Scotch," said Couzens.

"How is it," the colonel inquired as he poured the drinks, "that bourbon is supposed to be the American drink, but whenever you Americans have your choice, you usually take Scotch?"

Couzens started to tell the colonel that he had been living in the same shipboard cabin, or foxhole, or tent, with Mackenzie's bottle of Scotch for months, and that Scotch had become an obsession with him. But he decided not even to say the word, Mackenzie, or Dog Company, because that might be information for the enemy. Instead he said, "Scotch is more expensive."

"Do you Americans evaluate everything by money?" said the colonel.

"Since when have the Chinese been adverse to money?" Couzens said, grinning. "I always thought your wars were won with silver bullets."

"Chiang's way," said Colonel Chu. "Not ours. This war of the People's Liberation Armies will be won by lead, and blood."

"How about uranium?" asked Couzens innocently.

"Perhaps uranium too," said the colonel, his face dark under its smooth ivory texture.

Couzens noticed that his drink was stronger than a drink of Scotch should be, and he figured that Colonel Chu was trying to get him tight, and worm from him some fact. If the commissar wanted to try to get him tight on Scotch, that was all right with Couzens. This was the first drink of Scotch he'd had since they left the States. And the colonel was unaware of a flaw in Couzens' constitution. Couzens couldn't hold much whiskey. It made him sleepy, and he was sure he would pass out long before he said anything of value to the enemy.

Colonel Chu brought out a pad, and a long pen with wide point. "Now," he said, "there are a few questions. None of them military, you understand, lieutenant. Just things I'd like to know personally. I'm always interested in you young Americans. It's always strange to me that a country so obviously degenerate can produce, on occasion such fine, frank young men."

"Proceed," said Raleigh Couzens, taking another pull at his drink.

"Firstly, I wish to put a broad question. What do you think of this war?"

"It stinks."

"I beg your pardon?"

"It stinks. It's unbelievable that America should be fighting China. You're our traditional friends in the East. You ought to know better."

Colonel Chu made a note in his pad. It was brief. "But we're not fighting America. America is fighting us."

Couzens shook his head. "No. America is fighting Russia. The Russians don't have the guts to fight us, man to man, bomb for bomb, so they send you against us. Ever think of that, colonel?"

"Ridiculous. The aims of the Chinese People's Republic and the Union of Soviet Socialist Republics are the same, and identical. We fight for the liberation of all oppressed peoples, including those in the United States."

"We don't feel oppressed."

"You are oppressed, although perhaps you don't know it. You have been hypnotized, drugged by material things. You're fighting for washing machines and television wireless and Coca-Cola and Standard Oil and Buicks."

"Some guys may figure it that way," said Raleigh Couzens. "Not me. Know what I'm fighting for? I'm fighting for the principles of Thomas Jefferson. He wrote something called the Bill of Rights. You can see the original draft in the place where I went to school, in Charlottesville. He lived there. That was his college. Drop in and take a look at them, sometime."

Colonel Chu regarded Raleigh Couzens, to see if he was serious, and then made another note in his pad. "Now," he said, "do you think the other nations in the so-called United Nations are giving you sufficient help?"

"Hell, no."

"Well, why do you Americans maintain them as allies?"

Raleigh Couzens shoved his glass across the desk. "Mind filling it up again, colonel?" he asked. "Then I'll answer your question."

The colonel rose, and made another drink on top of the safe, and brought it to Couzens, and then took his own chair, but he was not comfortable, nor did he rest his hands across his stomach. He was eager for the answer.

"I can't talk very well," said Raleigh Couzens, "with that light blinding me. Mind moving it, colonel?"

"Why, not at all," said Colonel Chu, and shoved the reflector aside. "Now, you were about to say something, old chap?"

"I sure was. I was going to say I didn't think we were getting enough help here in Korea. Except, of course, I understand that the British have got to keep considerable forces in Hong Kong, and the French have got to keep most of their army in Indo-China because unless there were big forces there they might be attacked like the South Koreans. Still, they could give us more help. That's the way I figure it, until you figure Europe. You see, colonel, Europe's the crucial place."

"That so?"

"That's so, buster, and don't ever forget it." Couzens now realized he was feeling his liquor. He didn't care.

"I shan't," said the colonel, and then wondered what he was saying. He had to bring this interview back to normal. "Now," he said, with authority, "as regards your own country. I'd like your opinion about certain political personalities."

Couzens took another swallow. "Shoot."

"What do you think of Henry A. Wallace?"

"Corn."

"Eh?"

"Corn. I think he should stick to raising corn. He was probably an all-right guy, but he got taken."

Colonel Chu started to write something, and then didn't. "Well, what do you think of President Truman?"

"I don't think he knows which end is up," said Couzens.

"What's that you said?" Colonel Chu demanded, his cropped head projected across the table.

"Why, I said I wasn't sure Truman knew which end was up," said Raleigh Couzens, but not with the same emphasis. Something in the back of his mind told him he shouldn't be saying things like that. It was like a family. You could damn your family to hell and gone so long as there was no one else around except other family. But you didn't do it in front of strangers, and Colonel Chu was definitely a stranger.

The colonel wrote busily, his head bobbing up now and then to take a good look at Couzens, as if he were describing him. Couzens felt uncomfortable. He wanted to explain about Truman. He wanted to explain that he was only thinking of Truman's crack about the Marines a few months before, when the President had said the Marines had a propaganda organization like Stalin's. He wanted to tell the colonel not to take his crack about Truman so seriously. But he kept silent, because he feared anything he said would only make it worse.

Colonel Chu finished writing, and said, "Lieutenant, you've been quite helpful, quite helpful indeed, and most co-operative. How would you like to go back to your own lines?"

Couzens was speechless. He couldn't believe that he was hearing right.

"I said, would you care to go back to your own lines?"

"Why, sir, I'd like to." Couzens, like everyone else, had heard the poop of how sometimes the Chinese returned prisoners, well-treated, after indoctrination, but he hadn't believed it.

"Very well, I'll have you back tonight. You see, lieutenant, we are not fang-toothed barbarians, are we now?" The colonel smiled, to show his carefully kept teeth, with the gold inlays. "I want you to go back to your companions, and tell them what you have seen here, and tell them how you were treated. We do not want war with you boys, lieutenant. This war was not of our making. It was your capitalists, and Wall Street, that instigated the South Korean attack upon the people of North Korea, and the imperialists seized upon the fighting here to attempt a general war. But we do not want war. After your forces have gone back to Japan, or surrendered, we will not attack you. We are, most of us, simple farmers. We wish to return to the land."

"Me too," Couzens agreed, hoping this wasn't a joke, or a trick.

"Ah, yes. Now no doubt you need rest, and when night comes I will have you escorted back to the American lines." Above them the ack-ack began to throb, steadily, and then the cellar shook with the shock of bombs setting their teeth deep into the earth, the concussions bringing little spurts of dust from between the stones of the outer wall. Colonel Chu waited until the clamor subsided. "It is not safe to travel by day," he explained.

All that day Couzens slept on a straw pallet in another room of the building, and when night came the young Chinese officer who had escorted him into the colonel's office gave him food, and then they got into a Russian jeep, and started back the road by which he had come. On the previous night all the traffic had been towards the front, but on this night there was considerable traffic headed

away from the reservoir. There were horse-drawn ambu-
lances, and walking wounded, and empty ammunition
carts. Whatever had happened to Dog Company, it had
put up a fight, Couzens could see. He spoke as little as
possible to his companion. If they really meant to return
him, he didn't want to say anything that would jeopardize
his chances.

At last they came to the ridge of a hill from where
Couzens could see the village of Ko-Bong, and the Russian
jeep stopped. The tall young Chinese said, in his missionary-school English, "I will let you out here. From here you
will go to your own people."

"Who owns the town?" Couzens asked.

"I do not know. We don't. Perhaps there are Americans
in the town."

Couzens got out of the jeep and unkinked his joints and
muscles. "Okay," he said. "Goodbye, lieutenant, and
thanks."

"Goodbye, Yankee," the other lieutenant said. "Goodbye, and good luck." He whispered it, and he held out his
hand, and Couzens clasped his hand. Couzens started
walking towards the village, alone, and before he had
gone a hundred yards a weight seemed to remove itself
from his shoulders. He was free again, a free man. Whatever happened to him now could not be as bad as what
had happened before, because there is nothing so bad as
captivity. From here in, he could make a fight of it. He
would not be taken again, ever. Nobody would ever piss on
his legs again.

In the moonlight almost like the moonlight of the night
before, he approached the line of houses. He walked stead-

ily down the street until he came to where he had been ambushed. Then he stopped to think, and felt in the pocket of his battle jacket, and found his pack of cigarettes, miraculously unopened, and the lighter, and stepped in the lee of a wall for a smoke. While he smoked, he listened, and he learned from his ears that Ko-Bong was not deserted by all its sorrowing people, and neither was it occupied by troops.

Ahead of him was the American line. It would be a perimeter now. Obviously it was unbroken. The Second Platoon had not been penetrated. Couzens felt proud of that. They would be jittery, there in the line. They would shoot anything that moved. If they saw him at the foot of the street they'd know damn well he wasn't a ghost. They'd let him have it. Additionally, if he knew Mackenzie, Sam would be sending out a patrol. Sam never let the enemy rest, and Sam was never lax in his tactical intelligence. If the patrol found him, they'd shoot first and discover that he was an American lieutenant later.

So Raleigh Couzens decided, as a fact of survival, that he must spend the night in Ko-Bong, and approach Dog Company in the light of day. He ground out his cigarette and crept silently into the nearest doorway. Braced to spring, he illuminated the single room with his lighter.

A woman sleeping on a mattress of rags and straw, with a child curled under her arm, opened her eyes in quick terror. Before she could scream he lifted his finger to his lips in the signal for silence, and made a smile. The woman shut her mouth. She was a young woman. She was the same woman, he believed, that Beany Smith had tried to rape. He didn't move, for fear of frightening her into panic, and for a few seconds they examined each other. It seemed, then, that she understood she would not be hurt, for she motioned with her free arm towards the other side of the hut. There was a pallet there, empty. Once, no doubt, she had had a husband.

Couzens unbuttoned his parka, snapped off his lighter, and lay down. He couldn't get comfortable. There was a rock, or something, under him. He squirmed, and finally groped under the straw. His hand touched metal. He had found a gun. It was an M-1. He knew it from its contours, in the dark, as a man knows his wife. He brought it out from under him and flicked his lighter. The woman's eyes rolled in apprehension, but he was really smiling now and she relaxed. The gun was loaded. He was armed again. He was whole again. The fuel in his lighter would soon be gone, and he looked around the hut, and saw what he was seeking, a primitive brass lamp, and lit it and put his lighter back in his pocket.

Under the lamplight he saw that the gun was like his gun. It was filthy, yes. It had been dumped into the street's frozen mire, and fought over, and ground underfoot, and filthied. But wherever there was not filth, it shone like silver at a candlelit dinner party. Some Korean had found it after the fire fight of the previous night, and hidden it here. He found a rag hung on a nail, and a beer bottle half-filled with peanut oil, and went to work. The woman watched him in wonder, but at last her eyes closed, and she slept.

Whenever he touched the gun he thought of his home, for a gun was part of his home. A gun was what he remembered best of his father. It was before the dawn in Ko-Bong, so it would be yesterday's evening in Mandarin, and his mother would be watering the azaleas and hibiscus around the pool, and trimming the Australian pines that formed its backdrop. Now that he was gone, she had the duty. She would have stale bread for the bream in the pool, and balls of meat for his pet bass. Of course she couldn't catch frogs, and shiners, and live shrimp for the bass, as he had, but she would feed them efficiently.

Everyone agreed that his mother was a wonderful and brilliant woman, and a great beauty for her age. She played bridge like a man, with slashing bids of slam and double, and she was shrewd in real estate, and the price of fruit. She could speak fluently of the situation in Iran, and the new tax laws, and she called senators by their first names, but of her husband, who had killed himself with fine brandy, she never spoke at all. He was the blank in her life.

Raleigh Couzens wasn't sure whether he loved his mother, or hated her. He knew that only in the Marines had he escaped her, as he suspected his father could escape her only with alcohol.

And he blamed her, somehow, although his logic was amorphous and muddy, because he had lost his girl, his woman, Sue. His mother was always subtly sniping at Sue. It was that, he believed, that had caused their breach, really, although Sue hadn't said it that way. Sue had said, frankly and precisely, "Darling, when I want a toss in the hay I want it to be the real thing. And with us it isn't. You get all tense."

"No I don't."

"Yes, you do, Raleigh. You feel guilty about something."

And he'd protested, and called her dirty names, and Sue had been sweet to him, and told him to ask any good doctor. So he had. He'd asked several. They'd assured him it wasn't uncommon. For men in his social stratum, particularly in the South, where boys are carefully taught that there is a great difference between "nice girls" and "bad girls," it was more usual than unusual. He shouldn't worry. He'd outgrow it. But he hadn't, yet. He'd just joined up again, long before Korea. It had upset his mother, and she'd wept, and tried to bribe him with a trip to Europe. But once you volunteered, and were accepted, that was it.

And he continued to caress the rifle, and think of his home, and Sue, until the gray of the false dawn. It was better than thinking of the nightmare of his capture, and Colonel Chu.

When he knew there was sufficient light for him to be recognized—providing he got close enough to the outposts of Dog Company—he slipped out of the hut, and walked down the street of Ko-Bong. He passed the last house, and continued steadily until he knew he could be no more than two hundred yards from the line of foxholes, and knew that the machine guns, and the BAR's, and the Garands would be trained on him. Now that he was almost back, he felt miserable. He didn't give much of a damn whether they shot him or not, and he played with the idea of going straight in until someone said, "Fire!" But that wouldn't be fair to one of his friends. He shouted, "Hey there!"

One word cracked back, "Halt!"

"This is Couzens! Lieutenant Couzens!"

There was silence for a second, and then he recognized Sam Mackenzie's voice. "Come on in, Raleigh, you damn fool!"

Chapter Six

THE CAPTAIN had slept four hours, and when his field phone woke him, just before first light, he was fresh. "Signal from Regiment, sir," Ekland said. "Move out and join up at Hagaru. They've got a field hospital set up near the strip, and an air evac operating."

"Good," said Mackenzie. "Make a signal back. Tell 'em we can move at ten hundred hours. Tell 'em we've got twenty-four wounded."

"Twenty-two, sir," said Ekland.

Mackenzie knew that during the small hours two more had died. But those who lived would get out, if Dog Company got out. It was axiomatic, in the Marines, that you brought out your wounded. Sometimes it was costly. Sometimes it was not a fair trade. But it was a policy that helped make the Marines what they were. There was one certain thing in this world that a Marine could count on. He would not be abandoned by his buddies. "All right, twenty-two," said Mackenzie. He had to ask: "Who went?"

"Lieutenant Travis and Cohane, the corpsman."

"Too bad." The casualties among his lieutenants and

non-coms were distressingly high. This was always true. Always.

The captain rose, fully dressed, and picked up his carbine. There had been no new onslaught during the past night, and Dog Company was intact, but he hated to think of the good men he had lost. He suspected that the Chinese attack was a reconnaissance in force, or the objective may have been to capture the hydroelectric station. This they had done, although he had driven them out when daylight came. But they'd be back, and he was glad the move had been ordered. He could get the company out. He had sent a patrol into Ko-Bong during the night, and it was clear. Hagaru was only four miles to the south, and unless the Chinese had a block on the road, they'd make it easy. He might even punch through a block, if he could get air support, or an artillery barrage from the other end.

The captain checked his perimeter, and told his platoon leaders, and his sergeants, that the company was moving out. It was almost full light when he came to the Second Platoon, which had held the crucial point, the only road out, the night before, and had not been relieved since. It was just as he got there that the crew of a fifty-calibre machine gun swiveled the weapon, and waited, tense. On the road from the village, Mackenzie saw a figure walking, a figure with a rifle slung under his arm, insouciant as a hunter in the woods when the dogs range far.

"Nervy bastard, isn't he?" said the man squinting through the sights.

"Give him a squirt," said the loader.

"Naw. Wait'll he gets closer."

"You can knock him off from here. If you don't, somebody else will."

"Want to make sure."

"Sure of what?"

Mackenzie, behind them, said, "Hold your fire." He looked up and down the line of foxholes. Every gun was trained on this single figure. Mackenzie had a hunch that it might be a Chinese deserter, and deserters were valuable. "Hold your fire!" he called, louder. "Pass the word."

It was then that Couzens' first shout drifted down to the lines, and a minute later he had Couzens by the shoulders, and was beating him on the back, and shouting, "Where in hell have you been, you dope? Where've you been?"

"They jumped me in the village," Couzens said.

"I know. When the fighting started your men went up there after you. They found your three men, dead. They figured you were captured."

"I was."

"Well, then—"

"They turned me loose. They took me to their Army HQ, and tried to question me, and turned me loose."

The men of Couzens' platoon were now popping out of their foxholes, grinning, and crowding around them. "Get back where you ought to be," Mackenzie ordered. "You start bunching up and they'll lay a shell in here. They're watching us, you bet." He turned to Couzens. "They turned you loose? Why?"

"Beats me. Maybe they didn't want me. You should see how they operate. You should see how they move at night."

"We'll talk about that later," said Mackenzie. "We're moving out of this place. We're moving at ten hundred.

You got back just in time. You better come up to the CP, and get some chow, and help me get the stuff rolling. Everything's quiet this morning. It's been quiet ever since they hit us, that one time."

"What happened?" Couzens asked, as they walked along.

And Mackenzie told him what had happened. A detachment of Chinese had crossed the ice, using the white dress of Koreans as camouflage in the snow, and had fallen upon the squad bivouacked in the hydroelectric station, comfortable in their sleeping bags in the office on the ground floor, and probably not keeping a proper alert. "The gunnery sergeant was with them," Mackenzie said. "I didn't tell Kirby to take that detail, but he always picks a good, comfortable, dry place to sleep."

"What happened to Kirby?"

"He's dead."

"No!" It didn't seem possible that Sergeant Kirby would get killed in war. He was too old, and experienced, and careful.

"He couldn't get out of his sack. His zipper stuck. They bayoneted him, maybe twenty times."

"And the others?"

"One boy's alive. They shot him through the legs. He played dead."

"What happened then?" Couzens asked.

"It was more of a raid than anything else, as if they were after prisoners. This business across the ice wasn't much more than a diversion, and then they hit us frontally. Your platoon did real good. Your platoon counter-attacked. But when we went after that bunch in the plant, they were dug in, and we lost pretty heavily. Travis, Krakauskas, Phillips, and Scalpe dead. Simmons and Players wounded." All those he named were lieutenants, or sergeants. "Altogether, seventeen dead, twenty-two wounded."

"And prisoners?"

"You were the only prisoner."

Couzens didn't like the sound of it. He reviewed his interrogation by the commissar. He wondered what he had said that was wrong. If what he'd said was right enough, from the Chinese viewpoint, then it must have been wrong from the viewpoint of his own country. He was worried, and a little frightened. Some time he'd have to tell Mackenzie the whole story, and he was afraid it wouldn't sound right. He didn't think he'd be reprimanded or anything. After all, the important thing was that he was back in the line. But suppose he lost Mackenzie's confidence, and friendship?

Couzens, in the tent, began to gather up what he could take with him. Then he went out to check on the loadings for the Second Platoon, and the Third Platoon also, that had been the platoon of Travis. He relayed Mackenzie's orders that all vehicles be combat-loaded. Everything else would burn. He told the motor pool sergeant to start distributing gasoline for the burning.

Mackenzie sat at the table, and found the folder that contained the company records, and went over his roster, and carefully marked KIA, and the date, after the names of Travis and Cohane. And he scratched out the MIA he had written after the name of Raleigh Couzens. He'd heard rumors of the Chinese releasing prisoners, for propaganda purposes, or because of obscure oriental or Com-

119

munist reasons that nobody could fathom. But Raleigh Couzens wasn't one to fall for propaganda, and he wondered what had really happened. He also wondered when he'd have time to find out. It would be necessary to report the incident to Regiment. It was something for Military Intelligence—intelligence on a fairly high level. Raleigh was going to have to do a lot of talking, and perhaps some explaining.

He looked at the roster again. Seventeen dead, twenty-two wounded. He couldn't shake the feeling that it was his fault. He had fouled up. Oh, sure, the colonel had approved his dispositions. But whatever bad happened to a company, that was the responsibility of its captain, just as whatever happened to Regiment was the responsibility of the colonel. It was something you couldn't duck. He should have figured the Chinese would sneak across the ice, and hit the plant on the edge of the reservoir, and he should have had more men there.

Seventeen dead. Seventeen letters to write, when he got a chance. You couldn't be very original in those letters, because there always seemed to be so many of them, and everything that could be said in them, he had said before. He knew exactly what his pen would say. "Your husband was a fine officer, and an inspiration to his men. . . . I feel great personal loss. . . . Your son was liked by everyone in the company who knew him. . . . Your son was shot during a Chinese attack. He died painlessly." What a lie. Nobody died painlessly, not when you were twenty years old, or twenty-five, or even thirty, as he was. When you are young it always hurts to die.

A corporal, one of the cooks and the only fat man in Dog

Company, entered the CP. "What about the turkeys, sir?" he asked. "They've thawed. They've thawed fine, sir." In the fighting of the day before, of course, no one had thought of the turkeys.

"Burn 'em," Mackenzie said. He thought for a moment, and then amended this order. "On the way through the village, maybe you can drop off a case or two for the civilians."

"Yes, sir," said the corporal, his voice dreary, and he left, and Mackenzie was alone again.

He replaced the company roster in its folder, and shoved it down into his musette bag, alongside the bottle of Scotch, and the few personal possessions he carried there. There was an envelope stuffed with snapshots, and Mackenzie riffled through them, the way he often did when he was unhappy, or depressed. He came to a photograph of Anne, and Sam, junior, and himself, all united in a clinch at Hamilton Field, with a big Military Air Transport Service C-54 in the background. He examined its smallest detail, as a man often will when he possesses a picture with special meaning. The focus had been sharp, and Anne's clean features and the splendid line of her body seemed so alive that she'd move any second, although all you could see of the baby was a blob of nose and cheek, and his mop of blond curls.

It had been taken in the spring of 1948, during that thin slice of time when there was no fighting, and many people still spoke with confidence of peace, and everybody was getting on with business. In the photograph everybody was smiling, and nobody, not even Anne's mother, had guessed they'd had quite an argument at breakfast.

He had been ordered to Parris Island, to train boots, and Anne wasn't going with him. At first she'd said she couldn't go because of the baby, and then she'd said, "Sam, I'm just damn sick and tired of moving, and trailing you around the country. Why don't you get out of it?"

"Get out of what?"

"The Marines."

"I thought you liked it?"

"I did. I don't any more. I want to settle down. We're always moving, moving, moving. I want a home of our own. I'm tired of renting. I want some security. We owe it to the baby. You can make more money, outside."

"Doing what?"

She set down her coffee cup and said, "Well, for one thing, writing." An article on firepower had been printed in the *Marine Corps Gazette,* and he'd sold an eight-line piece of verse to *The Saturday Evening Post,* and he'd written a short story which had been rejected by eight magazines, but by three of them not very emphatically.

Sam laughed. "Well, if what you want is security, we'd better keep on taking the King's Shilling. Anne, this is a welfare state. Understand, I'm all for the welfare state. I think it's the greatest invention since sex. Look at what we get out of it. Medical care free, or almost, and cheap cigarettes and whiskey, and you can buy stuff from ships' stores at just about half price. But it isn't available to writers. When they make it available to writers, I'll quit the Marines, and be a writer."

"Stop being silly, Sam. I'm serious."

"I'm not being silly at all. Look at this egg." He pointed his knife at his breakfast egg, cozy in its cup. "I just read in the paper that for every egg eaten at breakfast the government buys another egg that nobody wants to eat. The government buys these eggs by the billions, powders 'em, and buries 'em underground, like the gold in Fort Knox. Who pays for that egg nobody eats? Taxpayers. Writers."

"You are too being silly, Sam."

"I am not either. The government has to buy eggs, transport 'em, pulverize 'em, process 'em, package 'em, and bury 'em. That costs a lot of money. Then there must be overhead, like a Bureau of Unwanted Eggs, or something. That's right, isn't it?"

"Well, then, don't eat the darn egg!" Anne said, angrily.

He decapitated his egg with a butter knife, and dug into it. "That wouldn't do any good," he said. "If I didn't eat it, then the government would just have to buy one more egg."

"Sam, you majored in literature, not economics."

"It doesn't take an economist to see what's happening. Look at potatoes. Up in Aroostook County, Maine, they're paying planters sixty-five millions a year to dig up potatoes, and paint 'em blue, because nobody wants to eat them."

Anne looked at him suspiciously.

"Now, if the government would just treat sonnets like potatoes, I'd quit the Marines and be a writer. I don't see why the government doesn't. What's a potato got that a sonnet hasn't got, if nobody wants to buy either sonnets or potatoes?"

"You don't have to write sonnets. You can write articles, or stories."

"I'll tell you when I'll quit the Marines and go to writ-

ing," he said. "Just as soon as the government pays me a
five thousand dollar advance on a book—providing I don't
write it, or gives me ninety percent of parity for not writing articles and stories. Parity, of course, will be the top
magazine price, plus twenty percent."

She laughed, finally, but she hadn't followed him East.
When he got back to the Coast, after three months, they
started talking about a house in Los Altos, not far from her
parents' home. They drew plans for it. The plan increased
in size in ratio to their dream, and the cost of building
materials kept pace. So it hadn't been built, and a shooting war had come.

Mackenzie slipped the photographs back into his musette bag. And now he was moving again, just when he
thought it was over. Well, he'd made his decision, back
there that spring morning in forty-eight. Perhaps it had
been a bad decision, but it was done, gone, past. Mackenzie called Ekland and said, "Bring your jeep over here. I'm
riding with you." He wanted to be in the radio jeep, in
case they ran into a block, and he had to ask for artillery or
air in a hurry.

Mackenzie lined up his column carefully. In the lead he
placed a jeep with a fifty-seven millimeter recoilless gun
mounted, and behind that a jeep with a fifty-calibre machine gun, and the radio jeep was third in line, and a
weapons carrier with a squad of riflemen and a bazooka,
fourth. Behind this point, sufficient for swift assault, he
put his six-by-sixes, two of them loaded with the wounded.
The other jeeps, and weapons carriers, were strung out
behind, with the rest of his heavy machine guns at the tail
of the column.

Dog Company began to roll out, and the squad he had assigned to burn the camp went to work with the jericans of gasoline. As they reached the village he stood up in the jeep and looked back. Flame and black smoke were shooting up from what had been the bivouac at Ko-Bong. Sherman had said it all, he thought, in three words. But then Sherman had been a captain, too. Sherman had been a company commander for a long time. Sherman knew.

As the column moved ahead, it began to snow again, at first only a few vagrant flakes, so he hoped the fall would not be heavy. Then the snowflakes grew smaller and more numerous, and the wind rose, so that Kato and Vermillion, the captain's runner, huddled down in the back seat. Somewhere in the distance artillery was thumping. "If that's their stuff," Mackenzie said to Ekland, who was driving, "at least they won't have direct observation—not with this snow."

"They're 105's," said Ekland. "They're ours. I can tell."

"I know they're 105's," said Mackenzie, "but that doesn't make them ours. The Nationalists surrendered plenty of them, back on the mainland."

"And they've captured more," said Ekland, "since this thing started in June. They got 'em from the South Koreans, and they got 'em from us too. Still, I think these are ours, just from the way they're firing. They just sound right."

Mackenzie listened closely, and agreed, and the firing grew louder, and presently they approached the battery. There were four guns, with Marines firing white phosphorus into the boondocks of a distant hill. Mackenzie had Ekland pull the jeep out of line, and they stopped for a moment and talked to the battery's captain. This captain said that as far as he knew the road into Hagaru was clear. They should turn to the right at the next crossroads. This captain said the hills were crawling with Chinese, and he would be glad to get back to Hagaru himself. He said that if they had wounded they would find the field hospital in the center of the town. The air strip was all the way through the town, and a bit to the south.

Mackenzie thanked this battery captain, and Ekland raced and bumped along the side of the road until the jeep was back in column. They reached the crossroads, and turned, and came to a Bailey bridge over a narrow stream locked in ice. There was an MP on the bridge. He looked good to Mackenzie. He was a sign of regimental authority, and strength. When you saw an MP, you weren't isolated any more.

The column passed three blocks of shot-up houses, and its center then came to a halt beside a building with a Red Cross flag stretched over the doorway. Mackenzie went inside, and found a medic, tired, harassed, wearing a bloody apron as if he worked in a butcher shop. "I've got twenty-two wounded," Mackenzie said.

"They been given penicillin, or aureomycin?" the medic asked.

"My corpsmen took care of them."

"Then you'd better get them out of here. You'd better get them on the air evac. We're full up. We're full up and then some." He hesitated, looking at Mackenzie. "Of course, if your corpsmen don't think they can make the trip. It's only two hours—"

"You'd better talk to my pharmacist's mate."

"Okay."

The Navy doctor, and the pharmacist's mate talked together for a while, professionally, and then the doctor said, "They'll all make it."

The column moved on, until they came to the air strip. Mackenzie took a good look at the strip. "It looks like a roller coaster," he said to Ekland.

"Those C-47's," Ekland said. "They can land anywhere. They're old, but they're good."

Planes were coming in, loading, and taking off through the snow. As his trucks filled with his wounded rolled up to the strip, Mackenzie timed the planes. One every ten minutes. He got out of his jeep, and watched to see that his wounded were gently handled. His wounded had to wait in line behind other wounded, and while they waited they were tagged, and checked by a doctor. Once in a while, when a man groaned, the doctor, or a nurse, bent over him with alcohol-soaked cotton and a hypodermic. All the medical people looked as if they were stumbling about in their sleep. Dog Company wasn't the only outfit that had had a bad time.

Mackenzie moved among the litters. "Tokyo," he said to some, "in two hours." And to others, who were worse hit, he said, "Tokyo, bud—and then maybe home."

Some of them, he knew, would be back home in two or three days, but most of them would soon be back in the line. In this war one wound wasn't enough. One wound would give you a week's convalescence, and perhaps another week's leave, and play, in Japan. And that was about all a man could hope for. Modern surgery was a wonderful thing.

That night Dog Company, by Battalion orders, dug in to protect the north end of the Hagaru air strip. Regiment wanted to keep the strip open as long as possible. The spearhead of the regiment was already moving south through Koto-Ri. Their battalion would be last to leave, and Dog Company, after passing through Koto-Ri, would have its mission on the secondary road, and pass under regimental command. This had not changed.

In the morning Chinese guns found the air strip. They were heavy guns, about 170's, Mackenzie guessed. But they were conserving ammunition, as usual, and while the strip was cratered in places, planes continued to land, and take off with the wounded. Finally the medical unit from the field hospital came down to the strip, and Mackenzie knew Hagaru was gone, and soon he must take the company on to Koto-Ri.

The snow had stopped falling, and apparently American counter-battery had found the Chinese guns, for they stopped too, and Mackenzie checked his vehicles, and then called in his officers, and his non-coms, to tell them what they might expect in the day. There was a lieutenant missing, and Mackenzie could not sort out which one it was, until he saw Sellers limping towards them, his face twisted, and his forearms outstretched. Mackenzie recalled that this was the first time he had seen Sellers since they left Ko-Bong.

When Sellers came closer, the captain saw that the hands at the ends of the forearms were blackened, frozen lumps. "I lost my gloves, sir," Sellers said. Sellers' face was shining with pain, or fear.

"You lost your gloves!" It was incomprehensible. A man

could no more lose his gloves than he could lose his hands, for if you lost your gloves there was a pretty good chance that in this cold you would lose your hands. And there were spare gloves. Mackenzie had always insisted on that, just as he insisted there be enough dry, clean socks so that every man could change morning and night. So it was not only incomprehensible; it was impossible.

Mackenzie's face was bleak as the sky, bleak as the ground at his feet. He started to speak, and then choked back the words. Sellers was a coward. Sellers was a malingerer. Sellers was a traitor to them all. What the captain started to say he did not say. All he did was point his finger at a C-47, loading, and say, "All right, get aboard!" And Sellers hurried away.

Mackenzie looked from one to the other of the silent faces in the semi-circle around him, and he said, "I'll shoot the next man who loses his gloves!"

And he turned his back on them all.

Chapter Seven

DOG COMPANY WAS relieved at noon that day, and pulled out. Battalion had messaged it was now situated in Koto-Ri. Division had assigned a battery—probably the one Dog Company had passed on the road from Ko-Bong—and two companies from another regiment, retreating along the track from Yudam-ni, to guard the Hagaru strip as long as feasible. Regiment wanted Dog Company to take up its mission at once, for Regiment, with its heavy equipment, was moving towards the coast, and needed protection on its northern flank.

Now Mackenzie placed the radio jeep at the head of the column. There was a maze of local roads around the strip, and only one of these was certainly clear and led to the main road south to Koto-Ri. Mackenzie had memorized a map of the area. It would not do to get on the wrong road. If they got on the wrong road, they would undoubtedly encounter guerrillas, and probably mines. Mackenzie hated mines. They were treacherous, impersonal, robot killers. You could not shoot back at a mine.

As the lead jeep bounced along, Sergeant Ekland noticed how morose Mackenzie was, how his long chin was tucked deep inside his parka, and how his eyes, usually so alert, so all-seeing, now seemed inattentive, and dulled as if by illness. Of course Ekland knew the reason for this. It is a terrible thing for a captain to discover that one of his lieutenants has bugged out, although Ekland, and most of the men of Dog Company, had known that Sellers was yellow. They had known it all the time.

Almost always, Ekland thought, the men knew a lot more about their officers than the officers knew about each other, or themselves. The men could, and did, observe and discuss their officers dispassionately; while officers' opinion of other officers was colored by rank and seniority, friendships and small jealousies, their manners at the poker table, the social graces of their wives, and the presumption that they were all born gentlemen, and all born brave.

Even so perceptive a captain as Mackenzie might not notice the flaw in Sellers, because that flaw was concealed when the captain was around. And when things got rugged, the captain and Sellers were always in different places. When Dog Company rested out of reach of the enemy, Sellers was everywhere, the busiest, most active, most talkative officer in the command. But when there was fighting, it was impossible to find him. Sellers' patrician New England nostrils could sense danger far off, as birds sense an approaching storm and take flight. Sellers couldn't openly bug out. That would mean court-martial and public disgrace, which for a fearful, hollow man can be worse than death. Sellers was ingenious, and smart, and energetic, and he used all these qualities to insure himself safe duty in the safest place. He had discovered that Dog

Company needed a liaison officer with a battalion of heavy artillery, Long Toms, set so deep in the perimeter that it could not be reached by enemy fire. At the Inchon landing, Sellers remained on the LST, to be certain all their gear reached shore, while Dog Company fought the T-34 tanks on the edge of Seoul. And when the first Chinese counter-attack came, the month before, Sellers had volunteered to race back to Regiment, in an escorted jeep, to help map the enemy deployment.

All these things the men noticed, and discussed, and it was strange that the captain never noticed them, the captain who could smell an unkempt gun barrel at twenty paces. It must have been humiliating to the captain, this business of the frozen hands. Company officers are fused together by the intimacy of war, the intimacy of those who sleep, wash, and eat and face death together for a long period of time. The captain must have felt as if one of his younger brothers had been proved a forger. Ekland felt sorry for the captain.

The captain raised his chin and said, "Don't take the right fork. Keep straight."

"Yes, sir." Ekland wondered what created a coward. There was a difference between being a coward, and being afraid. Ekland always sweated with tenseness, and nervousness, when they moved into battle, and when they were pinned down and shells were coming in he was almost paralyzed. He'd spoken to Molly about this fear, frankly, and she'd said, "John, don't ever let it worry you. Only a moron wouldn't be afraid when he was in danger of losing his life." For a girl her age she was awfully smart, Molly. She completed him. He needed her, all the time.

He'd always been able to control his fear, and not run. And once a fire fight started, and he was actually doing something, even something routine like encoding a plea for artillery, or sending out co-ordinates to the guns, then his fear miraculously vanished. A man wasn't afraid when there was a job to do, and a man took pride in doing a good job, whether it was hitching up the network to the stations, in Chicago, or keeping Dog Company in touch with Battalion, or digging gooks out of a cave with a flame-thrower. And there was another kind of pride, the pride of being in the First Division, with all its history; the pride of Regiment, and Battalion, and Company. A company was like a baseball team. One bad or lazy player could make the difference. Only a very selfish man would let down his company, so Ekland concluded Sellers must have been a spoiled and selfish man. Right now Sellers was safe in Japan, and in a few weeks he'd be back home, wearing ribbons. Ekland knew of self-inflicted wounds, and once he had seen a man incongruously blow out his brains in desperate fear of death, but getting yourself frostbitten was a shrewd and subtle way out. Nobody could prove frostbite was self-inflicted.

Far ahead of them Ekland saw another jeep approaching, behaving erratically. It swerved into the shallow ditch and a man piled out and scrambled under it. Ekland thought he heard the hiss of a burp gun, and then he saw thin gouts of flame from the second floor window of a house on the other side of the road from the jeep. He tramped down hard with his right foot, and the tires spun in the snow, and then gripped, and they lunged forward.

"What the hell?" said Mackenzie.

"Sniper," said Ekland, keeping his eyes on the window, and the road. "Got him marked."

Mackenzie put his carbine in his lap.

When their jeep was a hundred yards from the house Ekland braked, and grabbed his BAR from the rack on the dash. "Cover me," he said. "The window on this side, second floor. Kato, grenades for you."

Ekland hit the ground, running and doubled over, and left the road, with Vermillion and Kato behind him. Mackenzie followed, the butt of his carbine cradled in his elbow, like a boar hunter fascinated by the skill of his catch dogs. Nobody had to tell them what to do. They were good. They were pros.

This house, with cracked and flaking plaster walls, on the outskirts of Hagaru, like most Korean two-story houses, had no windows except in front, and so they rushed its blind side. They deployed in the shelter of the wall. Vermillion backed cautiously into the street, and as soon as the window was in his sights, he began to fire, methodically, to keep the sniper down. Mackenzie joined him, his carbine at his shoulder, to take up the covering fire when Vermillion changed magazines, and to watch the other window, and the door. Kato appeared, careful not to obstruct their fire, drew back his arm, and lobbed a grenade through the window with the smooth, easy motion of a warm-up pitch. While the grenade was still in the air, he turned and ran, in case the grenade should miss, and bounce from the wall. He had never missed, but some day he might. With the grenade's explosion, Ekland raced around the corner of the house, and through the door. Mackenzie heard four short bursts from the BAR, and then Ekland came out of the house, examining the breech of his weapon. "There were two of them," Ekland said. "Koreans, I guess."

The man under the jeep now crawled out, a pistol dangling from his hand. Mackenzie turned to Kato and Vermillion. "You two men go back and get the transport moving," he ordered.

The man with the pistol said, "Thanks. Pretty inadequate, isn't it—thanks?" He was a chunky man, older than a Marine at the front should be, and Mackenzie could tell from the condition of his boots and his greatcoat, and by the fact that he carried a pistol, that he was fresh from the States. A forty-five was not much use in this war.

"You hurt?" Mackenzie asked.

"No. They got a tire. That's all, I guess." They glanced at the jeep. There was a semi-circle of small round holes in the steel. "Not quite all," the man said. "I suppose you're Dog Company." He looked closely at Mackenzie. "You must be Mackenzie. Heard of you at Division CP. I'm on Division Staff. I'm Major Toomey."

"I'll have my men in the tail jeep change your tire, major. They can catch up with us."

"That's damn nice of you. I think I'd just as soon be shot as change a tire in this cold. I'm not exactly acclimatized."

"California?" said Mackenzie.

"Yes. San José."

"Los Altos," said Mackenzie.

"Do you know the Woodruffs?"

"Jim Woodruff? Sure. Lives on the Saratoga Road."

"Small world."

"Getting no bigger. What's the poop at Division?"

Major Toomey frowned. "Not very good. Not very good

at all. Navy's got a lot of ships at Hungnam, and more are coming in every day. We haven't been told yet, officially, but I think there's going to be an evacuation. I think there will have to be an evacuation."

Ekland, who had been listening, said, "Gee-sus!"

"You mean the whole Division?" said Mackenzie. It didn't sound believable. Only a few days before, the war had been over, and won, and now they were talking about evacuating the Division.

"The whole Corps, I should think," said Major Toomey. "Maybe the whole Army, the whole works."

Mackenzie drew in one long breath, and let it out with a whistle, but he made no comment. He could understand, because of the gap between Ten Corps and Eighth Army, that Corps might have to pull back into a perimeter around Hamhung, the industrial city, and Hungnam, its port. Certainly Corps could hold a beachhead perimeter, with all its artillery, and Navy big guns and the carriers, and all the air. What had happened? Were the Russians coming in, or what?

The communications jeep had now drawn abreast of them. Mackenzie sent Vermillion back down the line with orders about the major's jeep. Kato slipped into the back seat. Mackenzie saluted Toomey, as line officers often do when they encounter Staff, and said, "Glad to have met you, major."

Major Toomey smiled, returned the salute, and said, "I was gladder to meet you, and your sergeant here. Any time you're in San José—"

"Right. I'll drop around for a drink."

"Name's in the phone book. Toomey."

"I won't forget."

"Be seeing you, Mackenzie."

The column moved again. John Ekland, at the wheel of the jeep, had not ever been so cold—so cold, and frightened, and miserable. What in hell had happened to the United States? What in hell was happening when a bunch of gooks and Chinks could lick the United States?

If everybody bugged out on Korea, it didn't take a general or a genius to predict the final result. The United States had most of its infantry, and all its Marines, fighting these gooks in Korea, and if that Army fled and evacuated, and came back home with its tail between its legs, then the whole world would know that the United States couldn't hold Berlin or Vienna, or the line of the Elbe, or the Dardanelles, or the oil fields of the Middle East. It couldn't hold Japan, or maybe even England. They'd all be back inside their own borders, like squawking turkeys in a pen, waiting while the butcher sharpened his knife. "Like Thanksgiving Day turkeys," Ekland said aloud.

"Too bad about the turkeys," said Mackenzie.

"Yes, sir. Too bad about the turkeys."

And when the butcher was ready, when he was completely ready, he'd drop it on them. He'd certainly drop one—perhaps three or five—on Chicago. Maybe he'd aim for the Merchandise Mart, which was an excellent central location, or maybe he'd aim for the University, and its atomic research labs, where Molly worked. Ekland spit through the spokes of the wheel, as if to get a bad taste out of his mouth.

"What's the matter, sergeant?" asked Mackenzie. "Feel bad?"

"Sort of."

"It's tough when you have to kill somebody close up. Even a gook."

"Yes, sir."

"Makes you feel like a murderer. I know. You have to rationalize it. You have to get over it. It was either you, or them."

"I know, sir. It's either us, or them." If they had to pull out of Korea it was going to be us. Ekland was sure of that. He evaluated the future in the terms of his own experience. That's the way everybody thought of World War No. 3. It was natural. It was the only way it could be.

When a banker thought of atomic bombs on Manhattan, or in the river between the bridges and over the tunnels, he considered the dead and the maimed and the fire storms and millions of people clawing their way into the countryside, sure. But because of his indoctrination, and his profession, naturally he thought most of the financial chaos. He considered the billions in paper securities that would be irretrievably lost. Today a safety deposit box. Tomorrow an oven. He was shaken by the thoughts of accounts destroyed, and loans and mortgages never to be traced or repaid, and important clients missing in a cloud of atomic dust, and the gutting of Wall Street and the elimination of the Stock Exchange.

A doctor considered it differently. He thought of the helpless in the hospitals, burning, and no way to get them out. He thought of the splendid equipment, purchased by public contribution or painstakingly squeezed from state funds, wrecked and lost. He thought of oceans of plasma, and rivers of whole blood, and carloads of antibiotics and miles of bandages. He thought of the skin grafts they'd need, and couldn't get. You can't buy skin like rolls of wallpaper, but that's the way it would be needed.

A real estate man had to be real hep, come an atomic bomb. And he ought to prepare for it, in advance. He ought to sell in the cities, and buy the countryside, but with care. For instance, Seattle was finished. They could hit Seattle like snapping your fingers. Places like Miami and New Orleans were safe, unless, of course, they delivered their bombs via snorkel subs and guided missiles. Then Miami and New Orleans were finished too. One sure rule was Back to the Land. The ideal investment was a modern producing farm within commuting distance of a metropolitan area, and with its own water supply and generator. If the generator could be run by water power, and the house used solar heat, then the setup was perfect. For an ideal place like that, you could get three thousand an acre, and probably twenty-seven five for the house, if it had two baths and was liveable.

John Ekland considered it in terms of radio, and communications. When the butcher came, everybody who had relatives in New York, and Chicago, and L.A., and Washington would instantly pick up the telephone and call long distance to find out if they were safe. The telephone system would be screwed up beyond belief. He also suspected that the military lines, and Army and Navy radio, would be so overloaded by local commanders, and self-centered National Guard generals, that they would be useless for days.

And radio! Ekland would not like to be at the NBC control switches on A-Day, even if Chicago wasn't hit, which it certainly would be. If Orson Welles could scare the wits out of the country by talking about Men from Mars, what would happen when atomic bombs from Russia actually landed? First thing, of course, was that all the network stations would immediately be off the air. The listeners wouldn't hear any explosion. All they'd hear would be a click, and then nothing. Nothing at all. They'd think the power was off, and in the metropolitan centers it probably would be. But in other, smaller places they'd start turning the dial, and they'd pick up some local station, and listen to the usual hillbilly music and three commercials each quarter hour, and while they might wonder what had happened to the networks, it would all be normal—for a small space of time. Then a disk jockey would say:

"We interrupt this program—"

Ekland looked ahead, and saw a crossroads. Tanks were moving on the main road. They looked solid, good.

"We interrupt this program to bring you an AP news flash from Tarrytown, New York, by way of Poughkeepsie. There has been a tremendous explosion in the New York area. The Tarrytown chief-of-police believes it may have been an atomic bomb. We will have more details later."

Then the local station would go on, playing Flatfoot Boogie, or whatever, and the disk jockey would bespeak the qualities of Surf, The Boston Store, and Hadacol. Then, in his smooth, emasculated voice, "It seems that the news is true. There has been attack on a number of cities on both coasts. I have just called the mayor. He assures me there is no cause for alarm."

And then? Then the next amphibious landing of the Marines would be in Alaska, if Americans had the guts to shake off the shock of a hundred Pearl Harbors, and rise from the ashes of their cities. John Ekland could not see his own life clearly in this foreboding, for when he put on uniform again, he had renounced the privilege of making his own decisions. He'd be a sergeant, somewhere. That was all he knew for sure.

When they came to the main road, an MP raised his hand and stopped Dog Company. "I'll let you in here as soon as this mob of tanks passes through," he told the captain.

"Okay," the captain said. The MP would not break into a battalion of tanks to let an infantry company into line, even if Mackenzie told him they had an important combat mission. There wasn't any use arguing with an MP. An MP was the law.

There was something eerie, something wrong, about the way this tank battalion moved, and for a time Mackenzie could not put his finger on it. Then he knew. You might call this movement a breakout, or an attack in another direction, but fundamentally it was a retreat. Whenever you abandon ground to the enemy, it is retreat, however words coat and oil it, and there is a special sound to American troops in retreat. It is their wordlessness, their silence. All the sounds Mackenzie could hear were mechanical. All he could hear was the grinding of the tank treads on the ice and frozen ground, and the rumble of engines. It was as if the men were hypnotized, and the tanks retreated of themselves.

There was no shouting. There were no commands. There

were no wisecracks, or jokes, passed from tank to tank. The tank commanders stood in the ports of their turrets, their faces as impassive and gray as their armor. In their football-type helmets, each looked like a halfback who has just been taken out of the game, with his team three touchdowns behind. As the tanks passed Mackenzie, none of the commanders waved, and few of them even looked.

"Bow-wow!" shouted Vermillion. "Dog-faces!"

Mackenzie saw four tired men, two of them weaponless, jouncing on the back of one of the tanks. He recognized them as GI's, probably from the Seventh Division, hitchhiking to the sea. Mackenzie turned on Vermillion. "Shut up!" he said.

The last Pershing passed, and the MP blew his whistle, exactly like a traffic cop back home, and waved Dog Company into the procession.

The column moved at seven, sometimes four or five miles an hour, and Mackenzie fretted, but there was nothing he could do about it. That was the trouble with the American Army. It was conceived and designed in gasoline-land, lavishly painted with four- and eight-lane superhighways, where every hamlet was connected with its neighbor by a faultless strip of concrete or macadam, where if one road was blocked you could always use three alternate routes, and there were gasoline pumps always around the next bend. The men who designed the mobile equipment of the Army could not wholly shake their environment and tradition, even when they suspected the Army might have to fight in countries where hard-surfaced, all-weather roads were few. Like Jugoslavia. Like Iran. Like China. Like Korea. Maybe like Russia. There were only a few places in the world where the mechanized United States Army could fight with maximum efficiency. One of them was Germany, which it had proved. Another was the United States. What was needed in Korea were mules. Mackenzie had heard of the Army mule, but he had never seen one. He wondered what had happened to the mule.

Ahead Mackenzie saw the arms of the tank commanders fly up, one by one, in the signal for halt, and the column halted. "What's cooking?" he yelled ahead.

The tanker lifted both hands, palms up. "Don't know. They'll pass the word."

At this point Dog Company rested on the crest of a hill, and the line of tanks wormed downward before Mackenzie, so he could see the progress of the word, as the face of each tanker flashed back, and up. Finally the tank ahead got the word, and the tank commander turned to Mackenzie and shouted, "Road block. Chinks. Pass the word."

Mackenzie passed the word to the jeep behind, where a kid named Nick Tinker was swinging the fifty-seven recoilless around, like a small boy with a Roy Rogers pistol. He heard Ostergaard, the big, placid Swede driving this jeep behind, pass the word.

Mackenzie considered this wait ridiculous. It was absolutely stupid and ridiculous that a powerful formation of tanks should be stopped by a road block. There was firing ahead, about two miles, he guessed from the sound. He could hear a tank's high-velocity gun laying it in, and the dull thud of mortars which were probably Chinese mortars, and the dueling of machine guns. From the sound he judged that not more than two tanks were in action. This was a shame, but this wasn't tank country. On the right the tanks were barred by the cliff, and on the left they dared not venture across country, for fear they would crush through the ice formed over the paddy fields, and mire in the slush below. The tanks could not deploy, as tanks should, and race across country to take the enemy on the flank and rear. The tanks were chained to the road.

What was needed here was infantry. Mackenzie estimated the road. The Pershings and the Pattons stood astride of it so that not even a jeep could pass on either side. They had to move over. They had to get close to the rock. If they did that, he could bring his jeeps into action, his jeeps and his foot soldiers. "Vermillion," he ordered his runner, "you go on back and tell everybody but the drivers of the six-by-sixes, and the weapons carriers, that I want 'em. Right now! Tell 'em to hit the ground and move up. I want every bazooka man. Every one. And I want the jeeps."

Vermillion tumbled out, and Mackenzie yelled back at Ostergaard, "All jeeps follow me. Pass the word."

Then he turned on the tank commander in front of him. "Move that big bastard over!"

The tank commander stared back, surprised and uncertain.

"You heard me! Move it over!"

The tank commander said something into his mouthpiece, and the tank grated to the side of the road.

That was the way Mackenzie got Dog Company to the point of the Battalion. It was slow. It was tedious. It required much cursing, and excursions into the ditches. But eventually he came to a place where two tanks were firing. There was still another tank ahead of these two, but it was burning, and had slewed athwart the road. At regular intervals enemy mortar shells arrived, bursting around the burning tank. The road was efficiently interdicted, and part of Division was cut off.

Ekland stopped the jeep at what he considered a safe distance behind the two engaged tanks. Mackenzie said, "Think the ice on those paddy fields will hold our jeeps, sergeant?"

"Oh, yes, sir. Sure. I'm not sure the ice wouldn't hold the tanks."

"I guess their Battalion commander knows more about that. Those things weigh almost fifty tons. They go through the ice and they're finished. Tell you what we're going to do, sergeant. We're going to make a sweep. We're going to flank 'em. We're going to use the jeeps like cavalry."

"Very light cavalry," said Ekland.

"Very light indeed," said the captain. "But anything's better than sticking here. Pretty soon the Chinese will get wise. They'll find out we're stopped cold here, and they'll bring up some heavy guns, and we'll never get out. You and I are going to stay right here, sergeant. This will be the CP. The platoons have got walkie-talkies. We'll operate by walkie-talkie. You be my talker."

"Yes, sir," Ekland said. He brought the walkie-talkie from its case, and called in the platoons.

"Tell 'em I want a bazook on every jeep," said Mackenzie. "Tell 'em the jeeps are going to move off the road at an angle. The jeeps are going to do a left oblique, if they remember what that is. And when they're all deployed they're going to do a right oblique, and charge. The riflemen will follow the jeeps, and the machine-gun and mortar platoon is going to cover, if it sees anything to shoot at."

Ekland told them.

Mackenzie rummaged for his field glasses, and found them, and stood up on the seat, and swept the terrain a mile distant. Close to where the shells from the Pershings were bursting he saw what he believed to be the top of the turret of an enemy tank. A tank, naturally, would be the core of a road block. It was probably immobile, dug in. Behind the tank he saw no evidence of the enemy, but they were there. Mortar shells spoke their presence. "They've got a tank up there," he said. "You tell the platoons they're each to have two bazookas on that tank."

Ekland told them.

Mackenzie looked back over his shoulder and he motioned to Ostergaard to come up, and when Ostergaard came up he said, "I've got a special job for you with that mounted fifty-seven. I don't think that fifty-seven is a damn bit of good against all that turret armor. But when I give the word, you light out of here, but you stay behind the other jeeps, and open fire on that tank up there." He gave Ostergaard his glasses, and pointed, until Ostergaard too saw the turret.

"I see it, sir," Ostergaard said. "But what am I going to do with it?"

"You won't do anything with it," said the captain. "All you'll do is distract their fire, so the bazookas can slip in with a Sunday punch. Who's your gunner?"

"Well, that kid, Tinker, is our gunner, since we lost our gunner back to Ko-Bong."

"Can he shoot?"

"I guess so, sir. He says so. He brags he's an expert."

"Okay, let him shoot. Now look, Ostergaard, any time you think they've zeroed in on you, you move."

"Don't worry. I'll move, sir."

Ostergaard went back to his own jeep. Mackenzie said, "Okay, sergeant, tell them to get going."

Ekland spoke into his walkie-talkie, using the code name for Dog Company. "This is Lightning Four. This is Lightning Four Forward. Take off!"

Mackenzie watched as his jeeps swerved out on the frozen plain, with the brown stubble of last season's rice crop poking through the ice. There were only eleven jeeps, in the beginning, and they hadn't made their turn towards the Chinese block when there were only ten, because a shell from the Chinese tank found one. "This isn't in the book," Mackenzie said. "This may be all wrong."

"This isn't a book war," said Ekland. "Right, sergeant, but that won't help if I lose my company." Mackenzie noticed that a red beard had been sprouting on Ekland's chin since Ko-Bong, and that this beard was now stiff, like toothbrush bristles.

"You can call it a calculated risk," said Ekland.

"Captains don't take calculated risks," said Mackenzie. "Captains just make mistakes." A general could take a calculated risk. If it was successful, he wouldn't call it a risk, later. It would be a well-planned operation. If he failed, it was a calculated risk.

A cascade of mortar bombs enveloped another jeep, and when the brown smoke drifted away, that jeep was on its back, its wheels slowly spinning. Then the advancing infantry platoons walked through the mortar fire. They walked into it, and out again, but there were not so many of them walking out.

The two tanks ahead—the only tanks that could bring their guns to bear—now increased their rate of fire. Whoever was in command, in the lead tank, saw what the infantry was doing, and was co-operating as best he could. In the face of the burning tank, blocking the road, and the plaguing, dug-in targets ahead, he was almost helpless. But if somebody was sweeping the flank, he'd pour in his shells, and hope for a lucky hit. At least, he could keep the enemy partially occupied.

It is not often that a commander can watch the progress of a battle with clarity, as if it were a panorama that moved, and made sounds, and for the first time in his life this moment came to Mackenzie. Ordinarily a battle was confusion, and sudden noises close by, and the isolation that comes when you can see only a few of your men. But now he watched, not as comfortable as if he sat in an armchair before a television set, but with the same critical detachment. They're going too far out into the paddy, he thought. "Tell 'em right wheel," he said to Ekland.

"Lightning Four, right wheel!" Ekland said into the mesh of his microphone, and repeated the order, again and again.

The jeeps continued ahead. Mackenzie guessed the platoon leaders had missed the signal, or were too engrossed in their jobs to listen. It was probably simpler. Probably, it was just too noisy out there. From here in, Mackenzie knew, he could not influence the course of battle. He had committed his force in an unorthodox and desperate enterprise, and he was helpless. So he tried to concentrate on watching, through his glasses.

One of the jeeps stopped, and he recognized it, from its silhouette, as the one with the recoilless gun. He watched this gun begin to fire, and turned his glasses on the target, infinitesimal from this distance. He saw a flash of red, and a puff of white smoke, either on the turret, or very close. That kid, Tinker, was shooting good.

But the tank was still firing, and he lost another jeep. He lost the jeep with the gun. He didn't see the hit, but the jeep was overturned. The other jeeps spread in a semi-circle around the enemy's position. That was the way he had hoped they would operate, the way he would have ordered it had his communications been adequate. The men had never attempted such a maneuver before, nor was it anything you learned at Parris Island or Quantico. In military jargon it would be called initiative. Actually, it was as instinctive and simple as small boys spreading out for a pass in their first game of touch football. Mackenzie felt proud of his men. They could operate without the coach.

The Chinese would be frantic. Their high velocity gun would find the targets moving, spread out, difficult. Mackenzie watched tiny figures spill out of the jeeps, disappear, and appear again, always closer to the tank turret. Then he saw, clearly, the double-ended red spears of bazookas, firing, and the sound of explosions different from the crack of guns drifted back to him. Now his infantry was in the Chinese position, and beyond, and Mackenzie laid his glasses in his lap. "They made it," he said.

"I didn't think they could do it," said Ekland. "But I

heard the bazooks. Wonder how many bazooka men we lost?"

"Maybe one. At the most two. Maybe none," said Mackenzie. "They played it just right. Somebody was going to get that tank. You know what, sergeant?"

"No, sir. What?"

"Your men are always a little better than you think."

"Yes, sir." Ekland enjoyed it when the captain, often so reticent, chose to lecture him, particularly when the captain lectured on the elaborate lore of battle.

"An officer should realize that right from the beginning. He should understand that his men are good, and whenever they prove it he should tell them about it. Then they get better. They get better than they know."

The tanks ahead began to move, snorting like race horses held overlong at the barrier. The first one shoved the tank that had been hit, and was now burned out and charred. The motor roared, and its exhausts spit out streams of blue smoke, and it shouldered the dead tank off the road. When their jeep passed this dead tank, Mackenzie shut his nose and his mind to the smell.

Where the Chinese block had been, Mackenzie pulled off the road to re-organize his company. Couzens' platoon held the high ground commanding the road, and the others were now straggling in, bringing their wounded. Mackenzie was examining the twisted turret of the T-34 when two of his men approached him. One was very large, and the other very small, and he did not recognize them until the larger one spoke, for Mackenzie had never seen such a sight before.

It was not only that they appeared to have been hosed

by a stream of blood, but bits of flesh and splinters of bone were frozen to their parkas and gloves and boots. "We got hit, sir," the larger one said, and Mackenzie realized it was Swede Ostergaard, and that the small one was little Nick Tinker.

"For God's sakes, get off your feet until I can get a couple of corpsmen over here."

"We're not hurt, sir," said Ostergaard. "We're all right. It was Lieutenant Bishop. He got it in the belly."

"I guess that's what saved us," said Tinker.

"Yes, sir," said Ostergaard. "He took the whole load. We'd got in good range of this tank, here, and Tinker was aiming, and this lieutenant, he came up with his platoon, and he was standing right next to me when that shell came in and he just exploded. The jeep tumped over, and the two men in the back were hit, but we weren't hurt at all."

"No, sir," said Tinker. "Not at all."

"Okay," said Mackenzie, masking the revulsion and horror from his face. "When we get to Koto-Ri, change your uniforms. Find new parkas."

"Yes, sir," said Ostergaard.

"I was watching your firing," Mackenzie said. "You were doing fine."

"Yes, sir."

"Now get going. Find a ride on one of the six-by-sixes." Mackenzie turned away from them.

Dog Company reached Koto-Ri before dark that night.

Chapter Eight

THAT WAS a bad night for Mackenzie. He set up the company CP in a frame shack that had once been the barber shop of Koto-Ri. It was near the strip that had miraculously been bulldozed in by the engineers, and which now was being used to fly out the wounded.

There was a message for him in Koto-Ri, and a jeep, a present from Regiment. The jeep mounted a seventy-five-millimeter recoilless gun, and the message said he should carry out his assigned mission. He was grateful for the gun, and its crew. A seventy-five might knock out a Russian T-34 tank. He knew that a fifty-seven wouldn't, unless you got a lucky hit in the treads. As to carrying out the assigned mission, Battalion, and Colonel Grimm at Regiment, didn't know that Dog Company had come through another fight, and had suffered casualties which would be called "moderate" in the official reports, but which nevertheless reduced his effective strength below one hundred men.

Mackenzie first saw to it that his wounded were evacuated. Then he sent Ekland scrounging for additional supplies he thought they might need on the secondary road. He personally inspected his transport, and he was disturbed by the way the oil congealed, and the batteries lost their kick, in the darkness hours, even when the hoods were protected from the wind by tarps. The geography didn't show it, and therefore it would be hard to realize in the Pentagon, but at this time of year in North Korea you fought an Arctic war, if you fought at all.

At last Mackenzie thought of food, and he found a chow line operated by the ground crew of Military Air Transport, moving raggedly ahead on the edge of the strip in the rippling light of gasoline flares. Mackenzie got into this line. He got in at the tail end, as usual, but a young pilot saw him. This pilot must have thought Mackenzie looked especially hungry and gaunt, for he took him by the arm and escorted him to the head of the line, and a tired mess sergeant ladled his kit high with hot C-rations, and potatoes, and bread and peanut butter. An air evac nurse, her uniform incongruously clean except for blood spots stiffened by the cold, and her makeup still fresh from Tokyo, brought him hot coffee, and asked him about himself. He found himself describing the action of the day, and unburdening his mind of the bad moments.

She listened as if she were really interested, and probed him with questions when he thought he had nothing further to say. Finally, she put a hand on his shoulder, and he could feel her fingers tighten. "Be seeing you, captain. Good luck," she said, and she climbed into a beat-up C-47 heavy with the wounded, and she was gone out of his life. Walking back to his CP, Mackenzie savored the thought of her, but he could not for the life of him remember how tall she was, or the color of her hair or eyes, or what she looked like. But he would remember her, he thought. She'd made him feel better. She was a girl from home, and one girl from back home was like all girls from back home. They were with him.

It was almost midnight when he returned to the CP, but he couldn't crawl into his sack because there was a sergeant from a Graves Registration team there to visit him, and paper work to do. He sat in the crude, wooden, hand-carved barber's chair, and stretched out his long legs until his heels rested on the shelf that had once held the razor and scissors. He spread the company roster out on his lap. With the help of Kato and Raleigh Couzens he sorted out the names of the dead, and the wounded, and the missing as best he could. Twice he sent out Vermillion to check names with the leader of the platoon on security duty. When he thought his casualty list was correct, he gave it over to this Graves Registration sergeant.

This was a relief to his sense of military order, but it did not relieve the captain of further responsibility. It was no relief to his mind. There would be more letters to write, and in particular, at this moment, he disliked the thought of writing a letter to the wife of Lieutenant Bishop, Annapolis '49 and the most junior of his officers.

On the dock at Dago he had met Bishop's wife. Bishop had married two days before the sailing date, and the captain had been too busy to attend the wedding, but he had contrived to give Bishop liberty until the last possible moment. Then Bishop had appeared at the dock with his wife, both of them giddy at the discovery of each other.

Bobby Bishop was lean and tall, like Mackenzie, but

his cheeks were smooth and pink as a cherry not quite ripe, and his men had naturally nicknamed him "Babyface." But "Babyface" Bishop wasn't a baby. He was smart enough, and ambitious enough, to talk of getting into Staff School when this thing in Korea was over. And once he had questioned Mackenzie about the National War College, and how a man could make it.

The captain remembered Bobby Bishop's wife. That day on the dock she had been wearing one of those tailored suits of powder-blue wool which is standard uniform for brides on the first days of their honeymoon, and everything about her seemed fresh and new. The two of them together looked as if they had been hatched from a wedding cake, while Mackenzie was harassed, and sweaty, a clipboard under one arm and a sheaf of unscrambled orders under the other. Bishop had introduced her and said, "You didn't get a chance to kiss the bride, captain, so I brought her down here."

"You're very generous," Mackenzie said, and had kissed her. She had the lips of a child.

"You'll take care of him?" she'd asked. "You'll see that he brushes his teeth every morning, and gets his vitamins?"

"Sure." They all laughed.

"You will really take care of him, won't you? Because I want him back. He's nice."

"I promise."

And that was all Mackenzie remembered of her, except that there had been no tears, for she was a Navy brat. Now Bobby Bishop was not even a corpse to be given the dignity of burial, and Mackenzie had to write a letter to this girl he had seen only once, and whose first name he could not recall. He hoped he would find it somewhere in his records, and he began to stir around among the papers in his musette bag.

Ekland, whose radio jeep stood at the door of the shop, said he had a signal from Regiment. Dog Company was to shove off on the secondary road at dawn. He was to guard Channel Five while they were on the march. He was to report to Regiment immediately if they got into a serious scrap, or if it appeared the enemy was infiltrating through to the main road. The captain nodded and continued to prowl through the musette bag. Ekland ran the lines of a head set, and control switch, and speaker, from the jeep into the shop. Then he curled up in a corner, the headphones close to his ear.

"These blasted papers!" Mackenzie said. Once the paper work of Dog Company had flowed smoothly, but this efficiency had collapsed with the deaths of Sergeant Kirby, and before him, the company clerk.

"What's eating you, Sam?" Couzens said. Couzens had arranged himself for the night, setting out his coffee and his Colman stove and jerican of water, and gently bedding down his rifle within reach of his hand.

"Bishop," Mackenzie said. "I can't remember his wife's first name. I've got to write her."

"Well, you're not going to write her right now, are you?"

"No, but—"

"Get some sleep."

"It worries me."

"Well, if it's any help, her name's Frances, and she's living with her folks. They have a house on the Severn, near Annapolis. Her father's a retired four-striper."

"How do you know all this stuff?"

"Bishop talked about her all the time. He got a letter from her when we were in Ko-Bong." Couzens tried to recall how long ago that had been, but he could not, because it seemed so far behind them, although on the map it was only ten or twelve miles. "She's pregnant," he added.

Mackenzie beat on the arms of the barber chair with both fists, and began to swear, slowly and methodically. He used all the four-letter words that a soldier uses mechanically, and which are washed out of his mouth by feminine contact in normal times; and he used words that Couzens and Ekland had rarely heard before.

Couzens was concerned and shocked, not by the words but by the fact that they came from the mouth of Sam Mackenzie. The captain usually conserved such words for a proper moment and purpose. "Easy, Sam," Couzens said.

"Easy, hell! I've got to write that letter to that little girl. What am I going to say? 'Dear Frances Bishop: Your husband got a direct hit in the belly with a seventy-seven. There wasn't enough of him left to fill a cigarette carton. He made a tactical error. He stopped alongside a jeep that was drawing fire. So sorry. I'll try to get him a Bronze Star, so his kid will have something to remember him by'."

Mackenzie slammed his feet to the floor and paced the room. "Oh, no. You don't say that. You say they died painlessly. They were loved by their men. They died bravely."

Couzens stood up, looking tousled, and worried, and weary. "Easy, Sam."

"How would you like to write the letters? How would you like it, Raleigh?"

"Sam, you can't let yourself go like this. You've got to

get some sleep. Know what you need, Sam? You need a drink."

They both looked at the musette bag, hanging from the back of the barber's chair.

The captain shook his head. "No, I'm not going to touch it. I've needed it worse." He removed his battle jacket and his boots and his trousers and unrolled his sleeping bag and blew out the candles on the upper shelf, where there still stood a bottle that had once held cologne, and a cracked white mug.

Although he was exhausted, Mackenzie could not sleep. He was as uncomfortable as if he had lice in his clothes, and for a time he imagined he did have lice, and scratched and twitched and wondered whether his typhus shot was up to date. His muscles were taut, and would not relax, and while he commanded his mind to sleep, while he informed his mind of the necessity for sleep, while he tried to force his mind to allow his body the mercy of sleep, his mind would not obey.

His mind was mutinous and prankish, and it insisted on returning, wherever it wandered, to the bottle of Scotch. "Give yourself a break," his mind told him. "Take a snort. It'll relax you and let you sleep. It'll help the others, too. They aren't asleep yet. They're still awake, worried and nervous because you're worried and nervous. Bust out the bottle. It'll give you all a good start in the morning."

That's the way it always was. It was in the bad times that he considered opening the bottle, like the day he had come home from the Pacific.

The Corps had sent him home, after Peleliu, to help with training. He'd flown back on NATS, like an admiral or a

VIP, and of course there hadn't been time to tell anyone he was coming, even if he could have slipped a message past the censors. He spent an hour at Okinawa, and another at Midway, and another at Pearl, reflecting how American air bases all over the world looked the same, with the same snack bars and Cokes and peanut-butter crackers and Hershey bars—all wonderful and sparkling and refreshing after Peleliu. You could drop a guy down onto an American base, and he couldn't tell you, unless he already knew, what country he was in, or even what hemisphere. Then there was the last fourteen hours to San Francisco, and there'd been a crap game on the transport and he'd won seven hundred dollars, which once had been a lot of money, but to soldiers who hadn't been able to spend any money at all for months or years, except a few dollars at a PX, was just so much paper. When they landed at Hamilton he'd called her, and it was on that night—that dreadful night—that he'd come closest to opening the bottle.

When Anne heard his voice she'd seemed excited, and eager, after the first disbelief, but then she said: "Darling, of course come right on out. But I've got another date tonight, Sam, and I don't know how to reach him and call it off."

"Won't it be a bit awkward?" he said, with what he hoped was sarcasm.

She hesitated and said, "Oh, I don't think so, Sam. I hope not."

He went to the St. Francis, and bathed and changed, and discovered that his dress blues, which he had not worn for three years, were a bit too small for him, everywhere. A man could keep on growing, in his early twenties. But he wore them, because in December San Francisco was raw and chill, after the Palaus, and everything else he had was tropical. As an afterthought, he called the floor maid, and had a First Division patch, with its Southern Cross stars, stitched on his sleeve. He caught the train to San José, and took a taxi to the Longstreet home in Los Altos.

It was awkward, very awkward. The other date was an Air Force major with a guardsman's mustache and an Eighth Air Force patch on his sleeve and three rows of flashy ribbons on his chest. Mackenzie didn't know what all these ribbons meant, but he felt they must have been legitimate, because one of them was a Purple Heart. The major seemed completely at home at the Longstreets'. He knew where to find the cheese in the refrigerator, and the ice tongs, and he made a point of brewing the coffee, and he joked with the Longstreets familiarly as if he were a favorite nephew—or a son-in-law.

There took place between them one of those strange duels of patience that occur when two men are determined to have one woman alone, and are forced by the manners of the moment not to settle the matter in the way of cavemen, or cavaliers of the eighteenth century. The major won. The major outlasted him, and outwaited him. The major was fresh, while Mackenzie was tired from forty hours of flight across the Pacific. Or perhaps Mackenzie was not certain of his self-control, and feared he might blow up and cause a scene. Or perhaps he was deeply and secretly afraid that this was the way it would be, was bound to be, and was braced to accept it. And in addition to all this, Mackenzie's uniform was uncomfortable and tight, the collar biting into his neck, and his trousers climbing his legs whenever he sat down.

At midnight he gave up, and bade them goodnight with politeness as empty and insincere as a headwaiter's smile. The major obligingly called a cab for him, and courteously refrained from following when Anne escorted him to the walk. "Well, fly off into the wild blue yonder. Be seeing you around," Mackenzie told her, in parting.

And she said, standing there in the moonlight, straight and angry and maddeningly desirable, because of her jasmine, and her new maturity, and her lithe beauty, and his long need for her, "Captain, you are a damned fool."

He turned his back on her, and returned to the hotel, and in the lobby he ran into some others from the First. They told him they had some old phone numbers that had been good deals, if the girls were still in town, and some new ones that sounded promising, and they invited him along. But he went to his room. Now that he had seen Anne again he had no heart for other women. When he was in the room he took out the bottle of Scotch that he'd lugged across half the world. First he thought of throwing it out of the window, and then he thought of drinking it, and finally he thought of sending it back to her, done up in ribbons. That would tell her how he felt, if anything would.

So he ordered drinks sent up from the bar, and set them out in a row, a skirmish line of amber and crystal on the austere hotel writing desk. He killed the glasses in this line, one by one. He drank one, and then he wrote a paragraph he intended to enclose with the bottle. Then he drank another, and another.

That was the way she found him, at three in the morning, except by then he'd finished the drinks, and was wondering whether it wouldn't be just as effective to send her back the bottle—but empty.

She knocked, and when he yelled, "Come in," she walked into the room and straight into his arms. She found his mouth with her mouth, and tried to merge her body with his body, and for a long space of time neither wished to speak. Until he was tired, and out of breath. Then she said, "I love you, Sam. I don't love anybody else."

He said, "That guy."

"I sent Tom home. I was rude to him, I guess. I'm sorry, because he was nice to me. He's been nice to me for a long time." And she spoke of how lonely and fearful girls could get when their men were away to the wars; and how they were afraid for their men, and being afraid, sometimes tied to another man as an anchor, and a hedge against total loss. She said she supposed this was a weakness, but that was the way it was, and what was he going to do about it?

On that particular night Mackenzie wasn't in shape to do anything about it, except talk, and he couldn't talk very clearly. He sat on the edge of the bed and held his head in his hands, ashamed of his condition and his inadequacy, and tried to make straight words come out of a whirling brain. "I'm going to marry you. Right now. Right this minute. Call the preacher. Tell him to come up. Tell him to come up and have a drink and marry us and we'll get the license in the morning."

At last she persuaded him to lie flat on the bed, and she undressed him, stilling his protests with kisses. When she had him between the sheets she kissed him one last time, and although he clutched at her, and begged her, and raved of his desire for her, she left him.

That had been a bad night, a worse night than this. But his next night with Anne had been different, and so now again the next night might be different.

Maybe he'd wake up in the morning and discover that the Communists were all through, that Eighth Army had rallied and was driving them back, and that the retreat was at an end. Or it might even be that this war would end. All wars ended some time, didn't they? But some lasted for generations. Rome and Carthage. Greece and Persia. The Crusades. The Mongols and the West. England and Spain. America and Russia. No, that was wrong. That wasn't the way to say it. The way to say it was to paraphrase Lincoln. It should read, "I believe this world cannot endure permanently half slave and half free," for indeed in point of time, by which the space of the world was now reckoned, the world was smaller and more compact and one than Lincoln's country, all his awkward, gangling country, of 1861.

This war between the free world and the slave world could carry on for generations, as had other wars, but this one was more important, because it might decide things forever. This thing in Korea didn't look like much. It looked ridiculous. It was a skirmish over a piece of third-class real estate of no strategic importance. Yet it would be decisive, Mackenzie sensed. It was a clash of wills. What was the final objective of warfare? He brought it out of the textbooks, "to break the will of the enemy." Here in Korea, somebody's will was going to be broken.

And if this war was important, then Dog Company was

important, because Dog Company had the duty. It was necessary that the First Marine Division reach the coast intact, whether or not there was an evacuation. It was necessary his regiment get through, and this depended upon Dog Company's aptitude on the flank.

If the Marines were destroyed, or so battered they could not soon again be committed to combat, it'd make a difference. It would influence the Army commander, back in Pusan, and even the theater general, in Tokyo. They had little enough, the Americans. They couldn't afford to lose a division. They could afford to lose a company, but not a division. And if Tokyo was disheartened, then Washington would be shaken. Washington might decide it had all been a mistake, and draw back, and once having committed itself to drawing back, Washington might decide to draw back all the way—to the shores of North America. To isolation, on the shores of North America.

It was a damn shame that the young ones, and the good ones, had to die first. It was a goddam shame that a boy like Bishop got blown to shreds by a Russian shell out of a Russian barrel fired from a Russian tank, when Bishop had never had a chance to shoot back at Russians. But if Dog Company won out in the end, then Bishop had got in his licks, because it was to be decided here. Here, in Korea. Sam Mackenzie slammed his open palm on the floor hard enough to kill a man.

"Go to sleep, Sam," said Raleigh Couzens.

"Okay," Mackenzie said, and he slept.

Chapter Nine

DOG COMPANY PULLED out of Koto-Ri at 0600. Everybody
rode rubber. Mackenzie had eight jeeps, three six-by-sixes,
and two weapons carriers. The radio jeep led the column,
snaking out through the Koto-Ri streets until Ekland located the narrow set of tracks that Dog Company had been
instructed to follow to the sea. They left habitations and
paddy fields behind, and the hills rose slowly around them.
The sound of artillery defending the Koto-Ri strip became a dull thump, like distant drums, out of rhythm.

Then the sounds of war faded entirely, and Dog Company was alone. It was lonely on that road, lonely and
cold and desolate, and all of them were afraid, although
their fear was visible only in a negative way, by their silence. Dog Company had left the protective arm of Division, and Regiment, and Battalion. Dog Company was
on its own. Later, in the official action reports, it would
be called a Task Force, but it was a task force without
much punch or power. Even the private soldiers, the riflemen, who never were told anything, sensed this isolation,
this nakedness, and sought the comfort of a buddy's shoul-

der in the six-by-sixes and the weapons carriers. The private soldiers, almost all of them, were very young. They were so young that in the unusual and scanty periods of peace, referred to as "ordinary times," they would have been office boys and soda jerks and filling-station flunkies and Golden Gloves fighters and cowhands and grocery clerks. Yet there was this distinctive thing about them. They had volunteered. They were distinct and apart.

There was no sign of the enemy. And all the people, the people that armies call "indigenous personnel," seemed to have disappeared. This disturbed Mackenzie. "Where are the people?" he asked Ekland.

"Beats me," said Ekland. "Except—"

"Except what?"

"Except I haven't seen any civilian traffic. None at all. I haven't seen any ox carts, or anything. It isn't natural. There ought to be some movement on this road. You always see something, maybe only an old woman with a goat, or some kids crying."

"The poor kids," said Mackenzie. "They don't know what it's all about."

"I'd go crazy if I had a kid and he was lost and alone and hungry, like these Korean kids," said Ekland.

"Ever think of getting married?" said Mackenzie.

This was the first time that the captain had inquired about his private life, and it was not a usual thing. Usually, a company skipper avoided speaking of the private life of his men, for with some of the men it was a touchy matter. For some of the men the anonymity of a uniform was protective coloration, as in the French Foreign Legion, and they would resent it if an officer asked about their private lives. But since the captain had asked, and since the captain was sensitive to the thoughts and moods of his men, Ekland knew that he was genuinely interested, and not just curious, and Ekland felt he could speak frankly to the captain. "I should be married," he said. "By rights I should be married right now. I should be married and have my feet propped up on a hassock in my living room and be watching the Army-Navy game. Today's Saturday, isn't it?"

"Damned if I know."

"Well, if it's Saturday that's what I ought to be doing. I ought to have a wife and a good job with NBC, and not be wandering around some place at the rear end of the earth expecting to get my head blown off any minute."

"Well, why didn't you get married, instead of coming back in?"

Ekland laughed. "It was necessary that I save the world. Crazy, that's what we were. Nuts."

He twisted the wheel, and they skidded, and stopped, for in his thoughts of himself he had forgotten that he was at the head of the column, and those behind could not keep pace.

"Those civilians are hiding," the captain said. "Hiding like small game when the tigers are out."

"We're not tigers," said Ekland.

"They are," said Mackenzie. "They're tigers."

The jeep crept forward again, and both of them were silent, but they were thinking the same thing. They were under observation. They could see nothing, but they could feel it. When they reached a point where the road was wide enough for vehicles to pass comfortably, Mackenzie told

Ekland to stop. "I'm going to shuffle up the column," he said. "We want more firepower up front here."

He put the jeep with the seventy-five in the van, and behind it a jeep mounting a fifty-calibre machine gun, and also carrying Ackerman, his serious bazooka man. He himself, in the radio jeep, took station between the weapons carriers in the center of the column. He had a heavy machine gun bring up the rear. Then, as an afterthought, he sent a four-man jeep patrol far out in front. He wished he had skirmishers on his flanks, too, but there wasn't time for movement afoot. He had to keep pace with Regiment. And the terrain was nasty.

The terrain got worse. The road climbed interminably, but the mountains climbed faster on either side, and it developed, finally, that they were ascending through a gorge, a cliff binding their right, while on the left the road fell steeply away into a canyon. In this gorge the wind rose, and it seemed to grow colder. It was not really that it grew colder. It was simply that the wind provided the cold with a weapon, a thin blade to slice through the tiniest crevice in a man's clothes, and to stab at his mouth and eyes.

When a man is very cold, or very hot, it is difficult for him to stay alert for danger. The immediate discomfort is more pressing than the unseen threat. Mackenzie realized this, and so he forced himself to ignore the wind, and the cold, and concentrate on his job.

At noon he called for a break, and the men piled out of the vehicles, stiff and weary, and huddled in the lee of the cliff to their right. He walked among them, cautioning them on the care of their weapons and their feet and their vehicles. The C-rations in the six-by-sixes were frozen solid, and long ago the wood had been stripped from these mountains, so there was no fuel for fire except gasoline, and Mackenzie would not use gasoline for fires when he wasn't sure how much his transport would consume on the way to Hungnam. In any case, there was no time to thaw out food. The men ate combat rations. They beat out chunks of tropical chocolate and solidified cheese with their bayonets and thawed these chunks in their mouths. It was difficult, but it was food.

The captain inspected the map that Regiment had left for him at Koto-Ri. There was a steep peak across the gorge, to his left. It didn't have a name, but the map said it was two thousand meters high, and he believed it. He guessed the Chinese would have an OP on that peak. It was the logical place. He ordered Dog Company to move on.

The company crawled upward until it was opposite this peak, and then they passed it, and the road tilted downward again until the ravine on their left became flat plain, studded with clusters of rock and mounds of stones, as if they had been scattered by a careless giant. On this plain nothing moved, nothing stirred, until there was a single dull explosion, far ahead. His patrol jeep ought to be somewhere around that explosion, and he was debating whether to order his point up to their support, or whether to halt the whole company in place and prepare for defense, when the decision was taken out of his hands.

Out on the plain bugles blew, and cymbals clashed, and whistles shrilled, and incredibly the plain moved. It moved in waves. The waves were gray, like the plain, but the waves were men. It was incredible, and it was frightening. Mackenzie knew at once that this was the real thing. This was a mass attack by at least one battalion, perhaps two, and unless he was very lucky Dog Company would be destroyed right here, to the last man, and the Chinese flood would pour over him, and across the ridge to his right, and take Regiment on the flank. He began to give orders, Ekland relaying them through the walkie-talkie.

"Out of the vehicles! Keep away from the vehicles! Hit the dirt!"

The six-by-sixes and the weapons carriers were big and vulnerable targets.

Then, "Find cover! Find cover!"

Then there were special orders for the mortarmen, to emplace their weapons behind rocks, and start them going. But to the machine gunners and the riflemen there were different orders—to hold their fire. A mass attack, like this, should be met by mass firepower. The firepower should not be dispersed. It should be used, in the old-fashioned way, like a volley, a volley that in one blast of firing would throw back a wave. Like Wellington's thin red lines, throwing back the massed Continental infantry.

Ekland, relaying the captain's orders, found time to start his command set warming on Channel Five, and the captain noticed this and said, "We've got to have air. We've got to have air or we haven't got much chance."

The mortars began to speak, and Mackenzie saw them bursting with speed and precision in and in front of the waves. And he could see that the Chinese, even as they ran, were firing automatic weapons, but the range was too great, and they were firing wildly, and they were wasting

ammunition. They were screaming as they ran. *"Sha! Sha!"*
They were mad, and Mackenzie was grateful for their madness.

"You raise Battalion?" he asked Ekland.

"I think so, sir." Ekland began to speak on Channel Five.
"This is Lightning Four. This is Lightning Four. We're
under attack. We're under heavy attack. We've got to have
air."

Regiment acknowledged, and asked for co-ordinates.

"Tell him we don't have any co-ordinates," said Mackenzie. "Tell him about that mountain. Call it Hill 2000.
They've got the same maps. They'll place it. Tell him we've
just passed it, on the road, and the Chinese are attacking
across the open."

Ekland told Regiment, moving on the parallel road to
the south. Colonel Grimm, riding in a six-by-six fitted out
as a CP, heard it, placed Dog Company on the map with
his forefinger, and instantly saw the danger of the situation. He sent a request to Division, urgent, for air. He
sent a recommendation with it. After they bombed, the
planes should go in and strafe, and if it was at all possible,
they should maintain air cover over Dog Company until
the company was out of trouble. This was all Colonel
Grimm could do. Regiment had troubles of its own.

The message from Regiment went to Division, and from
there to Seventh Fleet, and from Seventh Fleet to Task
Force 77. In this task force was the carrier *Leyte*, with a
Marine Corps air group aboard. The Marines always were
supported by their own fliers. From the time Ekland gave
Dog Company's position, until the time the admiral found
that position with his dividers in the plot room of the *Leyte*,

six minutes passed. "How many've we got up?" the admiral asked the commander of the Marine squadron aboard.

"Eight, sir. With napalm."

The admiral had found it expedient to keep part of his ground support squadron always in the air, for just such emergencies. "Send 'em in," the admiral ordered. "And launch your others. With napalm." Worse than anything else, the Chinese feared napalm.

Presently the *Leyte,* steaming at flank speed out of sight of land, with four destroyers foaming alongside, turned into the wind to launch more planes. And unheard and unseen, ten thousand feet up and five miles to the south of Dog Company, eight Corsairs nosed over and plunged down through the overcast.

Dog Company slaughtered the first wave. Mackenzie tried to hold his fire until the Chinese were within a hundred yards, but before he was quite ready, a machine gun to the rear chattered nervously, and this set the whole company going, so that the effect he planned was not perfect. Still, it was terribly effective. There were no longer shrill cries, and whistles from the plain now. There were only moans.

Another wave came at them. Mackenzie could not tell from where they came. It was almost as if the dead rose to fight again. It was a fearful thing. When they came on, in waves like that, it was like trying to stop the sea, for they flowed and eddied around the mounds of their own fallen.

Mackenzie wanted to run, and because he was afraid he knew the others of Dog Company must be afraid too, he took time, from firing his carbine, to observe the behavior of his men. They were inching back, those who were firing.

They were huddling together. "Spread out!" he screamed. "Spread out!"

And so that they could see him, he walked towards the head of the column, pretending indifference to the snap and crack of enemy fire, and the wail of the ricochets off the rocks. Then he heard the whine of a high velocity shell coming in, and he threw himself on his face. When he looked up, he no longer had the jeep mounting the seventy-five, or any of that gun's crew. Dog Company received more shells, and from their timing and their crackling noise Mackenzie knew that they were from tanks, or SP guns, and that the Chinese somehow had brought up tanks or SP's out of those hills across the plain, and when they came at him again they could certainly break into his position. They would certainly wipe him out. He wondered about casualties, but there was no time to look. He re-loaded his carbine and rested on one knee. He had no thoughts and no further plans, except that he would hold his fire until they were very close, until he could clearly see their faces. He was tired, and he believed he was beaten.

Mackenzie didn't see the Corsairs diving in until they had reached their release point, and then suddenly, where there had been the third wave of men, there was a wall of fire. It was a wall of fire that did not subside, for napalm is tenacious. It sticks and clings to whatever it burns, until it has burned everything entirely. Out on the plain, a wave of men was burning. It was the most frightening spectacle of war that Mackenzie had ever seen. He became aware that the butt of his carbine rested on the ground, and that his men no longer were firing. Like their captain, they could only watch. They were awed, and paralyzed.

Another flight of Corsairs came down, and this time Mackenzie heard their air-scream, and they dumped on something out of his sight that sent up a pillar of black smoke along with the flames. Mackenzie spotted more Corsairs, flying in pairs so close it seemed their wingtips held hands, far overhead, and these held course in a great circle over the battle area. Mackenzie realized, at last, that Dog Company had held the flank, and that the Chinese had been thrown back, and the Chinese would be forced to stay back so long as those friendly Corsairs held the sky overhead. But he must act quickly, and Dog Company must move on while this protection existed, and it would not be there forever.

Mackenzie surveyed what was left. His first impression was that his company had been destroyed, and that perhaps only five or six of his men remained alive, and unwounded, but this was because he could not immediately see everything that was left on the road, and the smoking wreckage and human debris of the battle was what first caught his attention.

The radio jeep was a tangle of steel and twisted wiring and broken batteries. The weapons carriers were gone, and with them almost all of his mortar ammunition. He no longer possessed fifty-calibre machine guns, or the jeeps that had mounted them.

The pharmacist's mate who was the chief of his corpsmen appeared, and said, "We've just got to do something about the wounded."

"Do what you can, and do it in a hurry."

"I don't have any plasma, sir. It's all frozen, except maybe some that may have thawed when those there weapons carriers burned."

Mackenzie sensed that his pharmacist's mate was close to collapse, although he could not clearly see his face, and it was necessary that this man keep his nerve, and so Mackenzie said, "We'll get the wounded out in a hurry. Do what you can now. Where are the other corpsmen?"

"Wounded, sir. Both of them wounded."

"Well, treat 'em. Do something for them."

The face of the pharmacist's mate went away and that of Raleigh Couzens appeared in its place and Couzens' face was blackened with powder. "What've we got left?" Mackenzie asked.

"I can't tell exactly, except we haven't got Zimmerman or Sands."

"Wounded?"

"Killed."

Except for Couzens, Zimmerman and Sands were the last of Mackenzie's officers. "How are we for sergeants?"

"We've still got Ekland. I saw him back a ways, helping with the wounded."

"No others?"

"I don't think so. Those tanks laid it into the mortar platoon."

They walked together towards the tail of the column, continuing their evaluation. They counted, altogether, twenty-one dead, and forty-four wounded, and four men so dazed with battle shock they must be counted wounded, too. Mackenzie realized that he had come to the most important decision of his military career, and that whatever he decided would likely be considered wrong, if anyone ever bothered to examine his decisions and actions, later. Like any commander, whether of an army or a company, whose force has steadily been reduced by casualties, he had been deprived of alternatives of action. Eventually, such a force must have no alternatives at all, except death or capitulation.

"What in hell am I going to do?" Mackenzie said, his eyes taking in his wounded, holding in their pain, and his wrecked transport.

"Good God, Sam!" Couzens said, and Mackenzie realized that Couzens was shaken by his indecision, and that he must not display indecision again, or Couzens, and Dog Company, would shatter in panic. Well, there was one rule that he could go by, that superseded all others. He must not abandon his wounded. The six-by-sixes were still intact, and they would carry out the wounded, but even as Mackenzie thought of bringing the wounded along, on the six-by-sixes, he knew that they would never reach the sea alive, for at best it would be two more days before they found the sea. If the wounded were to be saved, they must reach an aid station this night. That meant returning to Koto-Ri, which he judged would be in American hands for another day or so. And it was impossible for Dog Company to return to Koto-Ri, for that meant deserting his regiment. It was improbable that Dog Company could be of much assistance in protecting Regiment's flank, henceforth, but there was always the chance, and so long as that chance existed, then the company must hold to the road.

Mackenzie reached the only possible compromise. The wounded would return to Koto-Ri in the six-by-sixes. He would send along a few men to help the pharmacist's mate. He would send with them four men in a jeep, to protect them from snipers. That was all he could do. The others, with all the ammunition and weapons and food that could be salvaged, would go on. Having reached his decision, Mackenzie began to shout his orders, and Dog Company took form again.

The Corsairs were still circling when it resumed its movement. It consisted of three jeeps heaped with supplies, and twenty-two men, all except the jeep drivers on foot. They had marched for only ten minutes when they reached the jeep that Mackenzie had sent on reconnaissance. Mackenzie had forgotten all about these four men ahead of the column, and it was just as well. The jeep had run across a heavy bomb planted as a mine, and that was the explosion Mackenzie had heard as the battle began. The crater was so wide the jeeps had to leave the road to round it. At dark Dog Company reached the village of Sinsong-ni, and here Mackenzie called a halt for the night.

Chapter Ten

Sinsong-ni was no larger than Ko-Bong, and more dismal, for few of its houses of mortar and clay, and huts of mud, remained intact. Some had been broken by bombs and rockets, and all had been holed by strafing planes. This seemed curious to Mackenzie, for he had heard of no ground fighting in this area. Sinsong-ni was merely an isolated village on an almost forgotten ribbon of road in a desolate section of an unimportant land. Then Mackenzie saw that the fronts of a number of the houses had been crushed in, as if by a great fist, although the roofs were undamaged, and he realized what must have happened here, some time in the past. Communist tanks, retreating from their defeats at Wonsan, must have chosen this village as a hideaway in the daylight hours, when American fighter-bombers, like swarms of hawks, sought them out. The Communists had discovered a quick and effective method for hiding a tank. You rammed it through a wall, and into a house. The tanks stayed in the houses until nightfall, like rabbits in thickets, but somehow they had been discovered, and the village had been shot up and rocketed and bombed.

Mackenzie saw smoke rising from only one chimney, and he chose this house as his CP, and sent in Kato and Vermillion to thaw out some rations, while he himself superintended the care of his vehicles. In the confusion after battle, the tarps for the hoods of the jeeps had been forgotten, or lost. But he found two sleeping bags, and protected the hoods of two of his jeeps with these, and the third jeep he drove into a house that had been bashed in by a tank. He assigned two men to each jeep, and ordered them to stand two-hour watches, and turn over the motors for five minutes in every hour. At this moment the jeeps were all-important. Without the jeeps Dog Company would lose its mobility in battle, its supply train, and whatever chance it had to push through to its objective.

Then Mackenzie went into the house with the fire. It was filled with his men. Like all Korean houses of its type, it was comfortably warm, for it had radiant heat, invented some four thousand years before the idea occurred to Americans. At the end of the larger room was the combination stove and fireplace, with its three holes to receive the great iron pots. At the far end of the house was the chimney, and the flue ran the whole length of the house, under the hard-packed clay floor, so that heat flowed everywhere evenly upward from the earth.

Some of his men already rested full length on the floor smoothed by the body oils and feet of generations. Others watched while cans of rations thawed and warmed in the pots. In the second room a lantern burned, and Mackenzie smelled the sour smoke of peanut oil.

In this second room was something he had not seen for so long a time that the sight of it startled him. It was a bed, a real bed with a mattress. It was true that it was a narrow, brass bed as hideous as if it had been imported from the back hallway of a four-dollar-a-week rooming house. But still it was a bed, and there was a spread on it, and it seemed as luxurious as a suite in the Waldorf. Raleigh Couzens was sitting on the edge of this bed, bouncing a bit, testing the springs and the mattress. "I saw it first," Couzens said.

"I rank you," said Mackenzie, shrugging his carbine and his musette bag from his shoulders.

"We can both use it," suggested Couzens. "We'll take turns."

"Like hell," said Mackenzie. "This one night, I'm going to sleep on a bed. If I get up to inspect the vehicles, and the guard, then you can use it while I'm gone."

"Don't you think it's wide enough for both of us?" asked Couzens, plaintively.

"Nope," said Mackenzie. "I don't." He noticed the old man sitting on the bench in the corner. The old man had been hidden by Kato's back. He saw that Kato was speaking to the old man, in what sounded like Japanese, and Mackenzie walked over and put his hand on Kato's shoulder, and took a better look.

He was a very old man, and the lines in his face were deep and dark, as if they had been burned in weathered wood, and he wore gold spectacles with square rims. He wore the cone-shaped hat, exactly like a Halloween witch's, that marks the Korean patriarch. His ankles seemed no larger around than a small child's, and his shoulders were bent and bony, and yet his shoulders carried his white robe with a certain grace, like a toga. "Who's this?" Mackenzie asked Kato.

"This is the old man who lives here," said Kato.

"Yes, but who is he?"

"Well, he teaches school here in this village. Or did."

"Ask him whether there are any Chinese troops around. No, wait a minute. He wouldn't know that. Ask him whether there are any North Korean guerrillas."

"I did, sir. He doesn't know. He says he never knows when soldiers are around until they come into his house. He doesn't leave his house. He just stays here and reads."

Mackenzie saw a wooden case in the corner. It was filled with paper-backed books. He picked up one of these books. It was in Japanese. Mackenzie noticed that the old man's eyes followed his movements alertly, and the old man spoke to Kato. Kato replied, and the old man nodded.

"I told him you weren't going to take his books," said Kato.

"Tell him we won't take anything that belongs to him," said Mackenzie. "And ask him about the rest of the people in this place. What happened to them?"

Kato spoke to the old man, lengthily, and the old man replied, and in replying he became excited, and his bird-thin hands twisted and shook. When he finished speaking the old man nodded at Mackenzie, as if he knew that Mackenzie would understand.

"Do you mind if I sit down, captain?" Kato said. "I'm pooped."

"No, of course not," Mackenzie said. Kato sat down on

the bench alongside the old man, and Mackenzie sat down on the other side.

Kato frowned, as if it required some thought to translate exactly. "Well, he says a short while ago the Communists came to the village with a great voice on a truck. I suppose he means the loudspeaker on a sound wagon. Everybody in the village had to come to listen. The Communists said that the Americans were invading the land, and would kill them all. So all the men between sixteen and forty had to enlist. Most of them did enlist, he said, but some didn't believe this loudspeaker, and ran away. None of them came back, and so there was a very small crop."

"A short while ago?" said Mackenzie. "How short?"

Kato asked a question and the old man replied. "Last summer," said Kato.

"What happened to everybody else?" asked Mackenzie.

"Well, apparently North Korean units, and later Chinese units, came through the village, and most of the young women disappeared. Then there came what the old man called 'the day of hell.' Seems that the Chinese when they used this road would stop in the village during the daylight hours and hide their tanks, but one day a lot of planes came over and blew this place apart and killed a lot of people."

"Not all of them?" Mackenzie said.

"Oh, no, sir. Not all of them. But those who were left alive were afraid to stay, for fear the planes would come back. So the older men had a meeting, and it was decided that the village should move. The older men, and the older women, and the children who were left, they moved to another place. The old man said he didn't move because

he could not take his books, and his books are all he has
left. Besides, he is ready to die. He is old and tired and
hungry and sick."

"Where did they move to?" Mackenzie asked.

Kato asked the old man, and there were a good many
Japanese monosyllables between them, and then Kato
turned to the captain and said: "He won't tell."

"Why not?"

Kato hesitated, and then he said, "Captain, he's afraid
we might go out and find them and kill them."

"You're fooling!"

"No, sir, I'm not fooling. He thinks the Americans want
to kill the Asiatics. He honestly does."

It was warm in this house, and Mackenzie took off his
gloves and rubbed his face with his fingers and discovered
that he had grown a considerable beard. He put two cigarettes in his mouth, and lit them, and handed one to Kato.
Then he thought of the old man, and offered him a cigarette, but the old man refused. "Where in hell did he get
that idea?" Mackenzie said.

"It's hard to put everything he said together," said Kato.
"But the way I figure it is like this. Most of his life, the
Japanese have been in control here, and everybody read
and spoke Japanese, and the Japanese put out a lot of
anti-American propaganda, I guess. He spoke about the
Oriental Exclusion Act, and the Greater East Asia Co-
Prosperity Sphere. He doesn't particularly like the Japanese. He said their administrators gouged everybody, and
the country was run for the landlords. But he said at least
the Japanese didn't think the Koreans were an inferior
race. They were the same color."

Mackenzie realized that the color of which Kato spoke was also Kato's color, and that Kato's ancestors probably, for the most part, were Japanese, and Mackenzie for a moment felt embarrassed. He decided to ask a direct question. "What do you think about that, Kato?"

"He's got something," Kato replied directly. "He hasn't got anything for me. I'm a Hawaiian, and a Hawaiian is probably better off than anybody else in the world. We don't have those problems. We don't have them at all. Except for one thing, sir. Hawaii is a part of the United States. Hawaii is a good sound part of it. But Hawaii isn't a state. We deserve to be a state. We're anyway as good as Mississippi, aren't we?"

"So far as I'm concerned," said Mackenzie, "better." He looked out through the door into the larger room, where Couzens warmed his hands over the fire. Somehow he was relieved that Couzens wasn't listening.

Kato spoke again to the old man, gesturing, and then said to the captain: "I told him I was part Japanese, and part Chinese, and part Polynesian. But he doesn't believe me. He says that's impossible."

Mackenzie said, "We really fouled it up, didn't we? I mean when people like this old man can believe like that? They don't know much about us, do they? They meet missionaries, and the Big Time Operators in Shanghai and Hong Kong, and the Standard Oil proconsuls. That's all they know about us."

"What's a proconsul?" Kato asked.

The captain considered Kato's question, and he realized Kato was only twenty, or at most twenty-one, and hadn't had much of a chance to absorb ancient history, and so he was careful in his answer. "Well, he's an official who performs executive duties outside his own country. He rules for his country outside his country. Like MacArthur. MacArthur's our proconsul in Japan. It's a Roman word."

"I see," said Kato.

The old man reached under the bench and brought out an ancient staff, polished and oiled by years of human touch, and the old man leaned on this staff, and spoke to Kato in Japanese, for a considerable time.

"This old man," said Kato, "he wants to know . . . well, sir, he wants to know what cooks. He wants to know what we're doing here. He wants to know what we want with Korea. He says he has read a lot about the United States, and he knows we are bigger than Korea, so what do we want with Korea?"

"Tell him—" Mackenzie began, and then he realized the futility of explanation, of the enormous and unbridgeable gap that separated their minds, and he said, "Tell him I don't know."

Kato spoke to the old man, and the old man replied, and Kato said, "He is tired and he asks your permission to lay down on the floor and sleep."

"On the floor!" said Mackenzie. "Hell, tell him to get into his own bed. I don't want his bed. I didn't even know he was here when I told Couzens I wanted the bed. Take him to the bed, Kato."

Kato took the old man to the bed, and Mackenzie sat on the floor to complete his day's duties. He opened his musette bag, and took out his company roster, and then he called Couzens and Ekland, as a precaution. "I'm recording casualties," he told them. "I'm checking off those I know were killed, up the road, and listing those who are still here. That bunch of wounded we sent back to Koto-Ri I'm marking wounded and missing, because there's no way of telling whether they'll make it back or not, and anyway I'm pretty sure some of them are going to hack before they get back. I'm making a special note on the corpsmen, and their escort. I want you guys to know this, because if anything happens to me you'll have to take care of the records."

"You give me the creeps," said Ekland.

"Well, it gives me the creeps to have to do this, but this is a thing a company commander has to do, when he's lost his gunnery sergeant and his clerk, and so you guys might as well know about it."

"I'm not an officer," said Ekland.

"Doesn't matter," said Mackenzie. "You never can tell. And both of you might as well know this too. You have to write the letters. You won't want to write them, and you won't know what to say, but you've got to do it."

Mackenzie replaced the company roster, and lay down and put the musette bag under his head, and sighed and wriggled until he was comfortable, and slept. Ekland went into the larger room and made a pillow of his parka and lay down beside Ackerman. All the others were asleep, but Ackerman was still awake, looking up through his spectacles at the smoke eddying under the thatch. "What's the trouble, Milt?" asked Ekland.

"Just thinking."

"What about?"

"Pris. You remember I wrote that letter to Pris, telling her to buy a car?"

"Sure. Why shouldn't she buy a car?"

"I'm thinking she won't be able to afford it."

"Why not?"

"I just don't think she will," said Ackerman, and turned on his side and pretended sleep, and Ekland, seeing that Ackerman had no desire to talk, slept.

Chapter Eleven

BEFORE DOG COMPANY pulled out of Sinsong-ni, Mackenzie ordered his vehicles re-loaded so that every inch of
space was utilized, and he could squeeze two men, in addition to the driver, into each of the three jeeps. He did not
like the way the men hung back when it came time to leave
the warm house of the old man. They had slept, and yet
they were tired, for on no night had they had sufficient
sleep since Ko-Bong, and their bodies were protesting,
even while their minds told them they must go on, out into
the cold and the unknown. In the process of re-loading
Mackenzie examined each carton of rations, and each
case of ammunition. He jettisoned the few mortar shells he
found, for he had no mortars now. He counted the first-
aid kits, and the bundles of socks, and the entrenching
tools, and he was disturbed at the shortage of cigarettes.
He eliminated whatever he was certain would not be
needed. He figured two days to the coast, if they were
lucky.

And he decided, in this re-loading, that Dog Company
could spare a case of five-in-one rations—food for five men

for one day—and he gave this case to the old man, and Kato explained to the old man how it should be opened, and used.

When they took to the road the headlights poked shallow holes in the yellow gloom of the false dawn, and barely illuminated the ice-sheathed ruts. Nine men rode while the others walked, with the six who had stood watch through the night riding first. The vehicles moved very slowly, because of the uncertain light.

A solid brown overcast shrouded the sky, and sowed fresh snow over these hills, and it seemed that the darkness clung tenaciously to the hours. The men grew stronger as they went along, but they were silent, which was not a good sign. Each hill and curve in the road ahead was an ominous and mysterious threat.

After the two hours Mackenzie called a break. The men propped themselves against rocks, and smoked. There was one walkie-talkie saved, and during the break Ekland tried to use it, nursing its batteries and cajoling its frequencies, in an attempt to raise Regiment, or Division, or anybody. The range of a walkie-talkie was too short to reach the other road. Ekland knew this. He knew it absolutely. Yet again and again he pressed the transmitter button and said, "This is Lightning Four. This is Lightning Four calling Lightning. Come in Lightning." There was never any reply, but Ekland continued to call. It was comforting to speak into a microphone. It gave him the illusion of being in touch with someone. Somehow there was a sense of safety in a microphone.

Mackenzie said, "Cut it out, sergeant."

"Sir?"

"Let it rest. You're not doing a damn thing but alerting the enemy."

"Yes, sir." Ekland dropped the walkie-talkie back into the lead jeep. Ekland hadn't been thinking about the enemy. The captain thought of a lot of things he didn't think of. He looked up at the sky, and listened, and the captain looked up and listened, too. There was no sound from the sky. On this day the sky was not their friend.

When the men had rested, and stretched, Mackenzie ordered them on, and he dropped back to where Raleigh Couzens trudged behind the last jeep, one hand resting on a jerican of gas so that the jeep helped him along. "How you doin', Raleigh?" Mackenzie said.

"Pretty good, Sam, but—"

"But what?"

"But I'm not going to make it, Sam."

"Don't be silly."

"It isn't going to work, Sam. We haven't got dick." This was a strange and fatherless expression birthed by the Korean war. It could mean many things but one of the things it meant was that they didn't have the stuff, the punch, the power. It was the opposite of another expression of this war, "Ammo's running out my ass."

Mackenzie thought that Couzens hadn't been quite the same since Ko-Bong, and he remembered that he had been wanting to talk to Couzens about his experience, and he said, "Raleigh, you never told me about being captured. What happened? Why'd they let you loose?"

"Oh, to hell with it," said Couzens. "It isn't important now."

"I think it's important," said Mackenzie.

"Sam, you're nuts. You don't think we're really going to get out of here, do you, Sam?"

"We're going to give it the old college try." He tried to look into Couzens' eyes, but Couzens' head was bent. "What happened, Raleigh?"

"Sam, it was terrible. I don't want to talk about it. I'm not going to talk about it."

Mackenzie had always realized that under Couzens' insouciance, his quick wit, and his skill in debate there was a dark area you did not dare touch, lest you destroy him. Now this sensitive area was exposed, and needed protection, for Dog Company needed Couzens and his genius in battle. So Mackenzie slammed Couzens on the back and said, "Forget it, Raleigh. There's plenty of time to talk, if you want." And Mackenzie lengthened his stride and moved up to the point of the column. Something bad had happened to Couzens. He was sure of it.

Raleigh Couzens' mind was cleft. Half his mind re-acted normally to the surging drive for self-preservation. The other half wallowed in his failures, and exaggerated his guilt. He had failed his girl. He had failed his family. And worst, he had failed his country. Why else would the Communists release him? Why else, except that he had given aid and comfort to the enemy? His flip cracks about the President, and the war, perhaps even now were being used as propaganda by Radio Peking, and Radio Prague, and Radio Budapest, and Radio Moscow, and was being monitored in Tokyo, and London, and Istanbul, and Washington. He could hear it:

"An American lieutenant of Marines, Raleigh Couzens,

was captured during the recent rout of the American forces. He admitted that, in his own words, 'the Korean war stinks.' He also expressed dissatisfaction, with profanity, at the aid given the United States in the Korean imperialist aggression by other countries of the so-called United Nations. He also cursed the President of the United States. In keeping with the humanitarian principles of the Chinese volunteers, Lieutenant Couzens was released and returned to his own lines."

Back in Mandarin, when she heard of it, his mother would be elated. He was alive. He was safe. His mother wouldn't consider it disgraceful, but his mother was a very selfish woman.

Others would regard it differently. He would have to face a suspicious, grim-faced intelligence officer, in Wonsan, or Pusan, or Tokyo, or even in Washington. He could hear the questions:

"Exactly what *did* you say, Lieutenant Couzens?"

"What did you say about the morale of the Marines?"

"What did you say about our Allies?"

"What did you say about the President of the United States?"

Couzens shivered, and not from the cold. And it would be necessary to have it out, if he got back, with Sam Mackenzie. That was the worst. He would rather lose anything than lose Mackenzie's respect and friendship. He would rather lose his life.

The gradient of the road sloped downward now, and Couzens realized they were entering a valley. The jeeps moved faster, and the men moved faster to keep up, and the drivers shifted into low gear, so all could keep pace, and distance. Ahead, Mackenzie held up his hand, and the column halted. "Come up here, Lieutenant," Mackenzie called, taking his map from his pocket, and Couzens went up to the van with his captain.

Mackenzie spread out the map on the hood of the lead jeep, and traced their route with his finger. The finger stopped a mile short of a town named Chungyang-ni. On the map a single-track railroad passed through this town. On the map the railroad was called the Shinko-Shoko Line. "Ever hear of it?" said Mackenzie.

"No," said Couzens. "Never heard of it."

Mackenzie called for Ekland. Ekland might know more. As the communicator for Dog Company, Ekland was privy to all the radio chatter and gossip. He reported to his captain what would be of direct interest, which was probably only one tenth of what he heard. But Mackenzie knew that Ekland had a good memory, a better-than-good memory. "Ever hear of the Shinko-Shoko Line?" Mackenzie asked, pointing it out on the map.

"Yes, sir. It doesn't work. The Commies have always held one end of it, and ever since we took Hamhung we've held the other. They've got the cars, and we've got the locomotives, so it doesn't work."

"Thank you, sergeant," said Mackenzie. "We've got to cross that line. Even if the trains aren't running, I think they must have some sort of guard on the crossing."

"I'd say yes, sir," said Ekland. "If there's going to be an evacuation I figure the Commies will be all set to grab the line, and start operating it again, and so they'll have a guard at that town there."

Mackenzie thought it through. He couldn't send Dog

Company into Chungyang-ni, and across the tracks, without reconnaissance. The Chinese might have a couple of hundred men in the village. If they held the crossing in strength, then Dog Company would have to take to the hills, and by-pass the village. He didn't want to take to the hills unless it was necessary. His men were tired enough already.

"Lieutenant," Mackenzie said, "this is your baby. You take a patrol up there. Take a jeep and a bazooka and four men."

Couzens looked behind him and called up four men from his own platoon, and told them to bring up the rearmost jeep. This jeep was loaded with rations, but it was better to use this one than the others, crammed with ammo and gasoline. "How close are you going to support me?" he asked Mackenzie.

"Five hundred yards," Mackenzie said. That was all it was necessary to say, between men who knew their business.

Couzens and his four men moved ahead of the column, downhill. The lieutenant, his rifle alive in his hands, walked in front of the jeep. In the jeep was the driver, grenades strapped to his chest and a carbine at his knee, with the bazooka man riding the seat alongside. Flanking the jeep were two riflemen. That was the disposition of Couzens' patrol.

Walking down the road, with houses appearing in the distance like toy blocks, Couzens felt better. It was good to seek action. Action would cleanse his conscious mind. He hoped they would find gooks. He hoped he could crack down on a gook with his rifle. In the sights of his M-1 he would like to have a gook like the jet-eyed officer with the wizened face who had defiled him. He hoped this so desperately that his gloved hands grew numb on his rifle, as if they were frozen there. His rifle. His.

Raleigh Couzens wanted to pray, but he couldn't remember any prayers. All he could recall were some phrases out of the Marine Creed. "This is my rifle. There are many like it, but this one is mine. . . . I must fire my rifle true. . . . I must shoot straighter than my enemy who is trying to kill me. . . . I must shoot him before he shoots me. . . . I will. . . . Before God I swear this creed. . . . My rifle and myself are the defenders of my country. . . ."

The houses, to Couzens, seemed much larger than toy blocks now. They were like boxes and cartons strewn behind a store, and a winding street ran through the village. Smoke came from most of the chimneys, so Couzens knew the village was still lived in, unlike Sinsong-ni. He neither saw nor heard the people until the patrol came to the first house in this village of Chungyang-ni. Then he heard voices, muted. The people were singing. They were singing inside this first house, and they were singing in the other houses ahead. They were singing "Auld Lang Syne."

Couzens thought he must be mad. Then he remembered. The Korean national anthem, their song of unity and freedom, was written to the tune of "Auld Lang Syne." It was absurd, but it was true. It was their "Star-Spangled Banner," their "God Save the King," their "Marine Hymn," their "Battle Hymn of the Republic," their "Dixie." They had fought the Japs to this song, and particularly in this wild and rangy country, which military strategists called a "redoubt area," they had fought, and never ceased fighting, the conquerors. Now Couzens realized they were fighting the new conquerors, the Communists, with this same song. Dog Company was being serenaded into battle with a song of freedom, but quietly, quietly, so Couzens knew the enemy was not far distant. The enemy would be at the crossing.

Five hundred yards from the crossing, short of the first house of the village, Mackenzie halted his main body, and prepared either to support the patrol, if Couzens met light resistance, or to flee if the company was out-gunned and out-numbered. He scrambled up a rise alongside the road, sat down on a rock, and brought out his field glasses. "Come up here with me, sergeant," he called to Ekland. When Ekland came up beside him he said, "I want you to see Couzens work. Watch him work this patrol."

A ragged boy darted from the door of one of the houses and grabbed at Couzens' arm. "'Ello, Joe," he said. He was no larger than a boy of nine, but he was probably thirteen, and excitement and intelligence shone out of his eyes.

"Hi, Kim," said Couzens, halting. All the little boys of Korea—the boys that the Army and the Marines adopted and fed and made their mascots—were named Kim. Couzens knew an American column had passed through this village before, although in the opposite direction.

"Joe, they up there!" The boy pointed.

"How many?"

The boy did not understand the words, but he understood the question, for it was the natural question for an American officer to ask. He didn't know the word for the answer. He held up nine fingers.

"Nine?" said Couzens. That would be par for the course. That would be a squad.

"Nine," the boy mimicked, shaking his nine fingers at Couzens.

"They got mortars?" Couzens extended his forearm at a forty-five degree angle and added, "Poom!"

The boy shook his head, no. "Macines!" he said. "Macines!" The boy held an imaginary sub-machine gun in his hands and swept the street with it, saying, "Ah-ah-ah-ah-ah-ah," just like the small fry of America, destroying gangsters, or Indians, or spies, or Men from Mars in their radio-stimulated world of dreams.

"Thanks, Kim," said Couzens. He rested the butt of his rifle on the glazed dirt, and removed a glove, and fished in an inside pocket until he found two bars of chocolate. These he gave to the boy.

The boy said, "Thanks, Joe. I come."

"Get the hell out of here!" said Couzens, smiling and aiming an imaginary kick at the boy, and the boy grinned and scuttled back into the house, where a woman's face waited anxiously.

All this Mackenzie saw through his glasses, and while of course he could not hear the words, he interpreted the pantomime accurately. He could even reconstruct the dialogue. He chuckled, and explained it to Ekland.

Now that Couzens knew the strength and location and armament of the enemy, he could make a plan. He walked back to the jeep, and called in his flankers, and said, "They're at the crossing—nine of 'em. They don't have mortars. All they've got is burp guns. Now they've probably got three men out on sentry duty and the others are probably in the station shack at the crossing, keeping warm." At a flag stop like this there was always a frame shack, built by the Japanese when they laid down the line, to serve as a freight and passenger depot.

"Now the thing to do," Couzens went on, "is kill the six men in the shack first. Then pick up the strays. That calls for surprise."

Couzens' bazooka man, Jack Kavanaugh, said, "Well, if this jeep pokes its head outside the village, so they can see it from the crossing, there won't be a helluva lot of surprise."

"You win the eighteen thousand in cash and prizes, Jack," said the lieutenant. "I was going to get to that. You and me and Cohen are going to hit the shack, and Seitner and Flynn are going to have the jeep behind the last house on the street—the two-story house. See it, Seitner?"

"I see it, sir," Seitner said.

"Well, you and Flynn stay behind it until Kavanaugh opens up with the bazook. Then you two whip out and take care of the watch."

"Yessir."

"We go quietly, Jack," Couzens said to Kavanaugh, the bazooka man. "You and me and Cohen. We go real quiet and we don't do any shooting until you get that bazook on the shack."

So Couzens and Kavanaugh and Cohen, a rifleman, stalked the shack. Smoke came out of the shack's chimney. They were in there, all right. Couzens led, stalking the shack carefully as if he sought deer in Palm Valley. He never took a step until he was sure where that step would carry him.

On the slope five hundred yards behind, Mackenzie said, "Watch this. It'll be wonderful." And he passed the glasses to Ekland.

When Couzens was a hundred yards from the shack he eased to the ground, and took a prone position that was correct for a target range. He brought his rifle to his shoulder, and balanced it delicately, and then with a half wave of his arm, motioned to Kavanaugh to fire. A rocket left the bazook and the shack heaved and smoke poured out of it. One figure came out of the door, legs churning, and Couzens' first bullet met him before he had taken two steps. The man writhed on the snow in front of the door and Couzens shot him again. Through the head. Couzens patted his rifle.

Couzens waited for others, but they did not come, and he motioned to Cohen and Cohen charged. He charged bent far over and with shoulders hunched as men do who do not want to get hit before they can use the bayonet. He looked awkward, but he moved fast. He went through the door like a sixteen-inch shell. Nothing happened. Nothing at all. There were no shots, and in seconds Cohen appeared again, beckoning.

Couzens ran to the shack. Inside were two dead from the bazook. One was dead outside. That left six. Where were they?

Five hundred yards back, on the slope above the road, Ekland stood up and screamed and shouted, for he had seen a disastrous thing. Tiny black objects had fallen from the second floor of the house on the far end of the street.

They were grenades, and they had fallen upon the jeep hiding behind this house, and the jeep had exploded and was burning. Ekland and Mackenzie jumped down the slope and into the jeeps. Mackenzie yelled, "Let's go!"

When the grenades exploded behind, in the village, Couzens guessed what had happened. His logic had been wrong, all wrong. The squad of Chinese assigned to guard the crossing had not maintained normal security. Instead of having three men out on watch, and six in the shack, which they should have done if they were good soldiers, they had assumed there was no enemy in the area. After all, had they not only to listen to the radio to know the Americans were defeated?

So the Chinese had been lax. Their watch on the crossing consisted of three men, and these three Couzens had destroyed. But they kept six men back in the village, sleeping and resting and eating in comfort. The house in which they bivouacked was easy to spot, because the jeep, its spare gas cans alight, blazed under it, giving out many colors of smoke. Couzens knew that Seitner and Flynn were probably dead.

And he knew that his calculations had been wrong. He had failed again. He had failed Mackenzie.

At this point Couzens should have waited. He should have waited for Mackenzie to come up with the rest of the force, so that the house could be surrounded, and riddled and blown apart by cross-fires, and the enemy destroyed without loss. For of course Mackenzie had seen what had happened, and what had gone wrong, and would be streaking down the road to help him. But at this point Couzens' cleft mind was not functioning rationally, and he called to Cohen and Kavanaugh. "We take that house," he said. "We take it." And he advanced upon it, and they followed him uncertainly.

This house had two windows on the second floor, and the flame of a burp gun flickered from one of these windows and Couzens' M-1 snapped to his shoulder and he fired fast as if he swung on a single quail bursting from a palmetto clump. "Got him," he said, but fire was returned from both windows. He waited for Kavanaugh to blow them apart with the bazook and when Kavanaugh didn't fire he looked over to where Kavanaugh should be, and he saw Kavanaugh, but Kavanaugh's face was flat on the ground, and he was hit. And he looked over to where Cohen should be and he was hit, too, and down on his side, his knees jerking.

Couzens went on. Whenever he saw the flash of a brown face or hand he fired.

Running down the road, with Ackerman and Ekland, Mackenzie saw this and he stopped and shouted, "Get back, Raleigh! Get the hell back!"

Couzens heard this shout, but he did not obey. He walked on.

Then Mackenzie saw his lieutenant bow his head and sink to his knees, as if to pray, and then slide forward on his face.

After his men had disposed of the survivors in the house, swiftly and efficiently, Mackenzie tried to evaluate his loss and reorganize the company and push on. He had little heart for it. Raleigh Couzens had five, maybe six, small calibre bullets through the stomach. He was unconscious, and his bazooka man and his rifleman, the one still alive, were badly hurt too. And the bazooka was riddled, so now there was only one bazooka. He and Ekland did what they could for the wounded, with sulfa and penicillin, and had them placed on litters.

The burning jeep was the jeep with the rations packed in its back seat, so now Dog Company had no rations except the combat rations the men carried in their pockets.

Mackenzie wished he could call a halt here, but he dared not. Now speed was essential. They must get out as quickly as possible. Another detachment of Chinese might enter the village, and anyway it was a place of ill luck. "Sergeant," he told Ekland, "have the litters strapped to the hoods of the jeeps, and let's get going."

"Yes, sir, except—"

"Except what?"

"What are we going to do for rations, sir?"

"We'll worry about that when we get hungry. Right now we've got to get out of here. The quicker we start moving the quicker we'll get to some place where these men can be treated, and we can get rations." He hoped this was true, but of course he had no way of knowing. It was the only thing to say.

And the column moved out of the unlucky village of Chungyang-ni, and crossed the railroad tracks, rusty under a veneer of ice, and trudged uphill into the loneliness of the road.

The road ascended steadily and the men walked with bent heads, and there was no sound except the laboring motors of the jeeps, and the pain of the wounded. They were all unconscious now, and Mackenzie was grateful for this, but still they made noises when the jeeps jolted in the ruts.

At noon Mackenzie called a break, and the men ate what rations they had left. Mackenzie wondered how long men could endure, and march, without rations in this cold, but of course he said nothing of this to the men. He called Ekland, and together they went over the map.

"This place up here," said Mackenzie, pointing to a black dot on the map which marked some sort of habitation, "this place is where we'll spend the night. Then tomorrow we'll make it to the perimeter, if there is a perimeter up there. How far ahead do you think that place is, sergeant?"

"This map is sort of crazy," Ekland said. "You look at this map and you'd say four or five miles to that little place, but the map doesn't show the ups and downs. I'd say four hours' march, sir."

"That's what I figure, too," said Mackenzie. "Anyway, that's where we'll stop."

As they marched, the character of the land changed. The paddy fields, and all sign of man, vanished, and there were no longer gentle slopes such as they had seen in the valley of the railroad. Sheer rock climbed at their right, and to their left the slope deepened and the jeep drivers became wary of the left, for if they skidded they could drop off three or four hundred feet. And this land was forbidding, and seemed to close them in. And it grew colder as they climbed, and in the narrow places between the walls of this gorge the wind screamed. This wind that had crossed the frozen steppes of Asia screamed like a live and fanatic enemy.

Just before dusk they came to a place where the road widened and the land grew more level, on the crest of a ridge, and Mackenzie said to Ekland, "This must be it," and he looked about him for houses, but there were no houses.

"This was it, sir," Ekland said. He pointed to blackened timbers not quite buried under the snow. If you looked closely, you could see that three or four houses had once been here, but they had all burned. How long ago, or for what reason, they could not figure out. It didn't matter. They were gone.

"Well, let's get on with it," Mackenzie said. "We'll find some other place ahead." He knew this wasn't true. He knew they would have no shelter in the night. But the further he could lead, or drive them, this day, the better chance they'd have of finding someone, or some place, the next day.

They moved on, slower. They moved even after darkness came. They moved until Mackenzie's legs would move no more. The collapse of his men was immediate. He had to kick them to their feet to force them to change their sweat-soaked socks, which would surely freeze in the night. The litters, with the wounded, he ordered placed under the jeeps, where they would have some protection from the weather. Then Mackenzie, numb and exhausted utterly, collapsed too. His mind was so tired, and so concentrated on his men, that he forgot an important thing. His jeeps needed warmth in the night.

After his captain slept Ekland crawled into the front seat of the lead jeep, and found the walkie-talkie. The map told him there was no chance of his voice reaching anyone. His logic told him too. But one could never be certain with radio waves. There were skip waves. There was the Heaviside bounce. And anyway it was comforting to believe someone could hear him. "This is Lightning Four," he said. "This is Lightning Four calling Lightning. Come in Lightning."

He repeated this several times, but there was never any answer, and at last he gave up, and got out of the jeep, and found a place for himself against the cliff, and slept.

Chapter Twelve

IT WAS DURING this terrible night that the three wounded died, and the jeeps froze solid.

And it was on the following morning that Mackenzie jogged himself, and his men, into movement with the promise of the bottle of Scotch. It was the morning they ate combat rations that Ekland found in the pockets of the dead. It was the morning they were shadowed by the Mongol horsemen watching them from the cone-shaped hills across the gorge, and the morning they were ambushed by mortars when they reached a place of danger where the road left the protection of the cliff, and ran out into the rock-strewn flatland to touch a frozen stream.

And now Ackerman, the quiet corporal from Pennsylvania, lay dead out on the flatland, and under Ackerman was Dog Company's last bazooka. Mackenzie had told Nick Tinker, the youngest of them all, to go out and bring back the bazooka, for without the bazooka he didn't think they had a chance for it.

As Tinker slid out into the open from the shelter of the rocks, and the defilade of the hill, Mackenzie disposed his forces. He backed out of his own point of vantage, and in it placed Ekland with the BAR. "You cover Tinker," Mackenzie ordered, "but don't open fire unless you get a definite target. Don't want to expose our position unless it's absolutely necessary."

He brought up Beany Smith, with an M-1, to support Ekland. Four men, under Heinzerling, he stationed further along the road, so that if a fire fight developed Dog Company would not be taken from the rear. For the others he found a secure place, around a corner of the hill, where they would be safe from fragments if the enemy brought the position under mortar fire. Then he himself squirmed up beside Ekland and Smith to observe Tinker's progress.

Tinker was trying to remember how a jackrabbit behaved in the sand hills. This place reminded him of a wild canyon where one winter his brothers had spread a trap line, and he had stalked jacks with his twenty-two. This place looked much the same, and was no colder.

A jack ran a little, and then stopped dead, and when he stopped he blended into the background, and you could not see him. So Tinker paid careful attention to his surroundings, and avoided placing himself between the drifts of snow and the hills opposite, where the enemy watched. And he ran a little and then froze, like a jack.

Tinker wished his brothers could see him now. Matt, Pike, and Bill had been much older than he, and bigger, and stronger, and wiser in the ways of the ranch and the wilderness, and they had held him in contempt. But they could not have contempt for him now, darting out under the guns of the Chinese with more wit, and speed, and guts than they had ever shown. Specially picked by his captain —picked above all the older men.

Nick was the runt of the family, a child of the depression. And whenever, at table, Old Matt spoke of the depression—from which the Tinkers had never fully recovered and upon which he blamed most of his troubles—he looked at Nick. Nick was given to understand that in the cruel days of the depression his birth had been one in a series of undeserved financial catastrophes his father had endured. And he was given to understand he was unwanted, and entirely the fault of a careless mother.

The mother shielded him from insult and brutality as best she could, but there was little she could do, because she herself was trapped and enslaved. Sometimes, when the others were gone, she surrounded him with her arms and wept, and said, "My poor little boy. My poor little Nick."

On his seventeenth birthday Nick saw a Marine Corps recruiting advertisement in a magazine, and was fascinated by it. The sergeant in the advertisement wore a splendid blue uniform, his chest was bright with ribbons, and the girl on his arm was incredibly pretty. His three brothers, when they had money, drove to Hyannis for the weekly Saturday night dances. They came back smelling of beer and boasting of girls. But Nick in all his life had never had a girl, or a drink, although of course he never admitted this to Dog Company. So he took a bus to Omaha, with his father's written blessing, and joined the Marines.

There were no girls, and no blue uniforms either, in his seven months as a Marine. There was hard training at Lejeune, and then a long ocean voyage, and at Inchon he found himself a replacement in the First Division. He was given the patch of Guadalcanal, with the design of the Southern Cross, to wear on his sleeve. He was proud of it.

Now Tinker was close to Ackerman's body. He had not yet been shot at. He hoped the captain was watching, to see how correctly he behaved.

The captain watched through his glasses. The kid was doing a wonderful job, and had not drawn fire. Sometimes the kid snaked on his belly, and sometimes he ran, and sometimes he vanished into the terrain. He wondered how the kid had learned it. Then Tinker disappeared entirely, and the captain shifted his glasses to Ackerman, because he couldn't tell how close Tinker might be to the bazook.

Something moved within Mackenzie's focus. It did not move like a man. It seemed only that a clod of earth shifted, but Mackenzie knew it was Tinker. Then, definitely, he saw Tinker bend over Ackerman, or what was left of Ackerman.

The two figures were fused, and immobile, for long seconds. Mackenzie found he was talking to himself. He was whispering, "Get the hell out of there, you dope. Get out, you stupid kid!"

At last, he saw the two figures in his glasses separate, and in that moment Ekland shouted, "Here they come!" Ekland's long-barreled automatic rifle began to speak, in short bursts.

Mackenzie watched three, then two, then three more Mongol cavalrymen debouch from a rent in the hills across the gorge. He said, quietly, "Aim low, sergeant. Get the horses."

He saw Tinker running, but at this distance it seemed

Tinker barely moved, but Tinker had the bazook, all right. And he saw the short-coupled, shaggy ponies eating up the distance like quarter horses, and he knew the boy could not make it. He shouted for his men, back of him, safe behind the shoulder of the hill. He shouted for them to come up. It would be all over, one way or another, in a minute, and he did not believe the Chinese mortars could zero in on him in that time, and he had to have more fire-power if Tinker and the bazooka were to be saved.

At the strip of ice that was the stream the Mongol horse-men slowed, and it was there that Ekland's BAR began to find targets. Two horses dropped. And Mackenzie was aware of the welcome bark of rifles behind him. His men were firing slowly and steadily, and he knew that it was aimed fire, and he hoped they had remembered to set their sights for range and windage. Often, in battle, men forgot. Often men forgot to fire at all. There was nothing he could do to instruct or guide them now. It was all a matter of their training.

Four cavalrymen got across the stream and bore down on Tinker, and the captain could see they'd be able to cut him off. Then another pony crashed, but its rider was unin-jured, and bounced from the ground and continued his charge. Although the range was extreme, Mackenzie be-gan shooting at this man with his carbine, and at the fifth shot the Mongol fell.

The captain saw that Tinker was on the ground now, crouched and firing. He had been run to earth, and three cavalrymen, dismounted, were closing in on him, and Mackenzie could faintly hear their cries, and the nasty snicker of their burp guns. Then two figures only were running, and the one in front must have been Tinker, because this figure was lugging a bazooka. Ekland's BAR jumped and rattled, and the second figure sank to his knees, and then sprawled backwards, contorted, and did not move thereafter.

When Tinker came closer Mackenzie thought he was purposely weaving, like a quarterback dodging through a broken field, but then he saw that the boy was badly hurt, and the captain left his concealment and ran out to meet him. The captain grabbed the bazooka, and then half-carried Tinker into the shelter of the rocks. "Litter!" Mackenzie called. "Litter and four men!"

Tinker lay in the litter with his legs spread, writhing like a fighter who has been fouled in the groin, and grinning in agony, but there was no time to help him then. It was time to leave this evil place. The captain motioned Ostergaard to take up the bazooka, and said, "Let's get out of here." He lashed his column with his tongue, and it moved. They had gone only a few hundred yards-when mortars began crashing in the place where they had been.

A mile further along the road, when they had put another ridge behind them, the captain called a halt. It was necessary to do something about Tinker. Tinker's cries were unnerving his men. One of the jericans was back there somewhere behind the hill, foolishly abandoned in the scramble, but the other had been brought out, and it held perhaps three gallons. His men built another pyramid of pebbles and stones, and saturated it with the gasoline that was left, and he had his fire. He edged Tinker's litter close to the fire. He took off his gloves, and flexed his fingers close to the flame until they were no longer numb. Then he went to work.

With such a wound as this he had no experience. If no large artery was severed, he guessed the boy had a chance. If he could be got to an aid station, or a doctor—any kind of a doctor—even a Chinese doctor. And if he did not die from pain alone. Mackenzie had never heard of such a thing, but he thought that in this case it would be possible. From his musette bag the captain brought his first-aid kit, which he had supplemented from medical stores of his own choosing. In the kit were two morphine syrettes. After his experience on the Tenaru River, he had never been without them in the field. He ripped the plastic cap from the top of one of the tubes, exposing the sterile needle. He slammed the needle into Tinker's arm, squeezing the tube flat.

The boy kept on screaming.

The captain ignored the sounds, but a few of the men turned away, white-faced. The captain dusted the wound with sulfa powder, and taped a dressing over it the best he could. Some of the men still watched in silence, but he sensed their nerves were going. He tried to force the penicillin capsules into Tinker's mouth. It didn't work. The boy couldn't close his mouth to swallow, because of his pain.

In a taut voice, Ekland said, "Give him the other shot, captain."

Mackenzie considered this. A half grain ought to be plenty. A half grain was enough for any man. All the morphine needed was a little time. It would work. It had to work. And in any case, there was only this one syrette left, and it might be needed later. Maybe Tinker would need it later, maybe somebody else, maybe even himself.

He thought of an alternative. He said to Ekland, "Hand me that bottle." He couldn't reach it himself. He was holding Tinker down.

"The bottle of Scotch?" said Ekland.

"Yes. The bottle of Scotch."

Ekland found the leather case in the captain's pocket, and pushed it into his hand.

"Tinker," the captain said, bending low over the boy, "look at me. Look at me, I say! I'm going to give you a drink. I'm going to give you a big drink of Scotch whiskey and then you've got to swallow this penicillin."

The men watched, wooden.

Tinker stopped making noises. He wet his lips with his tongue and said, "Sir, I don't want whiskey. I want water." He choked a little, and whimpered like a lost puppy and said, "I want my mother."

The captain reached for one of the canteens thawing near the dwindling flame. "All right," he told Tinker. "Water. One drink and then you swallow these." He held out the pills.

The boy drank, and gulped the penicillin, and then the captain allowed him to wash it down with more water. Tinker was easier now, but his eyes were still desperate. "Captain," he said, "you not going to leave me? You wouldn't leave me, would you?"

"No," the captain said gently. "We're not going to leave you. Not now, or ever." He brought out the cigarettes and counted them. "One to three men," he said, "and Tinker can have one all to himself. Off your butts! Come on! Get going!"

Mackenzie trudged at the head of Dog Company, sharing his cigarette with Ekland and Beany Smith. Somewhere ahead he began to hear the thud and drum of cannon, and he knew it must be either the defenses of the perimeter—if there was a perimeter—or the guns of the fleet. The Chinese had no guns like that, nor would they spend ammunition so lavishly. It was encouraging, but the sound was far distant, and every fibre of him was tired. He realized that the ordeal with Tinker, now swinging quietly between four litter-bearers, had sapped his energy. It had dropped his vitality and reserves a full notch.

Beany Smith was aware that the captain was faltering. Back a few miles the Skipper had seemed fresh as any of them, but now Beany Smith knew he was fresher than the Skipper, and this frightened him. For the first time in his life Beany Smith had learned to depend on, and trust, somebody besides himself. He trusted the Skipper, even if the Skipper didn't trust him.

Right from the first Beany Smith had hated Mackenzie, which was natural. Beany Smith hated authority, and the captain was authority. He began hating authority in his school, which was a very select school—selected for bastards, literal born-bastards, like himself. It was called an orphanage, and the papers referred to those at the school as "homeless waifs." But he had known what the school was, and what he was, ever since he was six.

He ran off at fourteen, and was caught and sent back; and at fifteen he ran away twice again and was caught both times and returned, and he began to hate cops. At sixteen he knew enough of the world outside to make good an escape. He hitch-hiked to Memphis and got himself a job as a bag boy in a serve-yourself grocery store. After a year in the grocery he knew all the tricks, including those of the manager. For the first time he was eating well, but the manager and the company cops called it pilfering, and he was fired.

So he drifted with the seasons, picking apricots in California and apples in Oregon, and even oranges in Florida. He fell for a tired dance hall hostess in Chicago, and married her. She was something of a tramp. She spent her afternoons in the bedroom, reading the confession magazines littering her dressing table, and fixing her flaccid face. At night she'd usually be drunk. One night he looked behind the dirty cretonne skirts of the dressing table. That was where she cached her empty gin bottles.

He got himself a job selling mutuel tickets at Sportsman's Park. When the racing season ended he hitchhiked to Reno and got a job as stickman at a dice table. It wasn't true about his palming chips, but he was fired anyway, and the cops took him to the edge of town. Then they booted him.

So he went back to Memphis because in Memphis he knew a few people who'd buy him a meal, and give him a bed for a night or two. He was in trouble again soon enough. He snatched a car, although the technical charge was reduced to "joyriding."

The judge asked his age and he said nineteen, although it was really twenty-two. That was smart. The judge gave him a choice—ninety days in the can or join the service. The Marines accepted him, after looking him over with tolerant care. His physical was good, and his mental test surprisingly high, and this seemed to have over-balanced his record, or what they knew of it.

This Skipper, this Old Man, had been rough on him, Smith thought, ever since they left the Stateside port of embarkation. But he'd got no more than he'd deserved. No phony raps. Mackenzie was rough, but square. Beany Smith sucked the last good from their cigarette, and said, "Captain, can I spell you with that musette bag, and the bottle?"

Mackenzie was startled. This was the first time that Beany Smith had ever volunteered for anything. The bottle, pulling at his pocket, had grown heavier, and the musette bag and carbine also seemed to be gaining weight. A man of thirty had already lost something. A march like this separated the men from the boys, and it was the boys, not the men, who could take it. "All right, Smith," said the captain. "You can spell me." He lowered his shoulder and slipped the strap of the bag, and he reached into his pocket and brought out the bottle and handed it to Private Smith. It was a surprising relief.

Beany Smith slung the bag over his shoulder, and cuddled the bottle under his arm, as the captain had in the early morning, when they started. And somehow he felt stronger. He felt he could carry the bag, and the bottle, forever. The Skipper had trusted him. The Skipper had made him part of something. He was part of Dog Company. He no longer hated the Skipper, or feared him, or was jealous or envious of him. "Captain," said Beany Smith, "the girl who gave you this bottle—she's your wife now, isn't she?"

"That's right—she's my wife."

"Get along pretty good with her?"

"Uh-huh."

"I had a wife once. We didn't get along so hot."

"That's too bad."

"But I wish I was back with her now." They walked in silence, matching strides, and then Smith said, "How come you didn't drink the bottle when you got married? That was the time, wasn't it?"

The captain's laugh was muffled in his parka. "We talked it over, and decided not. Anyway, there was too much champagne."

"It must have been a swell wedding."

"Not so swell, it was wartime." Even at that, it had been too fancy for his taste, and Anne's, but the Longstreets had insisted on the full treatment. The marriage was three weeks after he'd got home, three weeks after he thought he'd lost her to the Air Force major. There'd been everything, even an arch of swords, and a general to lift a toast.

Mackenzie looked down at the bottle, in its red leather case, firm under Beany Smith's arm. He recalled how they had the bottle between them, he and Anne, as they drove towards Tahoe that night, and how they talked about it. "Another reason we didn't open it on the night we were married," Mackenzie said to Beany Smith, "was because we decided to wait until V-E Day. We were sure that would be the biggest day in the lives of all of us."

"That was right, wasn't it, captain?"

"No, it wasn't right. It should've been right, but it wasn't. Anyway, we decided to postpone it until we had a baby."

"Have one?"

"We certainly did!"

"Well, why didn't you drink it then?"

Beany Smith was being awfully inquisitive for a second-class private, but Mackenzie found he didn't mind, and wasn't even irritated. "Well, when Sam, junior, was born we decided it wasn't the time, either. It wouldn't be fair to the ones that came after, if we drank it then."

"So you've got other kids, captain?"

"No, not yet." He found the men had been inching close to him, so they could listen. "Stop bunching up!" he roared. They fell back into column, as they should.

Mackenzie now believed that the walls of the gorge were not quite so sheer, and then he noted, through a gap in the hills off to the right, clouds of greasy smoke ascending to the glowering, slate-colored sky. He knew it was time to work out his problem on the map, and form a plan. "Take five," he ordered. Without a fire to warm them, five minutes' rest would be all they'd want.

He broke out the cigarettes, and distributed one to three men, as he had before, and posted his watch front and rear. Little Nick Tinker was asleep, or unconscious, so the cigarettes came out even. Then, as his men dropped to the ground, Mackenzie pulled out his map, and called for Ekland. Those fat columns of smoke, he knew from experience, came from burning fuel dumps. "Where do you figure those would be?" he asked Ekland, pointing at the pillars of smoke.

"Well, sir, Ten Corps has big ammo and fuel dumps at Hamhung. I think it must be those dumps burning." Hamhung was the grimy industrial city six miles inland from the port of Hungnam.

Mackenzie inspected the map, and estimated their progress on the road from Koto-Ri. It checked. The pillars of smoke told him other things. Hamhung had been abandoned, but very recently. So a perimeter probably existed, although it must be much compressed. Still, in three or four miles they might run into the American lines, or anyway encounter a patrol.

The main Communist effort would naturally be on the main road, and the railroad, that ran through Hamhung. There, also, would be their heaviest concentration of troops. If he knew them, they'd all be rushing to Hamhung anyway, for the loot.

Then Mackenzie saw something on the map that made him frown. At a point ahead which he could not see, with his glasses, but still not far ahead, where according to the map the hills dropped away, a heavier road crossed his secondary road. "What do you think of this?" he asked the red-bearded sergeant, and jabbed with his gloved finger at the map.

Ekland looked at the map, and then looked up and concentrated on the terrain. "That looks like a bad spot, sir. But we've come further than I thought. We've done real good."

"It doesn't matter how far we've come. It's where we're going that counts. Think we'll find a road block there?"

"If they have one anywhere, that's where it'll be. If they're bringing tanks on down from the north, that's where those tanks will be crossing our road. Right there."

The captain nodded. Ekland had confirmed his own

deduction. He turned to Beany Smith. "I'll take the musette bag, and the bottle, now," he said.

"I don't mind carrying it on, sir."

"Thanks, Smith, but from here on it's all downhill. And it isn't far."

He slipped the bag over his shoulder, shoved the bottle into his pocket, and yelled, "All right, off your butts!" And they moved forward again.

Chapter Thirteen

THE CAPTAIN NOW walked warily, his eyes traversing the ground ahead, from left to right and back again, alert for the smallest movement, the most obscure sign. A foot soldier's eyes must be more sensitive than radar, if he is to live, for his enemies include the microbes of war—the tiny plastic mine to blow off a leg; the booby trap, to blow off his hands; the sniper, to blow out his guts while his mind wanders in a far place; the rifle grenade, to seek him in his hole. There is a reason for this concentration on the foot soldier. He wins and loses skirmishes, battles, countries. He can even win, or lose, a world.

As they marched, the captain faced the full measure of their peril, and sought a solution.

The Chinese fought like Indians, while up to now the Americans had fought like Braddock and his Redcoats, trapped, ambushed, and cut to pieces in the Appalachian forests, while chained and bound by their transport to the roads and the trails. Of course Braddock had had a good lieutenant. Name of George Washington. A real good soldier, Washington. While Braddock commanded him he obeyed orders, and took his punishment, the hard way. He'd learned his lesson, the hard way, and never forgot it. And eventually the American frontiersmen, the Scouts and Rangers and Cavalry, had known more of bush fighting than the Indians, and won out in the end.

And the Americans would win again, for their tradition was to discard tradition, when necessary, and to improvise, and invent, and tear up the rule book and the military manual.

The captain was aware that he was walking easily, as if downhill. Truly the ground dropped off before him, and far ahead he saw where the gorge emptied into the plain beyond, and an unbroken vista of horizon opened; and he held up his hand, and halted his men.

Then the captain saw what he was looking for. Where the hills merged with the level land, something had moved. And although it was all over in a breath, he knew what it was. At that point, a tank had stuck its ugly snout past a projection, sniffed, and retreated. The captain marshaled his company, and prepared his mind and his will for a final effort.

He called Ekland to his side. "Sergeant," he said, "they're there, at the crossroads. They've got a tank there."

"Yes, sir."

"I think they've spotted us, and they're waiting for us to come down the road, like we always do. They think we're a patrol, and behind us there'll be vehicles, like there always are. The Americans always have vehicles, don't we?"

Ekland guessed what the captain was thinking. "So we take to the hills."

"Some of us take to the hills. One of us can't." The captain looked back to where four of his men had laid down the litter with Tinker in it, and then dropped to their haunches beside the litter, exhausted.

Ekland stared up at the hill flanking the road on their right, steep and forbidding. "We'd never get him up there, would we? I don't know that we can get ourselves up there."

"We can make it," the captain said, "but not with Tinker."

"So what do we do—make a fight of it?"

"We make a fight of it—but not the way they expect. We don't stick to the road, not those who are going to do the fighting. And some of us are going to get through and one of those who is going to get through is that kid, Tinker. And I want to put him in for a gong, sergeant. If I'm not around to do it, you do it."

"Yes, sir, but—"

The captain called for Ostergaard. "How many rounds you got for that bazook you're carrying there?" he asked Ostergaard.

"I've got one, sir, and Kato is carrying one, and Beany Smith has got one and Vermillion one, and I think somewhere there are two others." With everything else he had to carry, a man couldn't lug along more than one, or at the most two, bazooka rockets.

"You know much about a bazooka, Ostergaard?"

"Not much, sir. I fired one once in training, Stateside, and I fired three or four when we took that house apart back at that last town. That's all I know, sir."

"Okay, you be my loader, then. You take two rounds with you, and Beany Smith, he should have two rounds, and I'll take the bazook. Four rounds should be plenty. If there's one tank, one should do it. One should be enough, because if you miss, the tank always gets in the second shot. If there are two tanks, I doubt if fifty rounds would be enough. Still, we'll take a couple of extra rounds."

The captain looked about him, and summoned them all with his eyes. "Okay, you men," he said. "Now we're going to split up this force into two parties. One party will be under Sergeant Ekland, and this party will include Tinker and four litter-bearers, and four good riflemen. The sergeant's party is to march straight on down the road, Ekland leading, then the other four, strung out.

"Five men are to come up the hill with me and the bazook. Ostergaard, Smith, Heinzerling, Kato, and Vermillion.

"Sergeant, you give us time to get to the top before you start, because when you pass the crossroads I want to be sitting up there on the nose of the hill with the bazook."

The captain noticed that Ekland's red, stiff beard pointed straight out, as if in protest, and he knew his sergeant was shaken. "You mean, sir—you mean you want us to move right across that tank's line of fire, like ducks in a shooting gallery?"

"That's it, sergeant. That's it exactly. And I don't want you even to look around. I don't want you to raise your eyes from the ground. I want you to pretend you're unconscious."

"I will be."

"No, you won't. That tank will be backed up a hundred yards or so on the other road, at the crossing. That tank doesn't want you. That tank doesn't want the litter and

Tinker, and the bearers. That tank wants the jeeps, and the weapons carriers, and the six-by-sixes, and all the other fat targets that ought to be behind us, but aren't."

"I get it," Ekland said. But the sergeant's quick mind sought and found a weakness in the captain's reasoning. Had the Chinese, ahead at the crossroads, guessed the Marines' strength only by direct observation, or did they know it surely by radio from the Mongol cavalry and the mortar battery, back aways? The sergeant decided not to raise the question. It would only complicate things, and might stir doubt in his men. And at least the captain had a plan, and he didn't.

"Don't even turn your head," the captain said. "Not until you hear shooting. Until you hear my bazook. Then crack down with everything you've got, because we may need help to get off that hill."

Aboard a battleship at sea, within sight of the port of Hungnam so that its sixteen-inch guns could fire supporting missions, when called on, there was that morning a meeting of men, if not of minds, for an American army had never before been confronted with a situation like this, and it required study. The British had faced up to it, at Gallipoli, and Dunkirk, and Greece. They knew the word, evacuation, so it was fitting that a British Navy captain was included in the conference. And the Britisher was speaking:

"Gentlemen, I feel that the thing to do is pull back the perimeter gradually, in the darkness hours under cover of the guns. You have the guns. At Dunkirk, we didn't. You can lay down a curtain of fire that a mouse couldn't get through. Under this curtain you bring out the units that have been hurt, and you allow your fresh divisions—the Third Division and the ROK Capitol—to undertake the ground defense."

"Bring out the Marines!" said a general of Marines.

The Englishman inclined his head, and said, "Yes. First."

"We don't have to bring out the Marines," the general said. "Not yet."

"What are your casualties?"

"Three, maybe four thousand in the Division."

"Including frostbite?"

"No."

"General," said the Englishman, "with casualties like that, I don't see how your force can any longer be effective."

The general sat up straight, and beat his fist on the wardroom table, and started to explain about the Marines, and in particular about the First Marine Division, but the British four-striper smiled at him, and the general knew that the Britisher knew about the Marines, already, and was only trying to be helpful.

"We need the Marine Division," the Britisher said quietly. "We need them."

"Okay," the general said, "we bring them out. Now." He turned to his G-3. "Where are we?"

"Two regiments are in the perimeter," the G-3 said, "and the other is coming in. It's coming in with its guns, and its equipment, and its wounded."

"That doesn't sound like we have to be taken out of here, now does it?" said the general.

The Corps commander, who until then had held himself apart from the discussion, said, "We evacuate your Division. Now."

The general said, "Yes, sir," and turned to his staff sitting behind him and asked, "Everybody accounted for?"

For a moment, none of his staff spoke, and then a Major Toomey, recently arrived from Washington, said, "Sir, I think the last regiment has a company missing. It is called Dog Company. It was sent out on that secondary road there—" he looked up at the map on the wardroom bulkhead—"to protect the regiment's flank. It left Koto-Ri okay, but reduced in size, and it wasn't heard from again until last night. Last night, according to the action reports, someone operating a walkie-talkie at Regiment heard this company calling. This company's code name is Lightning Four, and that's what this man at Regiment heard."

"Did he contact this company?" the Corps commander asked.

"He tried, sir, but he couldn't raise them. These short-range talkies are tricky."

The admiral, who had not said a word, said, "What are we going to do about this company? Are we going to abandon them?"

Nobody spoke, but all of them knew the answer.

"We have to have air," said the general of Marines. "That's up to you, admiral."

"There isn't any air today," said the admiral, who once had been an air admiral. About the time most of the men fighting in Korea were born, this admiral was flying a boxkite onto the deck of the *Langley.*

"It'll take air to find that company, and support it, if it's still there," said the general.

"This whole coast is socked in," said the admiral. "I wouldn't send out a buzzard to fly in this weather. Specially over those goddam mis-mapped hills." He scratched his chin. "However, we might send out a pinwheel, just to look for them, to see if they're still there. Where's my air controller?"

A commander in the back row stood up and said, "Here, sir," as if answering roll call at school.

"How many pinwheels you got?"

"Well, right now, sir, all of them are out on air-sea rescue, or gun-laying for the cruisers. Except I think there's a one-place job standing by on the *Leyte*."

"What can it do?"

"I'm afraid not much for this job, sir. It's only designed for short-range reconnaissance, and spotting. It doesn't carry anything except a second lieutenant."

"Can't it drop anything?" the admiral asked. "Medical stores or anything?"

"Not very well, sir. The pilot's all by himself in a plexi-glass bubble in the bow. He can't do much except look."

"Well, what in hell is it good for, except spot?"

"That's about all, sir. But it does have a couple of basket litters rigged on the outside, to pick up wounded. It's picked up quite a few wounded."

The admiral scratched his chin again, and then he scratched the back of his neck. "If it can bring back wounded," he said, "it can bring up supplies. Ever think of that, commander?"

"No, sir."

"Well, have those basket litters filled with supplies, and send it out. At least we'll find out whether that company is still there, or not. What kind of supplies do you think they'll need, general, that is, if they're still on the road?"

"Ammo," said the general of Marines. "Ammo and food and cigarettes."

"What kind of ammo?"

"Rifle, M-1."

"Okay, get going," the admiral told the air controller, and the conference turned to other business.

In the Combat Intelligence Center on the *Leyte,* Second Lieutenant Slaton Telfair, III, who his friends called Pinky, listened closely to his briefing, and when the briefing officer finished he asked a question, tracing a pencil along the secondary road as the map showed it. "Who owns this real estate?" he asked.

"Reds. The Chinese."

"Then what's that company doing there?"

"I personally don't think it is there any more," said the briefing officer, "but higher authority thinks it's there. Higher authority thinks it sent out some sort of a radio message last night. On a walkie-talkie."

"So I stick my neck out along that road, in this weather, looking for some people who probably aren't there? Sir, do you have the correct spelling of my next-of-kin?"

The briefing officer grinned, and so did Slaton Telfair, III, and the briefing officer said, "If you run into small-arms fire you're to come back. We don't want to lose that pinwheel."

In a few minutes a helicopter rose straight up off the

deck of the *Leyte*, like a noisy blue fly, and headed towards the unseen land.

When he was sure the captain had reached the ridge
line, Sergeant Ekland ordered his men forward. Occasionally he looked behind him to make certain his men kept a
good distance. To the Chinese, his detachment must look
like a patrol, a considerable patrol. "Loosen up," he commanded over his shoulder. "Take it easy. Pretend like they
ain't there."

Mackenzie had reached the nose of the hill, with Ostergaard puffing behind him. "Load it!" the captain said.

Ostergaard loaded it. Beany Smith and Heinzerling
and Kato spread out, along this nose, to cover the captain.
They wormed themselves into the ground until they were
solid. They made sure their grenades were at hand.

From this point the captain could see the road, and the
heavier road that crossed it, and which had been macad-
amized, and although pitted and worn, in this part of the
world could be considered a main road. Far below him,
to the left, he could see nine men of his company, four of
them carrying Tinker's litter, marching steadily. He could
also see the enemy tank and ambush, exactly where he
had placed it in the map of his mind. Men were swarming
over the tank like ants over a beetle. He put his glasses on
it.

It was a Russian T-34, sleekly stream-lined. Its armor
would deflect most projectiles fired from ground level.
But Mackenzie wasn't on the ground. He was on top of
them. He wriggled forward on his belly until he came to a

place where he could steady the bazook upon a rock. "Don't let 'em see you," he whispered.

His men crept up beside him.

Mackenzie watched. He watched the sergeant and his men approach the crossroads. If I ever get back, he thought, I'll make the colonel commission him. I'll scream and shout until he gets shoulder straps. It sounded ridiculous. If he ever got back. He was lucky to have come as far as this. He aimed the bazooka until the sights steadied exactly on the spot where the turret joined the chassis. Then, hardly breathing, he marked the progress of his men.

He saw Ekland's tightly knit figure come to the crossroads, and Mackenzie said his luck aloud:

"He either fears his fate too much,
"Or his deserts are small,
"That dares not put it to the touch
"To gain or lose it all."

Ostergaard, working up beside him with an extra rocket, said, "What was that you said, sir?"

"I didn't say a damned thing."

"Yes, you did, sir."

"Okay, Ostergaard, so I said something. And if you are smart you will be quiet and when I let this bazook loose you'll say something with that M-1, and also keep that extra bazook round handy."

"Yes, sir."

The captain watched. The erect, miniature figure that was Ekland reached the cross of the road, and walked on,

from this distance cocky and confident as if he were leading a patrol into a waterside bar in Dago. Behind Ekland
came Tinker's litter, and behind them, well strung out,
the four good riflemen. The captain held his heart for
them. He waited for the Communist burp gunners, now
invisible in their hiding places around the tank, to open up.
They didn't, and he held fast to his fetish. What a ridiculous thing, the captain thought, that his fetish was a hunk
of poetry—an old double couplet written by Montrose, the
Scotsman, the wild and brash Scotsman. He supposed
every soldier must have a fetish of some kind, to be con-
sulted like a Haitian *ounga* before battle. It was a picture
in a wallet, a coin, a charm, a six-sided star to keep a man
from harm.

And all he had was four lines, written three hundred
years back.

Ekland's detachment passed through, all of them, without drawing fire.

Mackenzie's finger tightened around the trigger of the
bazook, slowly and carefully, as if he were instructing a
squad back in boot camp at Lejeune.

The bazook said, "Shooo!"

The tank shuddered and buckled, and Mackenzie heard
an explosion, muffled, for the shaped charge had exploded
inside the tank. Then he saw that what had been a T-34,
sleek, fast, and dangerous, was now an iron coffin leaking
smoke. "Okay!" the captain said. "Off your butts. Let's go!"

They charged down the slope of the hill, yelling. It was
ridiculous. It was like an old film of the U.S. Cavalry,
pennons flying, routing the redskins. It was San Juan Hill,

232

and Hill 609, and Washington's ragged Continentals rallying at Trenton. It made no military sense at all.

It seemed to Mackenzie that he simply floated down the hill, and it was not until he was almost at the bottom that he realized he still carried the bazooka, which he didn't need at the moment, while his carbine banged against his back. It was too late to stop, and do anything about it, and anyway the bazook might be needed again, so he kept on running. When he was almost to the tank he saw a figure rise up in front of him, and this figure had a gun of some sort and Mackenzie tried to swing his bazooka like a bat, but it was too big and unwieldy. Anyway the figure backed away.

Although he was within ten feet of the Chinese tommygunner when the man fired, Mackenzie never saw it. All he knew was that he was on his face, in a pile of icy shale and broken rock, and his knees were drawn up, because his stomach hurt so.

Ekland saw the whole thing. He had led his column, as the captain commanded, past the crossroads, keeping his eyes straight ahead, watching his crusted boots move. He did not so much as bob his helmet as they passed the Chinese tank. He tried to walk confidently, as if powerful support was not far behind. He concentrated on this bit of acting. This concentration allowed him to hold in his fear.

He walked like this until he heard the explosion of the bazooka's rocket, and then he wheeled, and the four men carrying Tinker's litter put the litter down, and with the other four they turned the other way. At first Ekland's detail walked, until they were sure the tank was killed, and then they started running. Ekland saw Mackenzie and the others leaping down the hill. He also saw that there were eight or ten of the enemy milling around the tank and he shouted, "Watch out!" but of course the captain couldn't hear him.

He saw one of the Chinese turn and cut down the captain. He saw it all.

Ekland knelt and began to fire his BAR, and his men were firing too. Ekland fired until there was no more ammunition, but by then there were no more targets either.

He ran to where the captain lay, and shoved the others aside, saying, "Don't crowd him!"

He saw that the captain still lived but he knew the captain was badly hurt, for every few seconds the captain had a spasm, or a fit, or something, and his arms and legs jerked and his face was shorn of color, and contorted. Beany Smith was thrusting an aid kit at Ekland, and he took it, and said, "Please, sir, hold still."

And by a miracle of will Mackenzie relaxed on his back and breathed and held still, and Ekland went to work on him.

There was only one bullet hole, high in the stomach, almost in the solar plexus. It bled, a lot. The bullet hadn't come out through the back.

Ekland looked around when he had finished his job with the sulfa powder and the compress. He looked at the faces of his men. They were all thinking what he was thinking—the captain was going to crap out. "Come on, we've got to get out of here," Ekland said. "There'll be more Chinese along this crossroad—lots of 'em. Where's the other litter?"

"Back with Tinker," said one of the litter men.

"Well, we can't give the time to get it," said Ekland. "We have to bring the Skipper over to it." He selected his two huskiest men. "Ostergaard, you and Heinzerling, you carry the captain. Give your guns to somebody."

For the first time since he had been hit, Mackenzie spoke, "Get the hell out of here, you damn fools. I've had it."

Nobody paid any attention to him. Heinzerling and Ostergaard made a cradle of their arms, and the captain was lifted into it, and then they found that he could not hold on, and had no support for his back, so Beany Smith held up his back, and they carried him across the road, and up the road to where Tinker lay, still unconscious. They carried him gently, as if they feared he would break.

They laid him down on the litter gently and Ekland said, "Sir, do you hear me, sir?"

"Yes. Water. My mouth is dry."

Ekland poured water into the captain's mouth and Mackenzie choked and spit. "Can't you hold it down, sir?"

"More." Mackenzie's voice was strained with agony.

Ekland gave him more water, and this time Mackenzie held it down, and Ekland wondered whether he was doing right. One thing he ought to do, he ought to stop the captain's pain. "Should I give you that last syrette, sir? It's in your bag, isn't it?"

The captain shook his head, no. "It might get worse. Besides I don't want to use it. So long as I don't use it we've always got it—we've always got that one. We've got something to fall back on. How's Tinker?"

"Still knocked out."

"He might wake up. If he wakes up and starts to scream,

then you use it, you hear me, sergeant? Then you use it."

The captain's head fell back, and they thought he was dead, but he kept on breathing. Ekland turned to Beany Smith, kneeling beside the captain. "Smith, give me that bottle! He needs it! He needs it now!"

The captain's hand moved, and closed on his pocket. "No!" he said. "Not yet! We don't open it yet."

"Yes, sir," said Ekland, for the captain still commanded. "Four men to this litter. Move!"

They moved, but they moved very slowly now. Their stomachs ached in emptiness, and their legs had been bastinadoed and beaten by the hills, and their shoulders screamed protest against each necessary strap across them, and they were aware of the weight of each round of their ammunition, what little was left. Their feet would no longer behave, such was their exhaustion. Their feet would no longer move straight ahead. And their heads would not behave. Their heads wanted to dream. Their heads told them to stop, and lie down, and dream.

After he crossed the coastline, Second Lieutenant Telfair, in his pinwheel, caught himself a little altitude. He crossed over those sensitive spots in the Ten Corps perimeter from where the massed guns thundered, laying a ring of fire around the evacuation. Unless you were in a pinwheel, you were pretty careful about flying over your own guns and anti-aircraft batteries. You made your recognition signals quite clear. This was not necessary with a pinwheel. Everybody knew a pinwheel, and knew only the Americans had them, and laughed at them as they proceeded across the sky like lazy dragonflies crabbing against the wind. Of course this worked both ways. Usually the Commies, the first time they saw a pinwheel, were frightened, and hid. But when they learned it did not carry bombs, or rockets, or indeed anything that could kill you from the air, they enjoyed shooting at them with small arms. They did not, however, use anti-aircraft guns on pinwheels, for they had learned this was an indiscretion. If they missed with the first shot, then the pinwheel would call down the wrath of God, in the shape of massed artillery, upon the anti-aircraft position.

After he worked the helicopter to a thousand feet, Second Lieutenant Telfair sat back and enjoyed his matchless view. He could see everything that was happening, and the burning of the stores and ammunition dumps at Hamhung especially intrigued him. He had heard about smoke rising six or eight thousand feet from an ammunition fire, and had not believed it, but now he saw it was true. There would be turbulence in that smoke, he thought, just like a thunderhead.

He looked at the map clipped to the board on his knee, and he saw how the roads were, and looked ahead and compared them with the map. The map was not exactly accurate, but it was easy to pick out the main road that ran down from the reservoir to the perimeter, because troops were still moving on it, and using the main road as a guide, he looked until he saw the secondary road. It wasn't much of a road. You could see that from the air. He didn't see anything on it, not anything at all, except a wisp of smoke at the crossroads. He got almost under this smoke, and then allowed the pinwheel to drop straight down several hundred feet.

When he was close to the road he saw that it could be a burned-out tank that smoked, and it was easy to see the bodies, about a dozen, he thought, lying around in the snow. But from the air, he couldn't tell whose tank it was, or discern the nationality of the bodies. He was pretty sure the tank and the bodies had nothing to do with the company he was looking for. A dozen bodies didn't make a company.

So Second Lieutenant Telfair caught himself some more altitude and headed up the road again, in the general direction of Koto-Ri. He soon saw he couldn't go far, because a few miles ahead the clouds butted into the peaks. And as he approached this point he saw tiny red sparks flickering. He swiveled the helicopter, and allowed it to dip for a closer look, and he saw that the people who were shooting at him were mounted on horseback. "What kind of a war is this?" he asked himself aloud. "What kind of a war is this when cavalry can scare away a helicopter? By rights they shouldn't have any cavalry, anyway."

Now Second Lieutenant Telfair, unknown to anyone aboard the *Leyte*, and against orders, carried with him several hand grenades whenever he went on a mission with his pinwheel. He had never found a desirable target for what he thought of as his bombs, but this was it, if he was ever going to find it. He waggled the pinwheel wildly to distract the horsemen's aim, and then went into what he considered a dive, meanwhile fighting to pry open, against the blast of wind, a section of his plexiglass cocoon.

When the opening was large enough, he pulled the pin of the grenade and dropped it towards earth, and banked the pinwheel to see what would happen. He saw that his bomb wasn't going to kill anyone, because the horsemen were racing off. They were no longer shooting at anybody. They were just running. "I wonder whether this pinwheel scared those horses?" he said, disappointed. When he was flying he always talked aloud to himself like that. Sometimes this made him think he was crazy, and once he had told a Navy doctor about it, and the doctor had just laughed at him. "Doesn't a pinwheel make a big racket?" the doctor had asked.

"Sure," Lieutenant Telfair had said. "You can't even hear yourself think."

"Well, that's why you talk aloud, so you can hear yourself think," the doctor had said, and the doctor had laughed until he cried. This, Lieutenant Telfair did not understand, but he knew that he thought better, on a mission, when he talked to himself. "I guess I'd better go back," he told himself.

So he stopped his pinwheel in midair, backed it around, and started towards the coast again, but he decided that on the way back he would take another, and closer, look at the burned-out tank, because nobody had bothered to shoot at him the first time. He swept along the road, low. He moved fast, too. His air speed was one hundred. A helicopter is deceptively clumsy, like a pelican. A helicopter is not really so slow. A helicopter flies faster than a duck, and enemy riflemen forget to lead them, for they are so fat and ungainly, and that is why so many second lieutenants like Slaton Telfair are still alive.

When he came in low over the tank he was pretty sure that it was a Chinese tank. It looked just like the turret of a T-34. "If that is a Chinese tank," he said, "then there must be Americans around. Maybe all those dead are Americans. Maybe they fought the tank and they killed the tank and the tank killed them."

He stopped the helicopter again, and allowed it to settle towards the ground, directly over the tank and the dead. He hovered twelve feet over the dead. The dead were Chinese, all of them. "Well, I'll be damned," said Lieutenant Telfair. "There ought to be Americans somewhere. Where are they?"

He began to look.

On the ground, Dog Company had seen the helicopter approach, of course, and they had screamed and yelled, and waved their arms. The helicopter had sailed over them, serenely, and on up the road towards their bivouac of the night, and the hill where they had seen the Mongol horsemen.

They cursed him. They cursed him, and the Air Force, and the Navy, and the high command. "Know what he's doing?" said Petrucci. "He's out looking for the Chinks. He doesn't give a damn about us."

"Why they don't even know we're here," said Heinzerling.

"Know what would happen if that screwball pinwheel saw us?" said Heinzerling. "He'd call down fire on us, that's what he'd do. He'd have the *Mo* laying sixteen inchers in our laps."

"That's all we need," said Petrucci.

Far back the road they heard the rattle of rifles, and then an explosion that could have been a mortar, or a grenade. "Hope they got him," said Heinzerling.

"They won't," said Petrucci. "Them pinwheel pilots are shot with luck. They live forever."

Apparently Petrucci was right, for presently they heard the pinwheel again. They looked back and they saw it stop over the tank, and then it started moving again, down the road towards them.

Ekland knew he had to do something, and he had to do it fast. He had no flares, or even any tracer ammunition any longer, or anything at all to attract the attention of that pinwheel. The pinwheel might just happen to see them on the road, but this was unlikely, because of the overhang of the cliff, and the condition of the road, icy mud churned and filthy and frozen, exactly like their clothing. They were almost perfectly camouflaged. They might be seen in clean snow, and he looked off the road, and he saw clean snow. "Follow me!" Ekland yelled, and he ran out into the snow-covered flat, where his filthy parka would be marked against the clean white, and the others followed him, and they waved.

When the pinwheel was almost overhead it slowed down, and then stopped, and then began a weird revolving motion. It was as if the pinwheel said, "Who are you? Who are you down there? Friend or foe? Make some sign."

"He wants us to make a sign," said Ekland, and then he thought of what to do. "We make an SOS. We make an SOS in the snow."

"With what?" asked Beany Smith.

"With ourselves," said Ekland. He detailed them. "You, you, and you, you're an S. You three, you're the O. You three here, you're the other S."

Nine men lay down in the snow, as Ekland arranged

them, and the pinwheel came down beside them, and a face in the pinwheel grinned, and a hand in the pinwheel jabbed down at the loaded basket litters.

They unloaded the supplies, and loaded Tinker into one of the basket litters, and they were about to lift Mackenzie when Mackenzie waved his hand and shook his head and said something, but they could not hear him, because of the noise of the pinwheel's engine. Mackenzie pointed to his musette bag, and then he pointed to Ekland, and they all knew what the captain meant. And then Mackenzie touched the pocket of his parka, and Ekland leaned over him and took out the bottle of Scotch.

They strapped the captain into the basket litter, gently. The pinwheel rose straight up, and was soon gone. Twenty-five minutes later it descended on the deck of the *Leyte,* and the trained crash crews, seeing its basket litters were loaded, ducked under the rotor.

Second Lieutenant Telfair went below for coffee. Adjoining the ready room, the *Leyte* maintained a snack bar, and soda fountain, for the men of its air group. The commander, Air Group, saw Telfair drinking his coffee there, and he said, "Well, what'd you get?"

"Two wounded," Telfair said.

"Three more and we'll make you an ace," said the commander, and everybody laughed.

Chapter Fourteen

Dog Company now had more of everything than it needed. It had more than it could comfortably carry, but Ekland insisted they carry it all. He insisted they bring the litters with them, and he insisted they load the litters with the extra magazines of ammunition, and extra cartons of food. He allowed them to eat all the combat rations they wanted, or all they could chip from the cartons with their bayonets, but then Ekland got tough.

He ordered them on, immediately. They no longer had fuel, so it was necessary they keep moving.

With a fresh magazine in his BAR, and his stomach growling at its work, John Ekland felt better. He walked at the head of the column, as Mackenzie had. He had unloaded his pack on one of the litters; and over his shoulder, now, he carried the musette bag with the company records. Under his arm was the bottle guard, as Mackenzie had carried it.

He counted his men, altogether there were now fourteen. It was awful. It was worse than Iwo. But so far as

Ekland could figure out, it was still an intact command, and he was at the head of it.

If necessary, Ekland knew, Dog Company could fight again. Back there at the crossroads they had had a small victory, although they had lost the captain. A victory was the richest and most stimulating food you could put in their stomachs.

Then Ekland saw a line of skirmishers coming towards him, backed by armor, hopelessly out-numbering him. Dog Company was cut off from the friendly sea. "Hit the ditch!" he yelled behind him. "Ostergaard, bring up the bazook! Who's got the bazook rockets? Bring up those damn rockets!"

Then, over the sights of his BAR, he examined the people coming towards him, and something in the way they moved, their steady and yet almost careless progress, heedless of ambush in the ground or enemies in the sky, told him they were friendly. He dropped the BAR, rose, and began to wave his arms. He didn't know it, but he was weeping.

"We heard noises up here," said the lieutenant from the Third Division, "so we came up to see what it was all about. Who are you people?" This lieutenant peered at them closely, as if they looked peculiar.

"Marines," said Sergeant Ekland. "We're from the First Marine Division."

The lieutenant seemed surprised. "Is that so? We didn't think anything would be coming down this road except gooks. That's the way I was briefed. That's what intelligence told us."

"Well, we're Marines, and we're poohed."

"You're being evacuated, you know. Your whole division is being evacuated. They're putting 'em on the ships right now. There's a rear guard, and a beachmaster, to take care of the stragglers."

The sergeant straightened. "These are not stragglers," he said loud and clear. "This is a company. This is Dog Company!"

The lieutenant looked them over. "A company?"

"Yes, bud, a company!"

And the lieutenant looked them over again, and he saw that as individuals they might all be casualties, but together they were still a fighting team. And the lieutenant realized that what this sergeant had said was true. They were a company. "I have transportation around the bend," the lieutenant said. "If your men can't make it, I'll order my vehicles up here to pick them up."

"My men can make it," Ekland said. This was the first time, he realized, that he had called them "my men." With the bottle still under his arm, he led them out.

Since they were the last out, they were the last aboard, which was only proper, and Ekland reported to the lieutenant-colonel commanding Battalion, and was told to get the company records in some sort of shape, if he could, because the Graves Registration people would be wanting to talk to him, and so would the new company commander. It was two days before he mustered them all together on the LST, purring out through the Japan Sea. "Well," he said, "we've still got the captain's bottle." And he held it

up, so they all could see. "So maybe it's time to open it."
He ripped open the zipper of the leather guard, and
brought out the Scotch. "What'd you say, men?"

Kato said, "I don't want a drink. I'm so full of rations I
could bust. All I want is some more sleep."

Heinzerling said, "I don't want a drink, not now, on
account of I'm going down and get a shower. They've got
a bath service on this boat, an honest-to-God bath service,
with hot water."

"Me too," said Vermillion.

Petrucci sauntered across the deck to where they were
passing out free cigarettes.

And they all of them left, for one reason or another, and
finally there was no one but Ekland and Beany Smith and
Ostergaard. Ostergaard scuffed his boot on the steel deck.
"Count me out, sarge. I'm superstitious."

"Well, Smith," said Ekland, "the captain promised it to
us, and that leaves nobody but you and me, and I guess
that leaves you alone, and you can have a hell of a toot
for yourself, because personally, Smith, I don't feel like
drinking it."

Beany Smith took the bottle, and examined it closely.
He rubbed it against his freshly shaven cheek, and looked
back at the bleak hills. "Me, I don't want it either," he
said. "This is our luck. We may need it again. We may
need it right here. I wouldn't drink it for nothin'." He returned it to Ekland.

A regimental sergeant saw Ekland and said he had
been looking for him, because the battalion commander
and Colonel Grimm wanted to see him. They were waiting
for him in the wardroom. The wardroom table was deep

in papers. "All day," said Grimm, "people have been looking all over this ship for you. Where've you been?"

"Between decks, mostly," said Sergeant Ekland, "working on these papers here." He asked the question he wanted to ask. "Sir, have you heard anything about Captain Mackenzie?"

"He ought to be just about landing in Hawaii now," the colonel said. "And tomorrow, if my times are figured right, he ought to be just about in a hospital in San Francisco."

"But, sir—"

"They don't lose many wounded, once you get 'em in a sick bay," said the colonel. "I'm glad they didn't lose Mackenzie." The colonel smiled, and it was so unusual for the colonel to smile, that all those in the wardroom, the staff officers and the communicators and the clerks, they all noticed it. "But that isn't why I've been looking for you, Ekland. I'm making you."

"Sir?"

"There aren't any officers left in your company, and we want to keep it on the rolls. I'm giving you the brevet rank of first lieutenant, effective when Mackenzie first recommended it. We'll just skip the second grade. Know what that means?"

"Yes, sir."

"You're acting commander of Dog Company from here in." He looked around him at his staff. "One of these gentlemen will dig you up a couple of silver bars. We've got plenty of them left over."

Ekland wondered whether it was expected that he should say something, but when he looked at the colonel's face he saw that it was not expected.

The colonel said something, "What's that you've got under your arm?"

"Why, that's a bottle of Scotch, sir!"

"A bottle of Scotch!" He sounded just as surprised, and incredulous, as had Dog Company when the captain had first brought out the bottle. "Well, if that's a bottle of Scotch, don't you want to celebrate?"

"Well, yes, sir, but not with this bottle of Scotch. It doesn't belong to me. It belongs to Captain Mackenzie."

The colonel looked at it, and Lieutenant Ekland could see that the colonel, himself, would very much like a drink of Scotch. "Mackenzie'll never miss it. He'll have Scotch by the bucket in a week or so."

"Oh, yes he would miss it, sir," said Ekland, "and if I opened it now, and drank it, I wouldn't have a company."

"Okay," said Colonel Grimm. A colonel usually thought he knew a good deal about his command, that is, if he was really a good colonel, an old colonel. And then every once in a while he discovered he didn't know anything at all.

Ekland said, "If you'll pardon me, sir—"

"Have to leave, lieutenant? Don't you want to mess with us?"

"I want to tell my men, sir," said Ekland. "And I have work to do and I might as well get started. I've got a lot of letters to write."

He saluted, and he left.

ABOUT THE AUTHOR

PAT FRANK (1908–1964) is the author of the classic postapocalyptic novel *Alas, Babylon*, as well as the nuclear satire *Mr. Adam*. Before becoming an author, Frank worked as a journalist and also as a propagandist for the government. He is one of the first science fiction writers to deal with the consequences of atomic warfare.

BOOKS BY PAT FRANK

ALAS, BABYLON
A Novel

Available in Paperback and E-book

When a nuclear holocaust ravages the United States, a thousand years of civilization are stripped away overnight. But for one small town in Florida, miraculously spared, the struggle is just beginning.

MR. ADAM
A Novel

Available in Paperback and E-book

One of literature's first responses to the atomic bomb, *Mr. Adam* is equally a biting satire and an ominous warning to society—that will resonate deeply with readers today as it did when it was first published in 1946.

HOLD BACK THE NIGHT

Available in Paperback and E-book

The riveting story of a Marine captain, his soldiers, and their arduous, difficult retreat from Changjin Reservoir to Hungnam during the Korean War.

FORBIDDEN AREA

Available in Paperback and E-book

A classic of science fiction and an eerie, cold-war thriller that is a cautionary tale of the dangers of nuclear power.